CW01338005

THE TROUBLE WITH

Quarterbacks

USA TODAY BESTSELLING AUTHOR

R.S. GREY

The Trouble With Quarterbacks
Copyright © 2020 R.S. Grey
Published: R.S. Grey 2020
authorrsgrey@gmail.com
Editing: Editing by C. Marie
Proofreading: Red Leaf Proofing, Julia Griffis
Cover Design: R.S. Grey
ISBN: 9798668491742

CANDACE
01

Oh, this feeling is decadent.

Sinful.

My hands dip back into the warm water.

My eyelids flutter closed, and the soothing sound of island music serenades me from all sides. I'm wearing an exotic lei. Oh dear, is that a handsome bloke walking my way down the beach? Tall and strapping? He's got a coconut drink in his hand, complete with a little paper umbrella. *For me?*

How did I get so lucky?

An ocean breeze rustles my hair as the handsome man steps closer—and then a screech pierces the air.

Reality is a knife, slicing through the center of my blissful daydream.

"Ms. Candace! Mika just BIT ME!"

"Did not!"

My private island is stripped away as I blink my eyes open again. Ah yes, my preschool classroom. I look down at the soggy pair of poo-stained trousers I'm trying fruitlessly to rinse in the sink. There is no tropical music or ocean breeze, but there are catchy toddler tunes playing incessantly over the speakers, as well as a portable fan propped up on the counter to assist in drying this morning's finger paintings.

I'm not on a beach; I'm on the Upper East Side.

There is no man walking toward me in the buff, kicking up sand. There hasn't been a man for many, *many* moons. I wouldn't be surprised to find I've forgotten which hole the penis goes in. There? *NO*.

Mika and Tinsley have come to join me by the sink to plead their sides of the argument.

Tinsley was playing with my toy! And I wanted it back! He bit me!

I've heard this story a thousand bloody times. I know how it ends.

I leave the pooey trousers to soak in the warm water (though I know it'd be best to just incinerate them), dry my hands, and crouch between the two warring toddlers.

I'm very good at my job. I have a special touch with children, like Tinkerbell or one of the Muppets. I check Tinsley's arms for teeth marks, and fortunately, there's nothing much to see. I still give her a little mermaid-shaped ice pack and a big hug then force out a meek apology from Mika. Once that's done, I draft an incident report and tack it to the outside of my door for an assistant to take to the headmistress.

The two tots hug and walk off holding hands, best pals once again.

I place my hands on my hips and peruse my classroom. Right now, the children are having free play, or as this snazzy preschool insists on calling it, "interpretive creative time", but a quick glance at the clock tells me we're five minutes late for our science lesson. That's right—the parents of The Day School expect their wee children to get a real education here, not just search for boogies and mutilate Play-Doh all day.

As such, I spent ten hours of my own time over the last few days constructing a blown-up version of an atom out of papier-mâché. It's so beautiful I could take it down to a trendy gallery in SoHo and they'd probably be able to sell it to some loaded art collector for more than my annual salary.

I'm meant to teach the toddlers what protons, neutrons, and electrons are. It's my planned lesson for the day. A few months ago, I would have laughed at this concept. Preschoolers learning about atoms?! What about colors and letters? Ha ha ha. *No*. These kids already know all of that. If put to the test, they probably know more than me. I shudder at the thought. Best to keep them thinking I'm the one in charge here.

"One, two, three! Eyes on me!" I singsong. The toddlers listen quickly, loving the game. "Toys down! Hands up!" Several pairs of hands shoot up into the air, fingers wiggling with glee. "Time to pause our play and gather round the circle table. We've got an important science lesson to learn today."

The Day School is *the* premier learning center on the Upper East Side. Parents put their children on our waitlist when they're little more than zygotes. There is nothing they won't do to ensure their child earns a spot here. There is no behavior too extreme. They've camped out on the sidewalk the night before registration day. They've hired private investigators to tail our headmistress. They've sent lavish gifts to bribe their way in. (This particular tactic I happen to really love. Please send more cookie bouquets! You won't hear complaints from me!)

There are no limits to what these loving (read: crazy) parents will do for their children. They assume this school is the best of the best, and well…they aren't wrong. Tuition is upwards of $40,000 a year (!), and every teacher here, including myself, has at *least* a master's degree in some fancy subject related to rearing today's youth: child development, adolescent psychology, astrophysics. The music teacher had a twenty-year run on Broadway! The chef in the cafeteria has won a James Beard award!

I don't quite belong here. I'm not all that fancy or brilliant, just a transplant from England with a Mary Poppins accent and a mound of grad school loans (*thank you, Columbia*) who happened to be in the right place at the right time. A few months back, I was working as an assistant *to* the assistant in the 4s classroom, and then the teacher in charge of the 3s room got fired for having a scandalous affair with one of the student's parents, which left me in a unique position.

Candace, we need you! Are you prepared to mold young minds into the leaders of tomorrow?

You mean pass out juice boxes and deal with incessant whinging? Er…I mean, sure thing!

At twenty-four, I'm the youngest teacher here. As if that's not bad enough, my short stature and general wide-eyed fairylike demeanor don't necessarily help my case. I look more like one of the students than one of the staff members. I've thought of ways to help this unfortunate circumstance: potentially dying my pale blonde hair a dark brown, wearing false glasses, trading in my Keds for no-nonsense Mary Janes. Last month, on a whim, I tried on a polyester pantsuit at Macy's and had to hold back a scream when I saw my reflection. I thought for a moment my gran had come back from the grave to haunt me.

Lack of respect and crazed parents aside, the arrangement I've got going here is quite nice. The toddlers are cute and too young to realize they'll grow up to become entitled buggers. Their parents have really set them up for it: Yates and Niles and Bronwyn and Margaux and Briggs. Their names might as well scream, *We're going to own all of New York one day!* They're signed up for ballet lessons and Mandarin lessons and piano lessons. Their eating habits are more cultured and refined than mine. They have drivers and nannies and masseuses. I'm slightly intimated by the lot of them—until one of them lets loose a fart or a burp and reminds me that they are, in fact, only three years old.

It'd be a nice life, really, working here on the weekdays, exploring the city with free time on the weekends, if I were able to swing it. Even though the school itself takes in more money than an illegal drug operation, somehow it doesn't quite get funneled down properly to us teachers. The pay here is absolute crap, so to afford my life in New York City, I've had to get creative. I split a flat with two other girls I met through a Brits abroad social club. The club itself was incredibly lame—full of old geezers moaning about World War II—so the three of us bailed after the first meeting (taking some stale biscuits with us).

To make ends meet, I also work a few other odd jobs. Two nights a week, I waitress at a trendy bar called District that draws in Wall Street types—guys with big egos and big wallets. I have to wear a sort of skimpy outfit, but I usually get loads of tips, and it's fun to take on a persona so different than the one I affect at The Day School.

I've also done maid jobs from time to time. My roommate, Kat, is an aspiring actress and needs money as badly as I do, so she has a nice gig with a luxury cleaning company. If one of her coworkers calls in sick, I usually volunteer to fill in if I can swing it with my schedule.

All in all, I'm a busy gal. I like it that way. I feel like I belong in this fast-paced city, hustling alongside everyone else.

I'm happy.

I think.

Oh hell, *my love life*. Right...

I haven't been on a date in quite a while. So long, in fact, that I can't remember if it's because I'm busy or because there's something wrong with me. Just in case, I give my armpits a quick once-over and am relieved to find a pleasant floral scent instead of cloying B.O.

My other roommate, Yasmine, goes on a date nearly every weekend. She has the time for it. She's loaded thanks to a trust fund and only crams into the small flat with me and Kat because she thinks it's fun to bunk together.

"It's just like my boarding school days!" she said when we strolled into the flat on the first day, alarmed to find it only had two bedrooms with dimensions more fit for a dollhouse. Yasmine claimed one bedroom for her own and volunteered to cover half the rent. Kat and I share the other room, sleeping on teeny twin beds and constantly waking each other up. She has to get up early for her cleaning jobs, and I sometimes get back late from District. We try our best to be quiet, but more often than not, stubbed toes or chiming mobiles negate our efforts.

My work at The Day School is almost over for the day, and I don't have to be anywhere after work tonight. It's a rare free evening, and nothing can dampen my spirits, not even the weather. The tail end of February is being a particularly cruel witch this year. Outside, it's bleak and horrid, and I can practically hear the wind howling even from inside the warm confines of my classroom.

It's nearly 3:30, and I try not to prance around with glee. I'll be out of here in no time. One good thing about the parents at this school is that they rarely pick up their own children. They leave that to the nannies and au pairs who are never, *never* late. They can't be! They don't want to jeopardize their cushy jobs by leaving little Winston III out on the curb shivering. So, at 3:30 on the dot, I wrangle the children into their jumpers, make sure they each have their respective lunch sacks, and pass out their dried finger paintings for them to take home, right as the sound of chatter fills the halls.

It's quitting time.

Two little arms suddenly hug my left leg and squeeze tightly. I look down to see Briggs with his mop of brown curls and doe eyes staring up at me.

"Do I *have* to go?"

I ruffle his hair and mimic the same pout he's wearing on his face. "Oh, c'mon. Cheer up, will you? I can't stand when you frown. You're much too handsome for it."

Then I pull a silly face and he erupts in laughter, but only for a moment before quickly remembering his earlier desolation.

"It's just so boring at home," he complains, and my heart breaks for him. I know how it can be sometimes. Palatial brownstones. Lots of staff. Not a lot of quality time with Mum and Dad. Then I remember something that will cheer him up. Something exciting is happening today.

"But you aren't going home today," I say, chucking him gently on the chin. "Remember? Your uncle—"

My sentence is cut off when Briggs glances up and emits an ear-splitting squeal of delight.

11

"UNCLE LOGAN!"

He lets go of my leg to dash off toward the classroom's half-open Dutch door right as I glance up. My brain does a little stutter step, forgetting how to operate as a normal human would. My jaw drops and my tongue sort of lolls uselessly. This man can't be Briggs' uncle, because he's most definitely the hunk from my daydream, the one with the coconut drink on the beach. He has the same unruly brown hair. Same tall, broad frame. Same chiseled jaw and roguish grin. I hear the call of the ocean for a split second before I shake my head and realize I've gone mad.

This isn't my fantasy man.

I've never met this man. I *know* I haven't. My brain would have tattooed it to memory.

This is just a man who bears a dangerously close resemblance to my fantasy.

I force my brain back into my body and head toward the door.

Briggs' uncle is one of the first to arrive for pick-up, so toddlers buzz around me as I reach to shake his hand and introduce myself.

"Hi there, I'm Candace."

"Ms. Candace! This is my uncle! He's famous!"

His uncle smiles good-naturedly and shakes his head like Briggs is only pulling my leg. Then he reaches over the bottom half of the Dutch door to accept my hand. "I'm Logan. It's good to meet you."

His hand is massive and quite warm compared to mine. I try not to crumble beneath the pressure of his tight hold.

Briggs groans in frustration. "He *is* famous! I can prove it!"

12

Logan seems intent on downplaying his nephew's claims, circumventing his praise. With a quirk of a dark brow, he asks me, "So you're Briggs' teacher?"

I beam, and then I realize we're still holding hands, so I force myself to steal mine back lest I get carried away.

"I am. Yes. I'm the 3s teacher here."

"Tough job I bet," he says, passing his gaze over the children dancing and wiggling and chatting around my legs.

"I know what you're thinking," I say, playfully rolling my eyes. "How *does* she manage it? Fancy clothes, posh office, absolutely *massive* paycheck." He laughs and I grin as I continue, "It's not something I like to brag about often. Guys get so intimidated."

"I'm not surprised. Look at you," he teases, waving his hand up and down my body.

Cheeky bastard. I can't help but laugh and shake my head.

I get it. My hair is up in a bun, and if I remember correctly, I still have an unused paintbrush stuck up there from earlier. The kids and I made a whole game of it during art time. *Has anyone seen my paintbrush?* I'd asked the class, turning in an exaggerated circle. *Now* where *has it gone?!* My soft blue dress is just barely fancy enough to pass staff dress code, though I've paired it with tight bike shorts underneath so I don't flash the kids my knickers throughout the day. My pale pink Keds complete the look, proclaiming the fact that I wouldn't hurt a fly.

Then his eyes flash back to mine, and I swear a spark of interest passes between us. "I'm intimidated," he says, all traces of humor gone from his tone.

A shiver passes down my spine and my cheeks heat to a very obvious shade of ruby red.

One of my coworkers passes behind Logan, and when she sees him, her eyes widen as she looks at me and mouths, "*Holy shit!*" before disappearing down the hall.

Oddly, it's her confirmation of his drop-dead gorgeousness that shocks me back to the moment.

"Yes, so…now you know about my job. What is it that you do?"

"I'm a professional foosball player."

I squint, wondering if I've heard him right. The level of chatter around us has reached an all-time high as students start to see their caregivers arriving. He's an awfully big guy, quite fit by the cut of his arms beneath that gray t-shirt. Professional foosball? *Really?*

"That's…wow. Good for you." I sound less than impressed, but it's not my fault I'm so caught off guard. "I didn't know there was such a thing."

He frowns, obviously confused by my odd reaction.

I've only been in the States a few years. *Is foosball a big thing here?* I wasn't aware.

Just to be sure I've got it right, I follow up with a question.

"So you knock that little ball around trying to score?"

He grins, looking down at me like I'm the oddest creature he's ever encountered. "I guess you could put it that way."

Huh.

"It's a big sport here?"

He tips back on his heels, and I swear I see a tiny tinge of color on his sharply tanned cheekbones. "Yeah, pretty big."

It's like he's embarrassed to admit it.

"See?!" Briggs says. "Told you he's famous!"

I make a mental note to look into America's professional foosball league when I get back to our flat. Even after living here for a while, I swear there's still so much about this country I've yet to learn, but if all the players in that league look like Logan, well...I've just found my new favorite sport.

"Uncle Logan, can we get a snack on the way to your apartment?!" Briggs asks, hopping from foot to foot impatiently.

"Sure thing," Logan says, glancing down at him with a smile before his warm brown gaze quickly snaps back to me. "I guess I'll see you around?"

Right. Our time has come to an end. We can't stand here all day chatting away. How horribly unfair.

"Sure. Yes. Cheers," I say, twisting the knob so I can open the bottom half of the Dutch door and let Briggs sneak past me. Logan steps toward me to help open the door as I step toward him to take my usual position at the threshold of the classroom, and the synchronized movement brings me right up to him, like *Hello, rock-solid chest in my face.* Our size difference is hilarious. It's like we're in some children's book about opposites.

For a brief moment, my mind wanders. I wonder how good he is at foosball. He must have a hard time controlling his strength while twisting that teeny pole around. His arms look like he could break the table like a twig. Break *me* like a twig too.

Oh yes, Candace, let your brain conjure up those images. That'll do you good.

Fortunately, Briggs steals my attention by demanding one last hug from me before he goes off with his uncle. I'm not surprised; he's eternally starved for affection. He'd cuddle all day if I let him.

"See you later, alligator," I say with a wink.

He beams, proud to show off our parting words for his uncle. "In a while, crocodile!"

Logan nods his head in farewell before tucking Briggs against his side and steering him toward the entrance of the school. I stand watching them leave for so long that I'm oblivious to the caregivers standing at my door, trying to pick up their respective children.

"Ms. Candace?" a shy au pair peeps.

I wave her away. Give me a second, *please*. It's been ages since I've seen anyone as handsome as Logan in real life. It's a true privilege, and I want to soak it in. *What a man.* Strong and kind and *tempting*. He's stepped right out of my daydream.

Logan reaches the exit at the end of the hall then turns back for a brief moment. Our gazes lock again and he smiles, but I barely catch it before I duck swiftly back into the doorway, praying he didn't notice how lovesick I looked watching him leave.

"Did he see?"

"The drool? I'm afraid so." The au pair frowns.

Just my luck.

I haven't got Logan out of my mind in days. As soon as the last student left my classroom on Thursday, I fired off a long text to my flatmates.

CANDACE: KAT & YASMINE! DO NOT DALLY! Come straight back to the flat after work. Kat, don't take the long route from the subway station just so you can pass by Cute Hot Dog Guy. This is important!

I've had *THE BEST DAY*. You won't believe it. There I was in my preschool classroom, washing a bit of poo out of some trousers (you know how it goes...), when this absolute *babe* came to collect his nephew from my class.

Truthfully, I thought I'd blacked out for a moment when I first saw him. He was a proper hunk with glorious brown hair that had a bit of wave to it, he was quite tall, and he had these *arms*. Are muscly arms supposed to make you damp all over? I'm panting just thinking about them.

Anyway, he told me he's a professional foosball player. At least, I *think* that's what he said. The tots can get quite loud near pick-up time.

YASMINE: *Foosball?* What are you on about, Candace? Have you gone mad?

KAT: Oh sod off. So what if I like to have a good look at Hot Dog Guy's arse on my trek home after a hard day's work in the city? It's called self-care.

CANDACE: Kat, I'm ignoring that. Yes, Yasmine—foosball! Y'know, the sport with the tiny ball you toss around the table? I suppose it's a big thing over here in the States. We must investigate and learn everything we can.

By the way, he's called Logan.

Logan + Candace. I think that sounds quite nice! I can hear the wedding bells now. *Dum, dum, dah-dum.*

YASMINE: Oh good grief. I suppose we can do some snooping when I get home. I'll grab wine on my way.

KAT: I'll grab hot dogs.

As soon as we all arrived back at home, I droned on about him for hours.

"Did I already tell you about his arms?"

"Loads of times," Kat said, quickly holding her hands up to her ears in case I decided to start in on it again.

I yanked them away so she could hear me properly. "And the hair? That dark brown color…like velvet. And just the right amount of curl! More like a wave. Do you know what I mean? Should I pull up an example on Google again?"

Yasmine swiped my computer off my lap before I could pull up my previous search.

"Please spare us. I'm sure he was hot, but who cares? It sounds like he's way out of your league."

I pulled a face like she was absolutely insane. "Out of my league?!"

I stood up to show her all of what I have to offer, confident she was selling me short. Though…as stray popcorn bits fell from my lap onto the floor, I realized *maybe* she did have a point. The TV remote fell out of my lap too—right on my toe. I winced and did a good bit of yelping and hopping around until I felt I had my pain better under control.

"Yasmine, *look at me*," I finally said, walking to the end of our tiny living room then posing like I was at the end of a catwalk. "There isn't a man on earth who's out of my league."

"You've got a bit of wine on your pajamas there," Kat noted, deadpan.

I looked down at my oversized t-shirt, which matched the ones they were wearing. We grabbed them in a gift shop on Coney Island as a total joke. It stretches all the way to my knees and features a caricature of a woman's body in a bikini top and bottom. The way it's cut, it makes it look like it's my body.

"I don't see it."

"There. Right near your left boob."

Ah yes.

I dabbed at the stain with my thumb, but it didn't budge. Old, probably.

"Chocolate too, just there," Yasmine joined in. "Does anything actually make it *into* your mouth?"

I smiled wolfishly at them. "Oh yes."

This is when—and I'm not *proud* of it, per se—I mimed a sort of blow job bit. They both rolled laughing, knowing I was totally full of it. Just like my nether regions, my mouth hasn't seen any action in quite a while.

"Anyway, ladies, I feel bad—I do. I'll have to break my lease when he whisks me off to some fairytale island to have his wicked way with me, but do send on my mail, won't you?"

Yasmine whacked me in the head with a pillow from across the room, which is quite impressive because she's the least athletic out of all of us.

Unfortunately, her pillow didn't do the trick.

I'm still thinking about Logan tonight, days later, while I work at District. I'm at the bar, waiting for the bartender to finish making drinks for one of my tables.

In the meantime, I'm picking a little red paint off my left thumb. It's evidence of the volcano I started constructing for another science lesson back at the flat before I had to rush here for my shift.

"It's not fair. You look adorable in this outfit. I swear to god, my breasts are one deep breath away from tumbling right out for everyone to see."

I glance over at the new girl standing beside me, the one talking. She only started here a few days ago, and she's really struggling with catching on to things. I swear she whinges on about something new every five seconds.

Why do they have to keep it so dark in here? I'm going to trip down these stairs!

What's with these slow-ass bartenders?

Are you getting good tips? Mine have been total shit all night.

This job is not hard. Take drink orders. Deliver said orders. Smile. Collect the tips.

"Do I look okay?" she asks, turning to me so I can assess her. "I feel like I look *horrible* in this uniform. Does the shirt have to be so tight?"

"You look great," I say with an encouraging nod and a thumbs-up, more than a little relieved when the bartender finishes loading drinks onto my tray.

"Thanks, Roger!" I say, sending him a quick friendly wink before quickly turning away from New Girl.

"Roger, does this shirt look like it fits me?" she asks, looking to him for input now.

Oh dear. Poor Roger. *But better you than me, mate!* I sprint as fast as I can away from the bar while keeping my drinks from spilling off my tray.

District is packed to the gills tonight. It's Friday, and the city is out in full force. I'm waiting on a few tables near the VIP section. They've all arrived within the hour, very thirsty and very demanding, but I handle it like a champ. The ladies are here to celebrate a friend's promotion at work and have very exact drink orders (shaken, not stirred—that sort of thing), but my memory doesn't fail me, and when I load up their table with Roger's cocktails, they squeal with glee.

"Candace, these drinks are perfect!" the leader tells me before turning to her friends so they can all clink their glasses together. "Before you go, would you mind taking our picture?"

I happily oblige. The shit lighting in here means all their flaws (of which there are barely any) will totally disappear in the photographs. They'll look slightly out of focus and decadent in this posh setting.

"Smile, girls!" I prod, holding the mobile up to snap a photo. I go ahead and take ten more—because someone will whinge about their eyes being half-closed in the first, no doubt—and then I pass back the mobile. They all lean in to get a good look at the screen.

"It's perfect!" one declares.

I smile and promise to be back to check on them soon before making my way to my next table. It's a group of lads here to celebrate a bachelor party, and they've been quite rowdy since they arrived. Very macho, very reminiscent of a herd of male peacocks.

They're the closest you can be to VIP without actually being in it, and when I wander over, they're talking extremely loudly about a guest sitting up on level two behind the red rope.

"That's definitely him! I think I know a Super-Bowl-winning quarterback when I see one."

"All you could see was the back of his head when he walked by, dipshit. It could be anyone!"

"Lads! Oy!" I interrupt them. "Can I get drink orders?"

I'm small, but my accented voice carries, and they all turn at once to lock their eyes on me. I stand at the base of their round booth, waving around the little notepad I use to jot down lengthy orders.

"Are *you* on the menu?" one of them asks, a bit under his breath, but they all hear it and so do I. A few of them snicker.

I take no offense. My main goal tonight is to earn tips, and I'll bet they're mostly harmless. All-talk sort of guys.

"That depends," I reply saucily, propping my hands on my hips.

They all lean in, interested.

"Shall I bring the bachelor boy a round of shots and we'll all have one?"

"Yes!" one of them shouts before the others have a chance. "Top-shelf tequila. Whatever you have that's best." He reaches into the back pocket of his suit pants and tugs out his wallet.

I hold up my hand; I already have their cards at the bar for their tab. He's forgotten, but I remind him.

"Right," he says, continuing to tug a crisp one-hundred-dollar bill from his wallet. "This is just for you then—if you take that shot with us."

For some, his offer might creep a bit too close to selling your soul. Putting up with these guys, joking and laughing with them…yes, they're leering at me like I'm a glossy rack of prime rib, but that hundred-dollar bill is too good to pass up. Besides, Roger knows the drill.

A few minutes later, we all take a tequila shot like pros, sucking it down and chasing it with a tart lime wedge. I use the back of my hand to wipe a bit of the juice from my chin and then unfurl a proud smile. They all watched me take mine, unsure of my abilities to hold my liquor. Of course, they don't know that Roger watered mine down enough that it barely had any bite to it at all. It's the only way to make it through a shift, especially with guys like these.

"She's my dream woman," one of them says, leaning in to take my hand. "Marry me?"

I laugh and play along, though his hand is a little clammy with sweat and he reeks of alcohol. It's barely masked by his expensive cologne, and though he's got a handsome enough face and a fat enough wallet, he's absolutely not my type.

"I appreciate it, really, but—"

"Candace?"

The sharp voice carries over the noise of the bar, drawing my attention toward the VIP section. Up on the second-floor landing, I spot Logan right away. It's not as if he's hard to find, standing up and facing me, as impossible to ignore as the sun. *God, what a bloke.* All tall and tanned in his black shirt and jeans. He's dressed way more casually than most of our patrons here, but he looks more like he belongs than anyone. His hair is just as perfect as I remember—short enough that it barely gets to do any of its marvelous curl, but long enough that my fingers could get tangled in it. *Easily.*

He curves around the tables to get to the entrance of the VIP section, and I watch him move, amazed by how fluid his steps are, how he commands his body and the people around him. They move and shift for him before he even has to ask. Noah parting the Red Sea, this one. Sheesh, quite convenient little trick that is. I'd never have to fight my way through packed subways again.

It's only been a week since I met him at The Day School, but I'd forgotten tiny details about him already. They coalesce back into perfect clarity as he comes to stand right in front of me.

I haven't had the good sense to wrest my hand away from Mr. Clammy Smells-a-Lot, and he hasn't finished the task either. Logan glances down at where our hands are linked, and a disgruntled frown takes over his handsome features.

"Are these guys bothering you?"

"I FUCKING TOLD YOU! IT'S HIM!" the original guy declares, and his friends all go crazy, crushing toward the end of the booth to get to Logan.

"Mr. Matthews. Truly, it's a pleasure. Oh my god. Dude, can we get a picture?"

My hand is released and I'm long forgotten, pushed to the side as they all try to get closer to him. I rub my shoulder where one of them not-so-politely elbowed me out of the way, and Logan is there, taking in every moment, completely unbothered by the swarm of lads surrounding him.

I looked into the foosball league like I meant to, but I didn't find much, and truthfully, it looked a bit...*silly*? Nothing like these guys are making it out to be. It's like Logan is really their hero. They want autographs and photos and "Can you call my girlfriend and leave a message? She's in love with you, man. You'd really be helping me out."

Logan doesn't take photos, but he signs a few cocktail napkins quickly and they get distributed among the group with a few grunts and threats and one solid punch to an arm.

"Dude, he gave it to *me*!"

"Candace?" Logan says, pinning the full weight of his attention back on me. My knees go weak a bit like maybe I'm not quite strong enough to handle him like this, looking at me from head to toe, brows pinched together, concern filling his brown eyes. "Come back to my table with me," he says, waving away the group's further requests and reaching out to take my hand.

With the contact, an electric current zings up my arm like I've just shoved the tines of a fork straight into a wall socket. I'd be shocked if my hair wasn't standing on end.

His hand is so big it engulfs mine completely. There'd be no chance of escaping him even if I tried, though I really, *really* don't want to try.

He tugs me along without confirming if I'd like to go with him, and I get half-dragged, half-carried up the flight of stairs into VIP. I've only been up here a few times and only before the bar opens to help shine glasses and lay out the bar. The veteran staff get to work this section every night, racking up tips and bragging about who they waited on. Even now, I briefly lock eyes with Simone—the waitress who trained me—at the VIP bar and shrug to let her know I have no idea what's going on. She sees Logan's hand on mine, and I think she realizes I'm not just waltzing up here to steal her tips. *Thank god.*

Logan's table is near the back, real secluded and tucked away. I expected a group of guys, but it's a mixture: two huge blokes and three absolutely stunning women, sitting between their dates in showy dresses I'd *die* to get my hands on. The one on the end perks up when she sees Logan approach again. Then her smile noticeably fades when she sees him and me holding hands. I try—immediately—to yank mine free, but he doesn't let go, not until we're right at his table.

"Guys, this is Candace. My friend."

Friend?! *Are we?* God, I hope so. Wouldn't that be lovely to have a friend like him? I'd never have to bother hiring a moving company again! Never have to struggle with an unopened jar of olives!

"Hey Candace," the group choruses, along with offering nods and smiles.

Logan turns to me and gives me another once-over. "Were they harassing you down there?"

I scoff and cross my arms over my chest, rubbing the elbow that's still smarting for a moment before dropping it. "What? *No*. C'mon, it's part of the job."

He frowns. "I thought you were a preschool teacher."

"I am." I grin. "But a few nights a week, I'm also Candace the cocktail waitress."

I wave a hand down my outfit, and he rubs the back of his neck like maybe he doesn't quite like it.

"That skirt's pretty short," he notes.

"*I'm* short."

For show, I flatten my hand to the top of my head then draw it across the gap between us until the side of my pinkie hits his chest, right between his pecs. When I try to pull it back, he lifts his hand to wrap his fingers around my wrist.

His bad mood finally lifts, and a soul-searing smile dimples his cheeks. "Yeah, I guess you are."

"Now are *you* going to stop harassing me so I can get on with my job?"

He peers down at me with a cheeky little look in his eyes. "Oh, now *I'm* the one doing the harassing?"

"Yes." I puff up my shoulders and chest like I'm going to take a real stand. "Dragging me away like that, all brutish and cocky."

His grin turns positively edible—or maybe it's his eyes doing that, making me think he'd like to eat *me* alive if given the chance.

"I saved you from them," he says, mighty proud of himself.

"Saved me from the absolutely massive tip they'll be giving me once they've knocked back a few rounds and become properly pissed?"

27

"Pissed," he repeats back, amused. "Your British words make no sense."

"Oh, right, let's see. Sloshed? Sozzled? In-*e*-bri-*ated*? That good enough for you proper Americans?"

"I like your words better," he says, all smooth and quiet, like he wants me to take what he's said and twist it into something a bit more sinister.

It's impossible to stop the flush from taking over. My fair skin means I color like an English rose any time someone pays me the slightest compliment, and well, when that compliment comes from Logan's lips, there's no sense in attempting to fend off the impending blush.

"Logan, is your friend going to join us?"

The question comes from a huge black guy with broad shoulders and a smooth bald head. Not many people have bald heads and still fall into the hunky category, but this guy certainly does. With his dark skin and big smile, it's easy to see why the girl beside him is crushed so close, staking her claim.

"There's not really room."

This statement comes from the girl at the end of the booth, the one who looked so miffed to see Logan's hand around mine. Owing to the numbers and the fact that with Logan, there's a girl to every guy, I'd imagine she's his date for the evening. Her snarky comment confirms it.

I feel bad for her, actually. She's clearly into him, and he hasn't looked her way this whole time. Cruel, really.

"Oh, no worries! I can't stay. I'm working." I offer up a big smile, and I sense, rather than see, the girl's relief. She wants me gone—yesterday.

"You could cover our table?" Logan suggests, and my eyes practically bug out of my skull.

"And offend Simone? Not on your life. She's been here for years, and I'm still a relative newbie." I rock back on my heels. "Relegated to the plebs, I'm afraid, but if you guys need anything and you can't find Simone, feel free to come grab me."

Let me tell you, it feels absolutely horrid walking away from Logan then. It's like I can feel his attention on my back as I walk away, and there's an invisible line I tug against with each step.

Things I'd rather do instead of leaving him:

1. Clean the rubbish bin down in the kitchens

2. Wash the mound of dirty clothes I've been ignoring all week

3. Go a week without having any sweets

Well...maybe not #3.

But a job is a job, and Logan isn't going to pay my bills. I rush back to my tables, checking that everyone's doing all right and refilling drinks for the next half hour before I finally get to take my break. I'm so, *so* tempted to run back up to VIP and squeeze into that booth beside Logan, but since that's absolutely mad, I take my mobile out through the kitchen and to the back alley behind the bar. It sounds sketchy, but there are always people out here on break. Even now, there are two busboys smoking a fag a ways down. I wave and they nod back before I dial my mum's number.

It's late back home, but she's always been a night owl. She's a sucker for those infomercials that drone on at all hours of the night: baking tins that magically clean themselves, head massagers. Every time I talk to her, she's buying something new that will ABSOLUTELY CHANGE HER LIFE.

The call connects, but for a few seconds, all I hear is the telly.

"Mum, you there?"

"Yes! Candace, hang on. Bloody remote's gone down between the sofa cushions and I can't get it."

The telly blares louder, she huffs in anger, and then finally, the noise cuts off and she sighs in relief.

"There. Now, I can hear you. How are you, darling?"

"Good. Yeah, on break at the bar at the moment."

"Busy night?"

"Not crazy, actually. Thank god. I might actually make it out of here at a decent hour. It was a bit mad a few weeks ago because of some football game. *American* football, I mean."

"Oh, yes. I heard about it. A club from New York won, didn't they? The Super Bowl?"

"*Team*, Mum, not club. They don't call them that over here. And yes, the team from New York won, which is why the bar was absolutely crammed full. I didn't get out till near three in the morning."

"And you had to go into school the next day?"

I rub my eyes just thinking about it.

"Yeah, but I mean, I survived, didn't I? And you got the money I sent back?"

I made a killing that night. It was well worth the lack of sleep.

"Yes, though I don't know why you insist on doing that. I've told you we're fine."

My parents are *not* fine. My mum is an eternal optimist. Their house could be up in flames, burned to bits, and she'd say, *Oh, not to worry. Let me just grab a bucket and fill it with the hose. I'll have this put out in a jiffy.* The truth is, my parents haven't been fine since my dad had a bad fall last year, broke his leg, and had to quit his work at the shipyard. Mum's cleaning job can't cover all the bills, and I feel so guilty staying over here instead of rushing home to help them more. Part of the reason I didn't is because Mum insisted I stay. *"We know how much you love it there. Don't come home on account of us. I'm taking care of Dad just fine."*

"I'll try to send a bit more at the end of the month. It'll depend on how well my shifts go this week. Speaking of, I'd better get back. I've got tons of tables and don't want to keep any of them waiting."

"Oh, right. Do be good and don't worry about sending anything back for us. Dad's physio is going well, and he swears he'll be able to apply for a job soon enough."

I don't bother arguing. I'll send the money home because it's the only way I can stay in America without being eaten alive by guilt. Also, I know they really need it. They barely scraped by before with Dad employed. I know my mum's insomnia doesn't just stem from her love of cheap gadgets, but because sometimes it's hard to sleep with all the stress she's got to carry for the family. It's why I have all the jobs, why I don't have any glitzy dresses like the girls Logan was with. Can't afford it. For now, I've got my District uniform, and that's all right. It serves me well enough.

LOGAN
03

I'm a real asshole the rest of the night. Sure, I sit in that booth, sip on my drink, and nod along with conversation, but I'm not really paying attention to any of them. I'm looking for Candace. I'm scanning the bar down below, hoping to catch another peek of her. I keep my eyes on that group of assholes who were taunting her before. I could hear them all the way up here in VIP, and it's what first drew my attention.

Then I saw her there with them and I froze for a moment, wondering if I'd gone insane. Sure, I've thought about Candace some since we met at my nephew's school. I thought of her in the weight room the next day and through a lunch with my agent that dragged on an hour too long.

She's a puzzle to me, and I've tried to figure out what it is about her that keeps bringing her back to the forefront of my thoughts. She's pretty, sure, but I've been around some drop-dead gorgeous women before, and it's not as if she's my type. I usually go for women who are more polished, women who know the game and how to play it.

Candace doesn't just seem like a novice in regards to my world; she seems wholly oblivious to it.

When I told her I play professional football, she couldn't have looked less impressed.

It threw me for a loop, especially because of the last few weeks. Ever since my team and I clinched the win in the Super Bowl, the attention from my fans has reached a whole new level. There's not a person on the street who doesn't know who I am. I can't go to the grocery store or the bank, or hell, even out to my car without getting stopped and congratulated on my stellar performance.

Except for Candace. She didn't congratulate me, and maybe that's why she's been stuck in my head.

Or maybe it's because she's British. Could be the accent paired with the sweet smile and the self-deprecating humor that forms a tantalizing combination of qualities I can't help but notice.

I want to spend more time with her. I wanted to ask for her number when I picked Briggs up from school, but I didn't because it seemed highly inappropriate. Instead, I've thought about her—so much so that for the first few seconds when I caught sight of her in District, I wasn't 100% sure I hadn't conjured her out of thin air.

Then I heard her speak and the accent thrust me into action. I pushed to my feet before I could stop myself. Melody shot out of the booth to let me pass, assuming I had to use the bathroom or something, and I didn't correct her. I only had one thought: get to Candace and rip that asshole's hand off hers.

It's all a blur after that. Did I really drag her back to my table? Did I invite her to wait on me and my friends? What an ass. I just wanted to spend another few minutes with her and she needed to work, so I was at a loss for what to do.

Now, everyone's ready to leave the bar, but I'm not. I haven't had a chance to talk to her again. She's been a tornado down below, rushing from table to table, smiling as she doles out drinks and passes out checks. She's good at her job, flirting and playing along with that group of guys but careful not to get too close or lead any of them on. Still, I bet one or two of them wish they could convince her to go home with them. They'd be idiots not to.

Melody drops her hand to my forearm, drawing my attention back to the table and my current date. I glance down at her manicured fingers, which are painted a delicate shade of pink. I wonder what color Candace would use on her nails. Bright orange. Yellow. Rainbow stripes. The thought makes me smile.

Melody misinterprets the gesture and sidles closer to me.

"Sorry I've been such a bore tonight," she says gently. "It was a long day on set."

I feel bad for Melody. This is technically our second date since we went out as a group last week too. Darius made us a reservation at a steakhouse and sprung her on me when I arrived.

"She's cool, man. She's been friends with Liz for years. She's not just some jersey chaser, and she's used to being in the limelight."

Liz and Melody both model. According to Darius, Melody is used to dating professional athletes and thus knows the drill. That should have been a plus considering that's partly why I've avoided dating in recent years. I've been burned by women who were with me for the wrong reasons. I've had women call paparazzi to ensure they're ready to snap photos at the exact moment we arrive somewhere, women who swore they were in it for the right reasons when in fact they were really only after fame and fortune. It's done a number on my ego and my general faith in the dating process.

Besides, it's not as if I have all the time in the world. Even now, in the off-season, I'm still expected to give my career my full attention.

That said, I can't seem to get excited about Melody. Sure, she's gorgeous and practically suction-cupped to my side, but there's no desire burning below the surface, no anxious excitement at the prospect of kissing her good night.

I try though. I try because my mother raised me to be a better man than I have been for the last hour.

"What were you shooting for today?"

"A designer jeans company. They wanted a really sexy feel so they had me in the jeans and nothing else." She wags her eyebrows teasingly. "It would have been fine except they had an Italian male model on set with me too." She assesses me then, looking for something. "You won't have an issue with that, will you? Me working with other guys?"

Why would I?

Oh right, because we're supposed to be dating.

I shrug. "All part of the job, right?"

She apparently doesn't like that answer, because she elaborates. "He was *obsessed* with me. Kept trying to get my number in between takes. And then it got so awkward because we were practically naked and pretending to be into each other. They had us take about a hundred photos where we were nearly kissing."

I take a sip of my drink, slightly worried she's going to continue if I don't stop her. "I'm sure you can handle your own."

She frowns, and I take a moment to glance back down and look for Candace, hoping she isn't at the table with the

36

guys again. A bit ago, I saw them force her into taking another shot. She's tiny—there's no way she can hold her alcohol that well.

"Are you guys about ready to call it?" Darius asks, stifling a yawn.

He and I both hit the weights early this morning, and I'm feeling as tired as he is. Even still, I'm hesitant to leave Candace here. Why does she work at a place like this when she has that job at The Day School? Why work two jobs? Then I remember her joke about her massive paycheck and it clicks into focus. She's hustling like so many others, just like my parents did back in Florida before I hit it big. I excuse myself from the group and promise to meet them out back, through the VIP exit, in a few minutes. Then I yank a couple bills from my wallet along with an old receipt.

I go down to the bar on the lower level, keeping my head down so as to draw the least amount of attention. It doesn't matter. I'm still noticed, but a quick shake of my head deters a few guys from coming closer. I wave down the bartender and ask him if he's seen Candace.

He frowns, thinking it over. "She's like a bird, man, flying around this place. I swear she moves faster than all the other servers combined."

He sounds fascinated with her and I narrow my eyes, wondering if he's just impressed with her waitressing skills or if it's something more. Then I shove aside the thought and ask him for a pen.

He hands me the one he has tucked behind his ear, and I jot down a quick note on the back of the receipt before passing it to him along with the cash.

"Make sure this gets to her, okay?"

His eyes widen at the sum of money in front of him. For a minute, I'm suspicious that he's going to pocket it all and forget my request, but then his gaze locks with mine and he nods reverently.

"Sure thing."

I'm expecting a call from Candace the next day, and when it doesn't come, I start to second-guess myself. Chasing women isn't something I've had to do since...*ever*. I was the star quarterback in high school, the star quarterback in college, and a first-round draft pick into the pros. Just because I haven't found a relationship that works long-term doesn't mean there's been a shortage of women ready and raring to give it a try.

There have been a lot of women, and then there's Candace. It's been two days and she still hasn't called.

"What if I wrote the number down wrong?" I ask Darius as I'm hunched over, gripping my knees and sucking in deep breaths. I feel like I'm about to fucking throw up.

We're doing sprint drills with our training coach and he's giving us hell because he's a sadist. Also because Darius was five minutes late.

"Are you serious? Logan *fucking* Matthews wrote his number on a damn grocery store receipt—that shit's worth a million dollars. I still can't believe you did that. What if the bartender had passed it around? If I were you, I'd change my number."

"I haven't had any weird calls. I think he really did mean it when he said he'd give the note to her."

"Uh-huh. Just wait. Tomorrow, your number will be splashed on the front page of Reddit."

He has a point. Maybe the bartender pocketed the cash and the note instead of passing it on to Candace. That would explain why she hasn't called.

Unfortunately, it doesn't explain why the hell I care so damn much.

"You two about recovered? We're going again in ten seconds!" Coach yells.

I resist the urge to punch Darius for being late. This day is going to suck.

CANDACE
04

Three nights ago, at the end of my shift at District, Roger caught me on my way out of the bar and slipped something into my hand.

"I don't know what you did for him, but he's pretty grateful."

I didn't get the chance to ask who he was referring to before he smirked and nudged my shoulder as he walked past.

I glanced down at the small fortune now resting in my palm. Then, at the grocery receipt.

Wait. *What?*

"Did you mean to give me all this money?" I shouted over my shoulder at Roger. "And is this your receipt from the store?"

He stopped and turned back, annoyed at my slow uptake. "Check the back—there's a note. I can't believe you got Logan Matthews' number." He shook his head like he was utterly dumbfounded.

I couldn't help it; my interest was piqued. I ignored the money and instead decided to shake down Roger for some valuable information.

"So you know him too then?"

He scoffed. "Who *doesn't* know him? He's the best quarterback in the NFL. Just won the Super Bowl a few weeks ago. Pretty sure he's on every cereal box in the whole damn grocery store."

My brows scrunched together. "Did you just say NFL?"

"Yeah, NFL. Football. You know, the most popular sport in America?"

"I thought he was a *foosball* player."

He barked out a laugh. "Foosball? Are you kidding? No. The guy plays football. You could hawk that phone number for a cool thousand dollars at the very least. Bet you could get even more if you found the right buyer."

I looked down at the receipt and slowly flipped it over. Sure enough, Logan had written me a note, and below it, there were ten aggressive black numbers. His mobile number.

"So then he's pretty famous?" I asked, unable to look away from the slip of paper.

"Extremely."

"How odd."

It certainly made much more sense—the physique, the VIP status, the models at his table. What a bloke! This is too funny. I wanted to phone him straight away and tell him all about my blunder. *You'll never believe it. Wait until you hear the full story. It's a riot!*

But I didn't call Logan because my attention slipped back to the wad of cash and I froze, absolutely stunned. He left me cash? Why in the world did he leave me *cash*?

Of course, I ask Kat and Yasmine about it, but not immediately. I give it a few days, trying to piece it all together myself. I scan back through my past conversations with Logan, searching for clues like a regular Sherlock Holmes, but I've got nothing and I'm growing antsy, so I enlist backup.

I should have known better.

"Does he think you're a sex worker or something? You didn't lead on or anything about maybe giving him a blowie?" Kat asks as she makes herself a cup of tea in our kitchenette.

"No! I absolutely, in no way made it seem like I was some kind of *lady of the night*."

"That uniform *is* pretty sleazy," Yasmine adds. "It wouldn't be out of the question that he got confused. Oh! Look! I found an even better angle."

She's on her mobile, scrolling down a Google image search of Logan Matthews. I've already seen more pictures than I care to: him on the field about to throw the football, all suited up in his blue and silver jersey; him dressed to the nines for some fundraiser; him on a beach, gripping his girlfriend's ass in a tight fist. It was after that one that I shot to my feet and said, *No more!*

My rear is practically on fire just thinking of him manhandling me like that. The obscene thoughts that flit through my mind are absolutely R-rated and perverse. It's not fair, really. His sheer size makes me go all swoony; he'd really know how to toss me around in bed.

I feel hot.

I push open the tiny window we've got beside the sofa and duck my head outside. The sounds of the city practically spear into me, the street noise and music and laughter. I close my eyes and breathe deep, and then a bird caws overhead and I scream as I feel a bit of poo drop onto my forehead and run down between my brows.

"It shat on me!"

Neither of my flatmates react properly. Yasmine is all, "That's why I never go in nature. It can be so unforgiving." Kat, at least, yanks off a wad of paper towels and attempts to toss them to me. They barely make it three feet, and she sighs as if to say, *Well, I tried.*

"It's an omen," I suggest as I dunk my head under the running tap in the kitchenette and decide whether or not I should phone a doctor. *Can I get rabies from bird poop? Is some of it in my eye now or is that just water?* I'm having a proper freak-out.

"Just calm down and come round over here so we can give the bloke a call. I can't believe you've sat on this number the last three days and done nothing with it. Look at him!"

I shut off the water and grab a vibrant pink tea towel to wrap around my sopping wet hair, leaving me looking like a turbaned palm reader when I walk back toward the sofa.

"You look lovely," Yasmine says with a dead-honest tone. "Pink is a good color on you."

"Oh shut it, will you? And pass me your mobile."

"Mine? Why mine?!" She immediately holds it up on the other side of her, out of my reach.

"Because I'm not going to call him from *mine*. That's embarrassing!"

Kat volunteers. "Whatever, use mine. But if he calls back and insists on chatting with me, well I'll probably have to give it a go because honestly he's the hunkiest man I've ever seen and I don't think you're adequately appreciating all he has to off—"

I yank away her mobile before she can finish her rant and phone him using the number I've now memorized by heart.

It rings for ages. I think I grow fifteen chin hairs by the time his voicemail finally kicks in. There's no deep voice there to greet me with an invitation to leave a message, just a stale robot insisting I wait until after the beep.

I don't, of course. I chicken out and hang up immediately.

"Well then, there you have it."

I pass Kat her mobile back, prepared to let the dilemma rest. *I've tried now, haven't I?* But then her mobile starts vibrating and the three of us shriek bloody murder so loudly our upstairs neighbor bangs on his floor, politely telling us to shut the fuck up.

"IT'S HIM!" Kat shouts, frantically waving her arms. She tries to pass me her mobile, but I don't want it. What am I supposed to do? *Answer it?!*

Yasmine groans and stands up to retrieve it, answering the call with a cool, clipped "Hello?"

I motion for her to put it on speakerphone, but she doesn't.

"Yes, hi. No, this isn't Candace. This is her friend, Yasmine."

I'm melting into a puddle of embarrassment. I can't believe I've let it drag on this far. He'll think I'm mad, and I am, actually, but I was hoping he wouldn't find out about that until well into our friendship, *after* he'd grown fond enough of me to appreciate my quirks.

"What's she doing?" Yasmine repeats. She eyes me up and down, clearly uninspired by my lackluster attire. Then her eyes land on the tea towel. "Oh, she's just…stepped out of the shower. Yes. That's why I'm the one answering."

45

Oh good thinking. Now he'll imagine me all wet and in my knickers. In real life, I've got on yellow cotton panties and a pale blue tank top I've had for so long it used to be navy.

"You want to speak with her? Sure, let me just make sure she's not still nude."

"YAZ!" I mouth, waving at her to cut it out.

"Oh good, she's got on this silky little robe. Barely decent, really—"

I yank the mobile out of her hand so hard I scratch her cheek. She winces in pain and I am sorry, but well, what choice did I have?!

"H-hello?" I say, immediately running toward my bedroom so I can barricade myself inside for some privacy. I get the door halfway closed before my two flatmates weasel their way in. Privacy is obviously not happening.

"Candace?" Logan asks, sounding a little amused.

"Yes, hi." I'm breathing heavily now, trying hard to get them to ease up on the door so I can force it closed, but it's two against one, and I'm the runt of the litter; there's no way I'll overpower them.

I sigh and let it swing open. They stand in the doorway, arms crossed while they listen, mighty proud of themselves.

"You sound like you're working out or something," he notes.

"No, just…showered, like Yasmine said."

"Huh." He sounds less than believing. "It's just that you called a second before I did. So did you call while you were in the shower?"

Oh bloody hell! So he's got brains *and* brawn?

"Oh…I don't…not sure. Maybe it was a butt dial?" My voice goes all high-pitched and squeaky. I'm making no sense.

"Right. Is this your number?"

"No. It's my friend Kat's. My mobile is…dead."

"You're acting odd."

I am odd. That's what I want to say, really. Just lay all my cards out there so there's no preconceived notions of me being fit for proper human contact. Best to just lock me up with some food and water and leave me be.

I sigh and rub my forehead—it's still raw from where I scrubbed away the bird poop.

"Truthfully, I think I'm a bit nervous." I tack on a laugh at the end that sounds absolutely mental.

Yasmine and Kat are both cutting their hands across their necks, trying to tell me to ease up on the weirdo, but they should know better than anyone that's a futile ask.

"Why's that?"

God, his voice. It's better like this, without his appearance distracting me. Like this, I can concentrate on how gorgeous he sounds…how easily he unravels me…

"I just…I found out who you are."

"Oh yeah? I wasn't hiding it or anything."

I rush to agree. "Of course. No. It's just—it's kind of a funny story. I thought…when you first introduced yourself as a professional football player at The Day School, I thought you said *foosball*."

His laugh sets me on a cloud. I'm floating.

"That explains so much," he replies, sounding a little relieved.

"Yeah, I really got confused. I looked into foosball and everything."

"Why would you do that?"

Oh right. Bugger.

"Just…I was curious about you. Is that embarrassing to say?" Judging by Kat and Yasmine's reactions, it absolutely is. "Oh well, it's true. I wanted to know more about you after you came to pick up Briggs from school, so I looked into the league and even watched a few matches on YouTube. Honestly, I thought it was the most ridiculous sport I'd ever seen, but I was going to make myself really like it if you and I became friends."

He's really laughing now, and I can almost picture him pinching his eyes closed and wiping a hand down his cheek like, *This girl. What a kook.*

"That's hilarious. I'll have to tell Darius about that. I've been complaining to him about the fact that you haven't called me since I gave you my number."

BLISS. My whole body lights up like a Times Square marquee. He's been waiting for me to call! This man with his hordes of models actually wanted to hear from me!

"Truthfully, it was the money bit that threw me for a loop," I reply, speaking truthfully.

"The money?"

"Yes, well, you left that nice note saying I should give you a call, but then you also gave Roger all that cash, and I don't quite know what to make of it. You don't…that is to say…you don't think I'm some kind of sex worker, do you?"

"Christ," he hisses. "No, Candace. *No.* Absolutely not. I'm an idiot."

I laugh, more than a little relieved. "Oh okay, good. It's just…I obviously can't accept that money, whatever it was intended as."

"I guess it was supposed to be a tip? Though now I see that it was pretty stupid. I just saw you on your feet all night working your ass off and knew you'd already been teaching all day. I felt bad."

Oh crap. Oh bollocks.

That's what this is.

He feels bad for me!

I'm Briggs' teacher and he sees me as this poor soul who's working hard and trying to make her way, and he gave me that money and his number because he felt bad. Oh my god, I wonder if he told his friends about the poor cocktail waitress and *CRAP!* Yasmine went on about the bloody shower and he must be so confused now.

"Right, anyway, I'll have Briggs take home the cash to return it to you. Or maybe that'd look odd, me sending a toddler off with half a thousand stuffed in his trouser pockets. Tell you what, I'll just—I'll put it in an envelope and maybe pass it off to the nanny who usually comes to collect him."

"Candace—"

"No, that'll work well. She's real polite. She won't steal your money. I actually…I've got to go now, but it was nice talking to you! No need to worry about me in the future. I'm doing quite all right. Bye now!"

I hang up before he can get another word in, and when Kat's mobile rings again, I shake my head and forbid them from answering.

"It's obvious now what's happened."

"You're not some charity case," Yasmine agrees. "You don't need his bloody money."

"Right. *God*, I'm glad I didn't get too carried away fancying him. Can you imagine how I'd feel then?"

Like an utter fool, crushed and embarrassed beyond belief.

I turn away from them and make some lame excuse about needing to get a bit of air. I throw on some joggers and shorts and yank off the tea towel, then I make my way down the stairs of our building, more than a little happy to get back out into the city. It's so blissfully noisy and chaotic out here, and my mopey thoughts nearly disappear altogether. Nearly.

I do just what I've promised and tuck Logan's money into an envelope for Briggs' nanny. The next day, at the end of school, I try to pass it off to her.

I've always liked her. Like the others, she's never late. She smiles and thanks me profusely whenever I hand Briggs off, though we never chat much beyond that. I always took it to mean she was busy and didn't want to dally, but now I realize there might be a language barrier. She's got a heavy Eastern European accent and is mighty confused when I try to explain to her who the money is for.

"Briggs has got an uncle, Logan. Have you met him?"

"No no." Then she smiles, trying to make up for her lack of English with politeness.

"Right. Er, well...maybe Briggs can help you get this envelope to him?" I try to shove it toward her, and she looks down at it like it's coated in radioactive green goop.

"Not good idea. You keep."

"I can't. You see, it's money—a lot of money."

I open it and flash her the bills, and she steps away quickly. Then she does the sign of the cross, gathers Briggs close to her side, and takes off down the hall.

Right, well, bloody good that did me.

That money burns a hole in my pocket the entire way from work to the market. Kat and Yasmine are already in the flat by the time I make it back home. I've got loads of healthy veggies and pasta to make for dinner, though I know we'll only ruin it with dessert afterward, but at least we'll have tried to give our bodies something nutritious, right?

"Get off your lazy arses and help me!" I groan under the weight of all the heaping sacks.

"Right right, we're coming," Yasmine says, getting up rather slowly, as if she's got ninety-year-old bones in her trim twenty-something body.

I threaten to aim a tomato at her head, and that puts a bit of pep in her step. We unload the groceries together then clear the bags. My purse is on the counter, and sticking out of it is the envelope I was meant to hand off today.

"Briggs' nanny wouldn't take it," I explain when they look at me questioningly. "I tried, though in the end I think she thought I was the devil or something."

Yasmine and Kat exchange a private glance. Yasmine's eyebrows waggle in my direction, and Kat shakes her head forcefully. Yasmine's eyebrows get a bit more aggressive, and then she adds in a pointed hand gesture as well. Kat's jaw locks as she intently shakes her head once again.

"Will someone just tell me what's going on?" I huff, rather annoyed.

"Yes, Kat, why don't you tell Candace about all the phone calls you've fielded today?"

My heart leaps into my throat, but then I chide myself and play it off as a bit of reflux instead of excitement. I did have a rather big cup of tea after lunch.

"Logan's phoned twice."

My heart does this silly little happy dance before I convince myself it's no big deal.

"And?" I ask, unloading some apples. "Did you answer?"

"Not the first time."

My breath hitches. "What do you mean, not the first time?"

"Well he was being quite persistent, you know. As I said, he phoned again, and I didn't want my mobile just ringing off the hook all day. He seemed rather eager to get in touch with you, so I answered the second time and he was awfully nice. Sounded so bloody hot, too, so I thought it'd be no big deal to give him your number."

And then, as if on cue, my mobile rings.

CANDACE
05

I don't answer it. I know that makes me the most cowardly coward on the face of the earth, but I felt like real crap yesterday and I hate that feeling. I've got a pretty good life going with my friends and my jobs; I don't need Logan Matthews coming in here and making me feel less than.

But maybe it wasn't such a good idea to ignore his call. I sort of thought he'd try again at least—up until now, he's seemed to be a pretty persistent bloke—but after that ignored call, he falls off the face of the earth completely.

No calls to Kat. No calls to my mobile either. Nothing.

A week passes in which I don't hear from him at all.

I do suffer through talk of him at school, though. Briggs goes on and on about a fun outing they had over the weekend. *We got pizza and ice cream and he took me to this arcade and he won me this huge stuffed panda and pandas are my favorite animal now and Logan is my favorite uncle but he's also my only uncle and*—at this point I was massaging my temples, praying my headache would dissipate on its own.

I have no choice. I can't call him, not after everything that's transpired. It's too far gone, at least that's how I feel until he shows up Wednesday afternoon to pick up Briggs from school. I'm a real mess, hair tucked up in a messy bun, red dress half concealed behind a paint-stained smock. I'm chatting with a nanny about early dismissal on Friday when Logan walks up behind her and pauses, waiting his turn at the door.

I go absolutely mute, like I haven't got a clue what to make of this turn of events. I knew he was going to show up here again. Briggs told me his uncle was going to be picking him up more in the coming weeks, and here he is, just as promised.

He's wearing a white Yankees t-shirt, a black ball cap, and jeans. His dark hair is just long enough in the back that it curls out underneath the bottom. He's so classically American and handsome it's like I'm staring at a propaganda poster. A mom passes him in the hall and does a double take. Oh right, yes, like you've never seen a man that hot before. *KEEP IT MOVING, LEEANNE!*

"So then, I'll be here at 12:30 on Friday. We'll see you tomorrow," the nanny assures me before taking Tinsley in hand and turning down the hall. Tinsley calls goodbye to me over her shoulder, and I spend a long time waving to her so I don't have to notice Logan step toward the door.

"Hey," he says, sounding a bit shy.

How a man like him has even *one* shy bone in his body is beyond me.

"Oh hello, you." I try to sound really cheery, as if nothing's happened between the last time I saw him and now. I slowly peruse him, trying not to be intimidated by our size difference.

"Do you have a second?"

I glance down the hall. "Truthfully, I've only got until the next caregiver arrives for pick-up."

He nods. "Right. Yeah. I just wanted to apologize."

"There's nothing to apologize for!" I say hurriedly, trying to emphasize how sincere I'm being. He doesn't need to feel bad that I'm so far below his league he thought of me as a charity case. "Speaking of, I actually have that envelope for you."

I dash off to get it while Briggs gathers his lunch sack, more than a little excited to see his uncle here again so soon. I'm back at the door quickly, shoving the envelope toward Logan and hoping he's not staring right at my blazing cheeks.

"Ah, well, there you go. That's all of it."

He takes it without me having to insist. *Thank god.*

"Candace, you have to know I'm a complete idiot. I thought it was a nice gesture or something. Hell, I don't know what I was thinking, but Kat told me yesterday that you thought I felt sorry for you, when in fact, I was just some guy with a crush who wasn't sure how to show it."

A CRUSH?!

I blink my eyes up at his. He looks less than impressed with himself.

"Whatever. Ignore me. I'm screwing this up." He adjusts his ball cap. "I swear, if you saw me on the field in uniform, you wouldn't even recognize this version of me. I'm usually pretty cool."

I laugh, immediately put at ease by how sweet he can be. He should be a total egomaniac stomping around the city like King Kong, but here he is, picking his nephew up from preschool, shoving that stupid envelope into the back pocket of his jeans like it's embarrassing him, and then gathering Briggs close when he runs over to give Logan a hug.

"Is there any way we could maybe start over?" Logan asks me with a lopsided smile. "You could pretend I didn't try to buy your affection like a fool?"

My heart melts a bit for him, and I nod quickly. "Of course. Consider it forgotten. And I'm sure there are tons of things I wish you would forget too. Probably, oh, I don't know"—I glance down—"how I look right now, for one?"

I arch my brows in hope as I look back up at him from beneath my lashes, but he only shakes his head, trying to hide his smile. "No can do, I'm afraid. You're too cute, paint and all."

Cute like a puppy? Or cute like a woman you desperately want to kiss?

Curse that bloody word and whoever invented it. Shakespeare, probably. Didn't he come up with all of them?

Briggs is tugging on Logan's hand now, insisting they go for ice cream, and Logan is pretending Briggs is really strong enough to carry him away. It's so cute.

"Hold on, buddy. I'm almost finished."

"Why do you want to talk to Ms. Candace for so long. Do you *liiiike* her?" Briggs scrunches his nose like the thought is as disgusting as a turd.

"Ignore him," Logan says, clearing his throat. "Now that we've started fresh, I just wanted to make sure to let you know Darius and I are having a party this weekend. Just a small group of friends—don't be intimidated."

I immediately drop my overtly intimidated expression and affect a cool-girl stance with my hand on my hip and my weight resting on the doorjamb.

"I assure you, I am *not* intimidated."

He grins. "Good. I'll text you the info if you feel like coming. Invite your roommates too."

He's halfway down the hall now, being tugged away by Briggs, so I throw him a wave and a nod.

"Yeah, cool! I'll see what I've got going on!"

If this were a movie, a godlike narrator would say to the audience, *Candace has absolutely nothing going on.*

He nods and finally turns to set off with Briggs.

It's not until he's at the door and I'm staring after him, lovesick, that another one of the preschool teachers comes up to me and tuts. "What a shame, right?"

"What?" I have to fight to pry my eyeballs off Logan's arse.

"That he's off limits."

In my head, a car screeches to a halt. "What are you talking about?"

"Don't you remember what happened to Tara? Fired for sleeping with a parent. How horrible."

"But he's not a parent."

She shrugs. "He might as well be. I'm sure the same rules apply."

She starts to walk away, so I'm forced to shout after her. "Do they though? *Do they apply?!*"

"What does it matter?" She laughs. "Logan Matthews isn't ever going to date any of us. A girl can dream though, right?"

I do dream. I dream and I dream and in every single one, Logan is doing very naughty, dirty things to me, things that make me wake up so embarrassed I can't meet my own reflection in the bathroom mirror. My toothbrush bristles say, *We know what you've been thinking about*, and as retribution, I dunk them under the stream from the faucet.

"You all right? You look like you've hardly slept a wink," Kat says, crowding into the bathroom alongside me. We've only got the one and usually I'm the first to wake up, but I'm dragging today.

"Shove over, you two," Yasmine says, cutting the shower off and reaching for her towel before she steps out to join us.

Now there are three of us in precisely one cubic centimeter of space. Yasmine's elbow catches the end of my toothbrush so it goes deeper into my mouth, nearly down my throat. I gag and only barely resist the urge to vomit before I catch myself.

"Watch it!" I hiss, hip-checking her.

"I was in here first. You two loons need to give me some proper space to get ready." She wraps the towel around herself tighter, and for a brief second, I'm flashed by her decadent curves. I'm so jealous I have the urge to vomit all over again.

Even Kat has a body guys fawn over, real tall and lean. She could be some runway model if she wanted, I swear.

Then there's me. Little ol' Candace.

NO.

I force that line of thinking right out of my head. I've never been weird about my looks. I've got good things going. My pale blonde hair always catches the sun, and my big blue eyes are the same as Mum's. I've got a small nose and a dimpled smile. My skin's pretty great, and I've got a petite figure, even if it's not overflowing with luscious curves. The only reason I've let these new insidious thoughts creep in is because I saw that girl Logan was with at District. She seemed to scream S-E-X from her hair down to her toes.

I'd bet on my life no guy has ever called her cute. Sexy, tantalizing, bodacious—yes. Cute—no way.

Whatever. It's not like it matters. As I learned yesterday, there's a good chance Logan is utterly off limits.

Oh, but doesn't that just make the whole thing even more tempting?

I yank off my pajamas and take my turn in the shower.

"Oh my god!" Yasmine gasps. "I think there's a tree between your legs!"

"Hush you! I'm going for a wax this afternoon so I've had to let it grow out a bit longer."

"Dear god. Have you checked for live critters in there? Maybe a squirrel or two?"

"Har har, very funny. Keep it up and I won't tell you about the posh party we've been invited to this weekend."

The shower curtain gets yanked to the side, and I don't even bother shrieking. I go right on washing my hair.

Yasmine and Kat stand there, prepared to interrogate me until I give them the truth. None of us cares a bit that I'm stark nude.

When I don't immediately spill the gossip—instead squeezing out another dollop of conditioner—Yasmine waves her hand impatiently.

I mime a zipper closing across my lips.

She growls in frustration. "Fine. Okay, look—if I hold my hand up a bit to block it, it's not so bad. There. It's like you don't even have a huge bush anymore. No need to go get that wax after all."

I grab the shower curtain and wrench it closed again.

"Kat, *you're* invited to Logan's party with me," I taunt.

"What?!" she screams.

"He said he'd text me the details. As soon as I know, I'll pass them along to *you*."

"Fine, okay. I'll get dinner tonight," Yasmine relents.

"*And?*"

"And wine."

"*And?*"

"What else do you want? This is called extortion, you know! It's criminal!"

"I'll take a slice of that cheesecake from the shop on the corner."

"It's like $8.00 a slice!"

"I suppose it'll just have to be Kat and me this weekend."

"Fine, you witch! I'll do it. Are you happy?"

I grin. "Pleased as Punch. Now pass me a towel, will you?"

I don't bother telling Yasmine or Kat about the minor, oh-so-small inconvenience wherein Logan might be off limits and if I so much as kiss him on the cheek, I might be fired and lose all my income and become destitute and have to move back to England and find work on the streets. Instead, I decide it's best to figure out as much as I can before bringing in the other two Stooges.

First thing Friday morning, I head straight for the headmistress's office at The Day School. I am not a rule-breaker. Truly. I once got pulled over while I was driving, and because I thought the officer was going to give me a speeding fine, I cried so hard he ended up consoling me through the window and then had to use my mobile to phone my mum to see if she could come meet me since I was no longer fit to drive. It was only later that I learned he just wanted to let me know one of my car's tail lights had gone out.

Anyway, I want to know for sure whether or not I have to keep my distance from Logan. I realize it might be all sorts of tantalizing to go after a forbidden man, but I like my job and I'm not trying to throw it away for a quick romp in the hay.

I round the corner and see Mrs. Halliday's office up ahead. Her secretary is already perched at her desk out front, and I greet her with a warm smile. I've brought them each a bribe.

"Good morning, Laura. Fancy a latte?"

She grins in surprise. "That's so nice! You didn't have to do that."

I very much did.

I pass her the Starbucks drink then offer a grin of my own. "Is Mrs. Halliday busy or could I have a little chat with her?"

Laura frowns after taking a quick sip of her latte. "Actually, she isn't here today."

"Isn't here? What do you mean?"

I'm sure all the color has drained from my face.

"Her husband is scheduled for a dental procedure, so Mrs. Halliday had to be there to drive him home after."

Bugger. Shite. Crap.

"But surely I could still reach her by phone?"

Laura takes another prolonged sip of that latte before shaking her head. "I'm afraid not. She's asked me to hold her calls today. Doesn't want to be disturbed, just in case."

It's dental work, not open-heart surgery. *For the love of—*

"Okay, I see."

I have half a mind to yank that half-empty latte right out of her hand. Some help she was!

This is worse than I was expecting. I thought I'd have a quick word with Mrs. Halliday and know one way or the other whether I'd be allowed to date Logan. Sure, yes, it's laughable that I would date him even if it weren't against the rules. I'm sort of putting the cart before the horse here, but it's in the realm of possibility at least!

Now, I have no way of knowing.

Now, I'll have to go into the weekend and be on my best behavior.

No snogging his face off. No doing a little striptease and showing him just how *not* cute I can be.

Could my life get any worse?

"OH MY GOD. UNZIP IT!"

"I can't! It's stuck!"

"Okay, hilarious. You two have had your fun, but seriously, get me out of this thing."

It's suddenly hard to breathe in this posh dressing room, like maybe they've done something to the air so we'll get a little lightheaded and forget we can't afford a single item of clothing in this store, not even a sock.

I twist away from Yasmine and try to get a good look of my back in the mirror. The zipper she had trouble getting up a few minutes ago is the culprit. It's what's keeping me in this dress that we saw in the window as we were passing by on our way to cheaper shops down the road, the ones that sell panties five to a pack.

It's a short red frock with thin crisscross straps in the back and a flirty hemline. A real showstopper.

"Oh my god, imagine if I wore that tonight?" is what I said, and Yasmine and Kat were all, "Oh, you'd knock Logan's socks off for sure," and then we sort of laughed and watched as this full-on glamazon walked out of the store with three bags in tow, a whiff of gentle perfume assaulting me as she passed by. I had a moment of absolute rage that I'd have to go to the party in a brown paper sack instead of this amazing red dress, so I whisked open the shop's door and strolled right in to find a sales associate.

"I'd like to try on that red dress in the window."

"Of course, but it's couture—" and this is where she said the designer's name, but it was all French and hard to understand, so I nodded along like I knew all about Pastrami Organza (or whatever his name was) and said, "Yes, that's the point. I only wear custom couture."

Oh, it was ace.

Yasmine and Kat kept high-fiving me while we waited in the dressing room for the woman to bring me the dress in my size. It was meant to be a bit of fun. Try it on, snap a photo of what I *could* look like if I had a few gazillion dollars to spare on clothes, and then immediately dash out of here.

That was before the zipper got stuck.

Before Yasmine and Kat both tried to pry me out of this thing.

I'm growing desperate. If the A/C weren't cranked down to arctic temperatures, I'd be sweating bullets.

"How are you girls doing in there?" the sales associate asks in her chipper tone from the other side of the door.

"FINE!"

"GREAT!"

"GOOD!"

We all shout over each other in a wave of panic, and she laughs like we're adorable before telling me to let her know if I have any issues with the dress.

Once she's gone, I do a good bit of pacing, which is relatively hard in the confines of the dressing room. Yasmine and Kat have to dart out of my way every few seconds.

"Okay, tell me again what this dress costs," I insist.

"$2,200."

"Right. But converted to British pounds, it's less, right?"

Kat looks like she's about to cry. "What does that matter?"

"I'm trying to find some silver lining! Now, Kat, you try the zipper again."

"I can't! My fingers have got blisters from the last time I tried!"

"Yasmine?"

She's the calmest out of all of us, sitting down on the bench and scrolling through her mobile now. "That zipper isn't budging. I've tried for ages already. Just tell the lady and see what she suggests we do. Surely, this sort of thing happens all the time."

"Oh, I'm afraid that's going to be a real issue. This *never* happens." is what the sales associate tells me when I cave and finally bring her in on my crisis.

Somehow, I find that very hard to believe. I'm the first person in the history of fashion to try on a dress and get stuck inside of it?

"On the plus side, it looks absolutely stunning on you. Red is definitely your color."

"That's what I told her!" Yasmine agrees.

My anger grows horns. "Right, of course. I am very glad it looks so amazing. The thing is, I've got about three pennies and some lint in my purse right now, so I won't be buying this dress. Please get it *off* me."

She does a good bit of trying with the zipper too, using all her tricks of the trade. The dress stays on, and the color drains from my face.

"I'm afraid we're in a bit of a pickle." She laughs.

I do not laugh.

"What are my options then?"

"Well…if you walk out of the store wearing the dress, I'll have to consider it shoplifting."

A horrid mugshot of me comes to mind—all bug-eyed and slack-jawed—and I shiver at the thought. I will not go to prison over this!

"And if we cut it off you," she continues, "you'll still have to purchase it. You're familiar with the 'You break it, you buy it' policy, I'm sure."

Which leaves the third option.

Fifteen minutes later, I slide my credit card across the counter toward her, trying not to cry.

"I'm so happy you decided to purchase the dress. It really does look lovely on you."

This is all my fault. This is what I get for not becoming some high-powered attorney or sugar baby or something. What about those girls whose sole job is to be "it"—y'know, just a girl who's always in fashion, or in the know, or in the cool spots around town. She gets paid just to live. I really should have applied to that job after school.

Once we cross the threshold of the store, I forbid either of my mates from discussing the dress any further. We're already late returning to our flat so we can get ready for the party. Normally, we'd walk, but I insist we spring for a cab instead since I can't exactly shower when I get home. They agree without much convincing; I think they're nervous I'm a hair's breadth away from a real breakdown.

In the cab on the way home, I calculate all the overtime hours I'll have to do at District to cover the cost of this dress. It makes me so queasy, I have to roll the window down and stick my head out. That really irks the driver. He's worried I'm going to get decapitated by an oncoming car, so I groan and bring my head back in. Probably for the best. Don't want to tempt the birds again.

I'm prepared to let my bad mood ruin the entire night when I feel my mobile vibrate on my lap.

I glance down to read the text, and my stomach flips upside down.

LOGAN: Hey C. What kind of chips do you like? I'm buying snacks for the party.

It's a silly question, and I wonder—or *hope*, rather—if he's only asking because he wants to ensure I'll actually be there. He texted yesterday with the address and time, but it looked so generic, like maybe he sent the same text to all his mates, so I only sent back a thumbs-up emoji in reply.

But this text is personal, and it makes me smile. He's called me C like we're old pals! I take my lower lip between my teeth and text him back right away.

CANDACE: Salt and vinegar, please! And they're called crisps, by the way. ;) Chips are what you get with a burger at a restaurant.

LOGAN: Seriously? Could you be more un-American?

CANDACE: Should I just don an American flag cape for the party? Maybe walk in with a twelve-pack of Bud Light on one shoulder and a bald eagle perched on the other?

LOGAN: Give me a second to regroup. That's quite the image...

CANDACE: Ha ha. Too bad! Don't go fantasizing. I've already got my dress on and it doesn't have blue and white stripes. It's red.

LOGAN: Red, huh?

CANDACE: I can practically see you salivating. You've got a bit of drool on your chin, I bet.

LOGAN: Can't help it...red's my favorite color.

The cab pulls up to our building then and we hustle up the flight of stairs to our flat. I don't get the chance to text Logan back because I'm too busy morphing into the version of myself who belongs in this fancy red dress. Yasmine goes wild with my hair, curling it and teasing it and then combing through it so it's this mass of blonde waves when all's said and done. I take so long applying my makeup that they start shouting for me to hurry up.

"We're already late! At this rate, we'll arrive just in time to help the lads clean up!" Kat warns.

"I'm coming!" I shout back, leaning in close to confirm my eyeliner is perfectly symmetrical on both eyes. I can't take any chances. It feels absolutely necessary. Then I swipe on some red lipstick—something I never bother with, but tonight it's perfect. It makes my lips look edible.

I'm buzzing in the back of the cab as we traverse Manhattan from our lowly borough to some otherworldly area where the streets are treelined and the flowerbeds are well manicured. Logan's apartment is going to knock my socks off. I know, because the doorman of his building is wearing white gloves and a little boxy hat as he ushers us in like we're royalty. He only lets us pass because we've told him we're here for Logan's party, and he has to check a list to confirm our names are printed there. They are! WILD! WHAT KIND OF PLACE IS THIS?! Another attendant guides us through the lobby toward a bank of lifts. He holds a keycard up to an invisible panel on the lift wall and then the doors glide shut. I feel absolutely out of my element.

"Is this real? People live like this?"

"Some people," Yasmine says, fidgeting with her hair. She grew up with wealth, sure, but nothing like this. This lift is probably inlaid with real gold and the blood of extinct leopards or something. It whisks us higher, away from the city and toward Mount Olympus, or so it feels.

Once we're on the twentieth floor, the doors slide open and here we are: out in a hallway with a single door that's propped open for guests. It leads right into the penthouse flat.

I see an absolute crush of people inside as we stroll closer. My heels carry me across the marble foyer as I hug my coat tighter around my red dress, but then Kat notices and her eyes widen.

"Off. Take it off. *Quick!*"

The coat gets yanked off immediately, and Kat takes it along with hers and sort of shoves them under her arm. Smart move, really, because when we walk in and see the guests, it's obvious my checkered coat wouldn't have really blended in. There're proper celebrities here—ones I know by name! There are beautiful women popping up around every corner, all dressed in slinky numbers or barely-there tops and skirts.

I think that girl there is a pop star I like, or maybe she just *looks* like a pop star? I can't be certain.

Before we make it past the front hall, we pass off our coats to an attendant, and our mobiles too after they demand it. Apparently, famous people have to worry about normal people like us snapping photos they don't want leaked to the press. I comply right away, partly because I understand their reasoning and partly because the attendant looks quite intimidating. I don't want him thinking I'm trying to break the rules or anything.

"Do *not* leave my side," I hiss to Yasmine and Kat after we're done in the entry. I'm worried we'll get split up and won't be able to find one another again.

Logan told me this would be a small gathering, but this is a circus of beautiful people all clamoring to have a chat with one another. They pay us absolutely no mind. We might as well be pieces of furniture. One man even tries to set his drink on Kat's shoulder while he's not looking, and she has to sort of yelp and leap out of the way to keep it from happening. You'd think he'd be bloody embarrassed about it, but he doesn't even notice!

"Let's just find Logan, yeah?" I suggest, though I'm not sure that will make things any better.

This is his party. He's the ringleader of this circus, and my stomach hurts at the thought. How is that possible? This place is so posh, so upscale, so bloody expensive! Have I imagined that text exchange from earlier? When he asked about the chips? He seemed so charming and down to earth, but this party is the exact opposite.

In one corner of the modern living room, there's a whole buffet that's clearly been catered by a world-class chef. The food is up on silver platters with heating lamps and delicate accoutrement I'd probably mistakenly eat only to find out after that it's only for show. It all looks amazing, and there are tons of tiny samples of tasty treats, but absolutely *no one* is eating. I see a woman pass by the table, stutter-step, glance down longingly at some pasta dish, and then dash away from it like it might make her arse grow two sizes right then and there if she doesn't get away quick enough.

But it's the sight at the very end of the table that catches my eye. It's like one of those childhood puzzles: Find What Doesn't Belong. Next to the fancy silver platters and serving dishes, there's a big red bowl of crisps. Salt and vinegar, just as I requested.

I nearly topple over in sheer bliss. Not only has he thought of me, it's obvious what he intended by leaving them out like that. I don't even bother cluing in Kat or Yasmine. They wouldn't get it. *You see the crisps are actually this huge romantic gesture!* But they're just crisps. *Right, but he asked specifically what kind I wanted!* He could have asked you for your favorite flower if he wanted to be romantic.

Besides, even if I thought they'd agree about how sweet the gesture is, I don't get the chance to bring it up, because just then, across the living room, I finally spot Logan.

The sight of him is a punch straight to my stomach. He's wearing dark jeans and a black long-sleeved shirt pushed up to his elbows. He's shaven his jaw so it's smooth and sharp. His hair looks divine, the short strands almost curly. He's so dark and moody you want to think he'd be a real arsehole, but I know the truth. I know he's put out that bowl of crisps for me. I know how sweet he is underneath all those layers of muscle.

The only problem is I can't quite get to him. There are half a dozen women around him, stuck to him like macaroni on a child's art piece. They're glued in place so that if he shifts an inch to the left, so do they.

If I want to talk to him, I'll have to join the queue.

I'm going to kill Darius. No, not just kill him—I'll be sure to torture him first. Slowly. This party was his idea. *C'mon, you need to celebrate your achievements! You're at the top of your game!*

I relented because I didn't want to be a stick in the mud, but I told him, firmly, that I only wanted ten people here.

He countered with fifty.

I told him twenty-five *max*.

He didn't argue after that and I assumed I'd gotten my way, but now I see that's only because the asshole wasn't listening to me anyway. He planned on doing it his way the entire time.

To say I'm uncomfortable with this many people in my apartment is an understatement. I keep glancing over to make sure no one is sneaking off down the hall toward my bedroom. In my life, practically nothing is sacred. The press knows every detail about every person, place, or thing in my world, sometimes before I do. This apartment has always been my sanctuary.

At least it was before tonight.

"I can't believe how nice your apartment is. Did you design it yourself?"

The question is asked by a pretty girl with a pretty face wearing a pretty dress. She told me her name when her friends cornered me a few minutes ago, but how am I supposed to remember it when there's a baker's dozen of them all talking at once?

"Uh, no. I don't even remember. Maybe it came this way?"

My move to New York was all a blur. I finished playing football in college, signed a deal with the pros, moved from Florida on a Sunday and was due at practice the very next morning. My agent helped me find this place and set up the move. I don't even think I unpacked a single box. I got home after practice and my life was set up for me, cable and all.

"Well the location is *great*. You've got the city at your fingertips."

When she says fingertips, hers reach out to touch my arm, and I glance down, more than a little annoyed. Where's Darius? This is his party. These are his friends. I know like ten people here, and they're all my teammates.

I hear a familiar voice and glance up to see Melody cutting through the crowd of women to get to me. I'm relieved to see her up until she wraps me in a hug then lays a possessive arm around my waist as she steps to take the place at my side.

"You sure know how to draw a crowd," she teases.

I let her keep her arm around me for a second, and then as graciously as possible, I step out of her hold.

"You have Darius to thank for that."

She laughs and crosses her arms, her expression tightening slightly as I pull away from her. "No, I mean these girls."

The jealousy is a little unwarranted considering I've made it clear I don't see us moving forward. After our second date, it was pretty obvious to me that I have absolutely no feelings for her. We haven't talked since then and I didn't even invite her here tonight, but I guess Darius took it upon himself to do that too.

"What have you been up to these last few weeks? Busy as usual?" She doesn't give me time to reply before continuing, "God, District was *so* fun."

Was it? I felt like an ass for ignoring her for half the night. I assumed she was as done with me as I was with her.

"Are you two friends?"

This question is asked by one of the women standing around us, and it's perfect timing, actually, because I spot Candace across the room and my heart starts to thunder in my chest. She came. She's here. She's over by the food and she's somehow managed to corral one of the circulating waiters. Instead of taking food from his tray, she's just talking to him, as if all the famous people in the room mean nothing to her. She'd rather spend her night talking with the hired help.

He throws his head back and laughs, and she's laughing too. Then he says something and goes over to load up his tray with more tiny portions he can dole out to the crowd. She reaches out for his tray, asking him something, and he passes it over, letting her hold it while he fills it up.

He nods in thanks and leaves to continue doing his job. Now she's left all alone.

I'm not sure if her roommates came with her, but they're not by her side now. She glances around and then, seemingly at a loss for what to do, she sort of starts to bob to the music before finally noticing me watching her.

She beams and lifts her hand, waving enthusiastically.

I wave back as my stomach clenches tight, and it's obvious why. She's so beautiful, like she's the only one in the room with a real pulse.

That red dress is a blaring fire engine drawing my attention. It's cut so short on her legs, and they look miles long even though they can't be; she's not that tall. Her blonde hair is curly and loose, framing her sweet face and red lips. She's a candy confection standing there all alone.

She keeps my attention and holds up her finger as she steps back to motion at the chip bowl. She makes a real show of reaching in to grab one then winks at me as she pops it into her mouth.

I'm totally enamored, a smile stretching so wide across my face my cheeks start to ache.

It's like she's the best TV show I've ever watched and I have to know what happens next.

I raise my drink to my mouth as she starts to dance. She lifts her hand to pinch her nose then shimmies low like she's going under water. Next, it's the Sprinkler. After that, she loads groceries into her cart. I'm smiling, and it feels like she's hijacked the whole party. No one else is here, just her and her ridiculous dance moves and her bright red lips—right up until a guy cuts her off mid-spin. He must compliment her because her cheeks burn bright pink. Then he says something else and she motions back to the chip bowl. He reaches in for some of his own, and just like that, they're talking.

I don't know him, but he looks like a wolf ready to eat her alive. He stares down at her in that red dress, and I can see his thoughts scrolling across his head like they're printed in a little bubble. *Where has this tiny red pixie been all my life?*

I'm moving before I'm consciously aware of it, not bothering to say bye to Melody or the other women I've been forced to endure for the last half hour. I'm across the room and in front of Candace, casting my shadow down on her before I've taken my next breath.

"They're so good, right? Definitely an underrated flavor."

That's the guy talking, trying to wow her with a discussion about the chips I bought for her.

"Do I know you?" I ask him brusquely.

His eyes widen and he pauses with a chip halfway into his mouth. Then he drops it back into his other hand, wipes his palm on his jeans, and extends it out to me. "Oh shit! No. I came with Paul, but I'm a huge fan. I mean *huge*. That Hail Mary pass you threw against Miami this season was just—" He mimes his head exploding.

Beside him, Candace mimes the same thing.

My sour mood lifts immediately.

She nods enthusiastically, playing along. "Right? Best pass I've ever seen. *Huge*. Really changed the whole inning."

"Quarter," I correct her. "Innings are in baseball."

"Are they? *Bugger*. I was so close."

I think I'll kiss her then, take her red lips for myself in front of the whole party, but I hold off for some insane reason. Maybe out of fear, maybe out of some desire to prolong the inevitable. I'll kiss her before the night's over; that much I know.

"If you'll excuse me," I say to the guy beside her without looking his way. "I need to talk to my date."

77

"Your date? Oh. Right." He takes a pointed step back. "Sorry, man. I had no idea. I wasn't flirting with her."

He gets the hint that I don't really care what else he has to say and wanders off. Candace waggles her eyebrows at me.

"Date, huh?"

"Yes. *Date.*"

"Am I one of the flock? You've got quite a few women over there shooting daggers at me. I'm not trying to step on anyone's toes."

"Even if you did, it wouldn't hurt."

"Tonight, it would," she says, pointing down to her heels. They're not sky-high, but they still have a thin spindly heel that could do some damage.

"Sounds like quite a threat."

"You'll do well to remember that whenever you feel like getting handsy. Are those crisps for me?" she asks, pointing over her shoulder.

"*Chips.* Yes. Who else?"

"I just wanted to be sure. It's a nice gesture, buying me *crisps.*"

"*Chips.*"

"Whatever, agree to disagree I suppose. I probably say quite a bit that would annoy you. For instance, you lot call them bathing suits, but we usually call them bathers or swimming costumes."

"Swimming costumes? Sounds like something you wear to cover you from neck to knees."

"The ones I wear do," she quips with a wink.

"Oh yeah?" I nod outside, to the pool on the outdoor balcony. "I can't wait to find out."

Her eyes go wide. "You're kidding! You've got a pool all the way up here too? What in the—" She shakes her head in disbelief. "That's it—in my next life, I'm coming back bloody *loaded*. No rearing children for $2 an hour. I'll be a Saudi sheikh or some warlord, just you wait."

"I can see it now. You seem just the type."

She reaches out and throws a punch at my arm as retribution for teasing her and it's probably supposed to hurt me, but I don't even flinch. I catch her hand before she draws it back, and I twine our fingers together. We're touching palm to palm. Blood rushes south. It's such an innocent touch, like something two teenagers would do, and yet, standing here, holding her hand in front of everyone feels as intimate as anything I've ever done in the privacy of my bedroom.

"You're overwhelming, y'know," she says, blinking her blue eyes up at me. "I already thought you were too good to be true with the hair and the face and the arse, but then I come here and it's like you're a real prince, fancy palace and all. You'll make some girl really happy someday."

She tugs her hand free and turns away.

I frown, not quite sure what she means by that. Everything I've done, every flirtatious move has been to show her I'm interested in her, to show her I'd like to make *her* happy if she'd give me the chance.

"There's Yasmine and Kat!" she says, waving them over. "They went to find the loo ages ago, but they probably got lost in the west wing or something."

Once they reach us, any chance I have of getting a private moment with her will be gone. I can't let it happen like that, her slipping through my fingers, quick as sand. I've been in motion for so long, on and off the football field, going from one play to the next, listening to my coaches and my agents and my financial advisers and my nutritionists and my trainers. I'm so good at shifting from one task to another that I've completely left out this huge chunk, the personal part of it all, the *life* part of living.

"Candace, are you seeing anyone?"

She barks out a laugh. "When have I got the time? *Before* or *after* my shifts at the school and District? Oh right, maybe I can pencil the bloke in for a quick lay on Sunday evenings. Then it's lights out by ten so I'm not a total snooze at school on Monday morning."

Her friends are approaching, and I only have a few more seconds. I have to know—do I even have a shot with her?

"So that's it? You're too busy for me?"

"For *you*?"

"Don't act surprised. I admitted my crush the other day."

She looks like she needs to lie down or maybe soak herself in an ice bath.

She's rubbing her forehead and looking away, frustrated. "I do remember that, though I thought my brain was having a go at me. Listen, you're lovely, just the sort of guy I'd go for if I could, but I can't."

I reach out for her hand so I can grip it and assure myself she's real.

"Why? Why can't we try this?"

Her blue eyes pierce through me when she replies, "Because you're off limits, I'm afraid."

Oh dear. Logan looks like I've just shot him straight through the heart with an arrow.

Maybe this is how David felt right after he hit Goliath with that rock. How in the world have I managed to inflict pain on a man as gorgeous and charming as Logan? I feel horrible.

My hand shoots out to grab his arm. It's a real hulking muscle, and I do get distracted for a moment, squeezing it under my fingers and feeling just how bulky it is. God, he must eat loads of protein. Hopefully he's not one of those wankers who shoots raw eggs down his gullet in the morning though. Blech.

Then I drag my attention away from his hard-earned muscles and up to his eyes…the lovely brown eyes that look utterly wounded right now. I feel bad all over again. I don't want to be David.

"Listen, okay, it's not that bad. It's just I don't know the rules at The Day School yet. This teacher got axed last year for having sex with a student's dad, and I know you're not Briggs' dad, but you're his uncle, and maybe that's just as bad? I tried to—"

"We're back! *Finally*. My feet hurt just from walking to the loo and back. This place is huge," Kat says, sounding as if she's just climbed Everest and she needs to take a load off.

"It really did take forever what with all the doors. I swore we went into like fifteen bedrooms before we ended up in the line for the loo," Yasmine agrees. "Anyway, who's this?" She looks Logan up and down, her brows shooting up to her hairline like she's mighty impressed. "Oh right…"

She's finally connected the photos of him from Google to the real-life thing.

"This is Logan," I say, motioning between the three of them. "Logan, these are my flatmates, Yasmine and Kat."

"Right. So you're Logan, Mr. Celebrity Athlete and all. Real pleasure to meet you." Kat extends her hand. "Quite a nice set of bricks you have here. What's the square footage on a place like this?"

Yasmine groans and cuts in before Logan can answer. "Kat, you can't just ask someone that. It's so crass."

"What? Seems like if someone is going to spend this much on a flat, they'd want to show it off."

He shakes her hand then looks to me with a pleading expression, as if hoping I'll explain that these aren't my friends at all, but rather two psychos I plucked off the street as a joke. *Funny, right? Anyhoo, they'll be leaving now.* But alas, it is what it is. Crazy attracts crazy, and we three come as a trio.

"Now that my friends have introduced themselves, I think you should take us out to your pool."

"Yes!" Kat agrees, clapping her hands together enthusiastically.

82

"Okay sure. Let's go," Logan agrees. "Let me just grab a drink first."

We head to the bar, and he asks the bartender for a water.

"Are you sober?" I ask, trying to keep my voice down. "No judgment or anything. I've got an uncle who did AA."

He looks confused for a second before seeing my gaze on his water. "Oh no. I just don't drink much. I already had a beer earlier, so I'm cutting myself off. My trainer can always tell if I've been drinking the night before a session, and it's not worth the extra sprints."

"Right. Then I won't drink either." I turn to the bartender. "Water for me too. On the rocks."

He looks thoroughly confused. "What?"

I fidget a bit. "I was just being cheeky. Can I just get it with some ice, please?"

He still doesn't laugh, but he does get me a cup of water with loads of ice. Once Yasmine and Kat have their wine, we set off toward the porch. I expect it to be freezing once we step outside, and I nearly run back in for my coat. But then, instead of icy air blasting my face, I'm met by pockets of warmth. There are huge heaters set up around the perimeter of the balcony, making it so you can stand anywhere outside and still feel comfortable, so much so that there are a good number of people in the pool. They're brave souls who've stripped down to their knickers and are splashing around in the water. One of the guys shouts for Logan to come over, and Logan waves to him before turning to us.

"Make yourselves at home. I'll be right back."

I watch, feeling bereft as he walks away.

With Logan by our side, we belong. With him gone, I suddenly feel like a fish out of water. At least we have each other, I suppose. We circle the pool until we reach the side of the balcony opposite the flat. There, we dare each other to stand at the very edge, right against the glass railing that seems much too flimsy to support my full weight. I manage two and a half seconds with the city hovering below me before darting back to safety with a little squeak.

"That's mad! Look way down there. I think that's a dog!" Kat shouts, pointing down to the city street.

My stomach rolls at the sight of her leaning over like that. "Do you have to stand over there? I swear you'll topple over if a decent gust of wind blows past."

At my warning, she pretends to slip, and I nearly lose my stomach. Then she and Yasmine roll into a fit of laughter, and I threaten to excommunicate the pair of them.

While we're over there, more people flood out onto the balcony, and I think it's because Logan's out here now. He's still with his friends, a group of guys taunting each other near the edge of the pool. I smile as I watch him with them, so carefree and confident. It's clear they're all a bit in awe of him. I suppose I am too.

I drift over to the edge of the pool closest to me as I consider how lucky Logan is to have so much outdoor space this high up off the ground. It really looks nice too, not just concrete and glass. There's artificial grass laid down between the pool edge and the glass railing of the balcony. He's also got huge trees in planters dotting the sides, so it's like we're in a proper garden instead of on some floating space-age balcony.

A huge splash draws my attention back to the pool, and I look back just in time to see Logan surface from the water. He whips his wet hair back and he's got a huge smile on his face. His friends are laughing, though not for long, because another two of them get tossed in next, and then the whole lot of them splash in. Even way over on my end, my legs get sprayed, and I take a step back, just in case.

"I'm going in," Kat says, already in the process of yanking off her dress.

"Ditto. The pool is heated and lovely," Yasmine says with a groan of pleasure. "I haven't been swimming in ages."

I'm ready to join them and strip too then look down and remember I'm still wearing the expensive red dress that's now fused with my body. There's no getting it off, and I certainly can't wear it into the pool. Given how much I paid for it, I suppose I'll just be wearing it forever.

"You coming in?" Kat asks, laying her clothes on a lounger behind us. She looks lovely in her black knickers and bra set, real tall and lithe.

"I can't, remember?" I fiddle with the edge of my dress. "You two go. I'll sit on the edge, over there by the stairs. Come swim over to me."

They take each other's hands and leap in together, laughing while they do it. I envy them as I curve around to the other side, watching everyone bobbing up and down in the water. I've never wanted to swim as badly as I do now. I bet the water feels good, and even with the heaters on, I'm still a bit chilly in my lightweight dress.

The stairs are all but abandoned since most of the crowd is gathering in the deep end. I take full advantage, hiking the skirt of my dress up around my upper thighs and stepping down until the warm water laps up to my calves.

I hear someone swim closer and glance up, expecting Yasmine and Kat, but it's Logan, alone, wading through the water in my direction.

He looks as threatening as a shark, mostly hidden under the surface, coming straight for me. I freeze for a moment, watching him as he gets closer, and then he stands, peeling his tall frame out of the water, droplets dripping down his body. His dark hair is pushed back off his forehead. His shirt is stuck to his chest, showing off every ridge and contour of his pecs and abs. My jaw drops a bit before I can help it.

"Not getting in?" he asks.

"I can't."

"Worried about taking your clothes off?"

"No. Well, not exactly. I literally *can't* take this dress off."

He furrows his dark brows. "What do you mean?"

"It's a long story and I think it'll only make you laugh, so I can't say. I'm trying hard to make sure you take me seriously, so it's best if I don't tell you."

He comes closer with a sinister look in his eyes. "Tell me or I'll dunk you, dress and all."

"No!" I hold my arms out to keep him at bay, though I know it's futile. He could do whatever he wanted with me and I couldn't stop him. I shiver. *What a thought.*

His wet hand shoots out to wrap around my forearm, his grip closing around it so easily it almost scares me.

"Logan!" It's no use. Even the serious tone I employ with the naughty toddlers at The Day School doesn't earn me his respect.

"One…"

He starts to count, and I know when he gets to three, I'm going in.

"I can't! It's embarrassing!"

"Two…"

"Right okay. Just hold on, will you?!"

"Three…"

"LOGAN!"

He tugs me and I'm in the water, dunked under so I'm wet from head to toe when I surface again, sputtering water in my absolute rage.

"OH MY GOD! YOU RUINED THE MOST EXPENSIVE THING I OWN!"

I think I'm going to cry. Really. My bottom lip is quivering. Logan swims over and doesn't stop until he's right in front of me, touching me, gathering me close. His body is so warm, and I don't push away even though he more than deserves it.

"What are you going on about?" he asks, pushing my wet hair off my face. "Is the dress really that expensive?"

My stomach squeezes tight as I admit the truth. "Over twenty-two hundred dollars with tax and everything. Don't look at me like that! I didn't want to buy it. Don't think I'm some girl who spends money she doesn't have, but I tried it on as a laugh, and well, the zipper got stuck and I couldn't exactly cut myself out of it. It's couture—custom! And now it's ruined!"

I look down at the material in the water and ignore the fact that the red chiffon looks quite pretty floating up all around me. This is no time for frivolity!

I'm right up against Logan now, wet chest to wet chest. He has his arms wrapped around me and we're bobbing while he listens to my hysterical rambling.

I'm faintly aware of him repeating my name, trying to get me to calm down, but it's useless. I'm going to go haul myself over that glass wall. It's the only solution. Yaz and Kat can use my life insurance to pay off my dress debt.

Logan's hand drifts up to my chin, and he lifts it gently until I'm forced to look him right in the eyes. His dark lashes are wet and thick, and his brown eyes sear into me in such a lovely way. If I had any talent for art, I'd want to paint him like this, right up close so the world could see him from this angle and we could all collectively swoon.

"I'll buy you a new one," he promises.

Then his hand leaves my face and snakes around the back of my dress, our gazes staying locked as if he's put me under a spell. I'm only half aware of everything going on around me: the soft feel of the wet fabric against my skin, the way our hips keep bumping together beneath the surface of the water, how much he overcrowds me when I'm not even backed into a corner. Then his fingers find the top of my zipper and he tugs, not gently. He pulls like he's on a mission, one he completes much too quickly. I hear the telltale sound of expensive fabric tearing and the dress splits in two, filling with water and starting to slide off my body.

I look down in absolute shock. A delayed reaction if there ever was one.

"I'll buy you a new one," he swears, again, stripping the material away.

"Well now you'll have to! You tore it!"

"What was your plan, exactly?" he says, tipping his head in such a boyish way that I almost, for a second, forget how intimidating he can be.

"Simple—to wear it every day until I die."

"Uh-huh."

"Please go get your checkbook right now," I say, pointing back inside his flat. "I'll wait. Make the check out to Candace Williams. That's C-A-N-D-A-C-E. I'll cash it in the morning."

"Sure thing…right after we're done swimming," he says with a cocky smile as he finishes yanking my dress off me.

I've been unclothed by a few lads in my day, and there's always been a lot of fumbling fingers and nervous laughter. Not this time. Oh, no. Logan is stripping me in front of a crowd of people, and it's like he's done the gesture a thousand times before. Very practiced, this man.

I'm highly aware that my knickers are not at all modest. They cut high up along my arse so that most of it is exposed, not quite a thong, but not that far off. Thank god I went for that wax! My bra is no better. I wore a strapless one when we went dress shopping, and the nude material has gone nearly see-through.

"I'm practically naked!"

"Hardly," Logan says, a wicked look in his eyes as he gathers my most prized possession, wads it into a ball, and tosses it out of the pool. Red fabric heaps beside a lounger, and now I'm stuck, in here with him, with barely any clothes on.

"Give me your tee!" I say, swimming closer and starting to pry the wet material off his abs. "It'll cover me well enough. Probably go down to my ankles with any luck."

"Sure thing," he says, reaching back in that ultra-sexy way to yank his shirt up and off in one fell swoop. Then he holds it out for me, and I reach for it. As soon as my fingers touch it, he jerks it away and tosses it out beside my dress. "Actually, why bother? It's sopping wet. You don't want to put it on anyway."

My eyes are wide as saucers. I'm pretty sure my jaw is dropped so low my chin is skimming the surface of the water. "I *did* want it, you cow! Now look what you've done. You're there, all nude and glorious and tan, and I haven't got a stitch of clothing to put on. We're basically in a porno!"

He grins. "Want my jeans?"

"Oh har har. *Funny guy.* Sure, give me those and let me put them on so I don't moon everyone and give them a fright on my way out of the pool."

89

At the depth we're standing in, his chest is up out of the water; meanwhile, I'm up to my neck, basically treading water to stay alive. It's getting a bit difficult as I've got the upper body strength of an infant. He sees me starting to struggle and reaches out for my hand, dragging me toward the shallow end. I let him, right up until my breasts are about to crest the water, and then I yank my hand back.

"That's enough, you rascal. I know what you're after. Trying to get a peek, are we?"

He shrugs as if he's not even a little remorseful, and then he sweeps his wet hair off his face. "Can't blame a guy for trying."

"Good to know what you're really like under all that charm and hair—a naughty little bugger. Now give me your trousers like you promised."

He reaches down to undo the button on his jeans, and I go a bit lightheaded from watching him. Water sluices down his toned abs. They are, without a doubt, the best set of muscles I've ever seen. He's so tall and lean, but built too, like every part of him is in tip-top shape, not a centimeter gone to waste. He's got this fabulously sharp Adonis V that basically draws my eyes down to where I should not under any circumstances look, but well, *sue me*, because I do. I have no choice. My eyeballs are glued to him as he starts to take off his trousers and reveals a pair of navy Calvin Klein boxer briefs. I'd bet they pay him a million dollars to wear those and represent their brand. They'd be stupid not to.

In my head, I'm quite a perv, so obviously I try to get a good look at what he's got going on *down there*, but everything below his waistline is under the water and it's fairly dark out here. *Oy, someone turn a spotlight on, will you?*

Once my eyes go a bit cross from all the struggling, I finally blink and force my gaze up to his face. He's looking right at me, like he's been waiting ages for my eyes to get to his. He's grinning. The bastard.

"Seen enough?"

"Quite," I snap, snatching his jeans away from him and trying to struggle into them.

It's not possible to do it at this depth. I'm not some aquatic acrobat who can balance and float and don clothing all at once. I huff and start for an even shallower section of the pool, but then cool air hits my chest and I duck under again, sending Logan a searing glare.

He shrugs, like he had absolutely nothing to do with my faux pas this time, but from the gleam in his gaze, I can tell he's benefitted from it.

I learn my lesson and trudge forward a few more steps, this time with my back turned to him so my hair acts like a curtain against my skin. I shimmy into his jeans, and once I've got them pulled all the way up, I realize there's still half a leg of material dragging on the pool bottom. I groan and lift each leg to roll up the denim so they fit nicely. Then I cinch the waistband in my hand and turn around.

"How do I look?"

"Like you're wearing a pair of men's jeans that are about ten sizes too big."

"It's not my fault you've got a fat arse."

It's an obvious joke since Logan hasn't got an ounce of fat on him.

"Cute. You look cute," he amends.

I groan. "What is it with me and that word?!"

"You don't like it?"

"A hamster is cute. A fat little gerbil—*aw, it's so cute.* For once, I want to be called something other than cute."

"I didn't think I was allowed to tell you what I really think."

His voice has gone all menacing and romantic. Oh dear.

"That's right," I say, starting to back up, because he's getting rather close again. He's got this feral look in his eyes, like he's not quite sure what he'll do with me once he catches me. "You can't. It's against the rules."

"Whose rules, exactly? Do you have an employee handbook I can take a look at? I bet there's nothing in there about dating a student's uncle."

I'm flustered now, because he keeps getting closer and my back hits the edge of the pool and I'm stuck, waiting there for him to devour me. My stomach tumbles around like I'm on a rollercoaster or being chased by a hulking beast. My free hand shoots out right as he reaches me, and my palm flattens against the center of his chest. A little more pressure from him and my arm bends like a spaghetti noodle. *So much for attempting a bit of distance…*

His leg slides between mine and he sandwiches me against the edge of the pool. Thank god I put on his jeans or we'd be skin to skin down there. My wet knickers wouldn't protect me one bit.

I'm losing myself quickly. I feel my sanity slipping as his hands reach out below the surface of the water to grip my waist so he can position me against his hips. Oh Lordy. I'm done for.

His head tilts toward mine, and I even lift my chin a bit on impulse before remembering the rules.

"We can't kiss," I say, my voice little more than a whisper.

"Right," he says, moving his head farther toward mine. "We can't kiss."

His lips hover there, so close to mine it's like we're kissing without kissing, toeing the line so closely we're millimeters from tipping over it altogether.

My heart is in my throat.

My legs are wrapped around his hips, holding him captive against me.

His hands tighten on my waist and he looks like he's in pain, staving off our attraction like this. Then he groans and makes it clear he is.

"Who are you, Candace Williams?"

"Just some loon from across the pond."

The corners of his mouth rise in amusement. "You're maddening."

I frown. "Oh no. That doesn't sound good."

"It isn't. You're not good for me. You know there's a whole party full of people watching us right now. I've never kissed a girl in public. Now I have a hundred people staring as I pin you against the edge of my pool."

"Well when you say it like that…"

I damn near shiver.

"I won't kiss you," he promises, his gaze on my mouth.

"It feels like you're about to."

He hitches me up higher on his hips so he's got a proper hold on me. God, it's perfect—how strong he feels between my legs, how hard he is right now even though we're not technically doing anything, just touching each other, just absorbing each other through our pores.

His mouth nears again and my eyes flutter. It's coming. Every fiber of my being knows Logan is about to kiss me and ruin me forever. I expect it. I want it.

Then…it doesn't come, and I'm the one in pain now. Real pain. My chest is aching from it. I let out a little whimper, like some sad dog whose tail's just been stepped on, then I lean into him, wrap my arms around his neck, and hug him as tightly as I can. It's not a kiss. It's not mouth to mouth, but it's the closest I've been to him and it's heaven all the same. He's warm even now, like a heating lamp beneath my fingers. I can't get a proper grip on him as he's so much bigger than me, but I try. I let my head fall to the crook of his neck and my lips graze his skin.

He groans and gathers me close, tangling his hands in my hair.

"What are we doing?" I whisper, genuinely perplexed.

What. Are. We. Doing.

This isn't normal.

Proper humans don't act like this. I've been on plenty of dates in my day. Good ones. Bad ones. Long ones. Short ones. They've never consisted of stripteases in a pool followed up by playful banter that quickly devolves into a hug that makes me feel like the world will end when it ends.

"It's just a hug, Candace."

It sounds like he's assuring himself as much as he's assuring me.

"*Oy!* You two!" Kat shouts from across the pool. "Ever going to snog, or are you just going to do a bit of touchy-feely mumbo jumbo? We're all getting a bit restless over here, waiting for *the* moment!"

My face goes red. Hideously red. Oh dear.

"We've been found out." I laugh.

"We were never hiding all that well in the first place," he counters playfully.

"Right. Whatever. I suppose it's time we rejoin the party? Take a bit of a breather?"

It's the absolute last thing I want to do, but we have no choice. We're not alone out here. We're in a crowd of people. We can't run off and hide away in his room. We aren't allowed. We're stuck breaking apart and cooling off, and I hate that I feel like crying. Even though we haven't *technically* done anything wrong, it certainly feels like we have.

"Let's go, wankers, or we're going to be late!"

"I don't think you ought to call us wankers right before we go to church!" Yasmine shouts from inside the shower.

Kat dips her head out of the bathroom with her mascara wand in hand. "I still don't understand why we've got to go in the first place. None of us are all that religious."

I rifle through my closet, looking for the most modest outfit I own, something with long sleeves that I can button up to the bottom of my chin. "It's important! I've got a lot of repenting to do after last night. I'll ask for forgiveness, and then once my soul is cleansed or whatnot, we can go out for some coffee and avocado toast—a proper Sunday brunch."

"I hope God is okay with us being a bit late," Yasmine adds. "I've still got to shave my legs."

"Don't bother!" I groan. "Jesus doesn't care if your legs are silky smooth!"

"Do you think there'll be any cute blokes there?" Kat asks.

"*Kat*," I hiss in annoyance.

She shrugs, unbothered. "Doesn't matter. I've got my eye on one of Logan's teammates anyway. We chatted for ages last night."

"He only asked you where the loo was," Yasmine points out, contradicting her.

Kat rolls her eyes, as if exasperated. "Yes, and then I pointed him in the right direction, and he said, 'Thanks,' and I said, 'Cheers.'"

"Then what?" I ask, flipping through shirts, angry that they all seem to be something a sinner would wear. Red?! Spaghetti straps?! *Really, Eve?!* Where are all my denim dresses that reach the floor? My paisley tops with the ruffle neck detail? Oh right—I don't own any.

"Then he walked away and went to have a piss, but I could tell we had a real connection. A sort of back-and-forth wordplay, if you will."

"Sounds like it. Hey, I'm borrowing your blazer!"

It's all I've got. I'll throw it on over a white button-down and do it all the way up if I have to.

The church itself is just the closest one I could find to our flat with a service starting in the middle of the morning. We're late, thanks to Yasmine's shaving, but we tiptoe down the aisle and toward the first empty seats we can manage in the third row from the back.

The catholic priest is already up on the stage with his flowing robes, chatting away in a thick New York accent. I swear I can barely understand a thing he's saying, but I'll

98

have to nod along convincingly all the same and hope God can't tell the difference. It's a solid plan up until Kat trips and tumbles into me so that we both end up going down onto the red carpet in the aisle with little yelps. When we stand and dust ourselves off, we get quite a few sidelong glares from old grans.

"*Sorry!*" I whisper under my breath.

One of them holds her finger up to her mouth and shushes me, and I shove Kat and Yasmine into their seats before they can cause any more trouble.

The Catholic mass is great. I learn a lot, I think. I couldn't quite repeat it back to someone if they asked, but I'm sure I've absorbed it all like a sponge. Right, well, except for the bit near the end. It's not that I meant to nod off; it's that Logan kept us at his house so late last night that I didn't get much sleep. It seems I must have missed the part about forgiving sins because before I know it, it's over and we're supposed to stand and leave.

"Where am I meant to confess?" I ask Kat and Yasmine. "You know 'Forgive me, Father, for I have sinned.' That whole spiel."

I look around for the confession box but don't see one. Maybe we should try that Buddhist temple around the block.

"What have you got to confess? What on earth have you done wrong?" Kat asks.

"She's right. You teach snot-nosed toddlers all day, for Christ's sake."

"I don't think you're meant to say *Christ* like that in a church, you know."

Only now *I've* said it louder than she has so *I'm* the one who gets a glare from the woman in front of us in the queue down the aisle.

"Honestly, you're so good all the time," Kat continues. "You never leave your dirty dishes in the sink like the rest of us, and you always empty the rubbish bin."

"Yes, but I've broken the rules, haven't I? Canoodling with Logan in the pool like that."

"Oh, sod off. You can't be serious. So the two of you sort of flirted a bit. Surely your headmistress can't take issue with that?"

I suppose I'll find out.

First thing tomorrow morning.

I have plans to go round to Mrs. Halliday's office and give it to her straight as soon as I arrive. She'll admire my bravery and tact. She'll think I'm a wonderful representation of her staff. Maybe she'll even use me as an example in front of the rest of the teachers. *If only you lot were half as wonderful as Candace.*

Except I don't get the chance because of Yasmine and her insistence that we try out a new sushi place on the way back from church.

I should have known from its location that we were in for it. A dimly lit alley—*really?*

To me, the restaurant looked like it'd serve you something one step above food you'd find behind a dumpster soaking in street juice, but Yasmine insisted all the best haunts look like this. *Real hole-in-the-wall* is what she said. Now it's Sunday night and we're all sick. Worse, we've only got the one bathroom.

"This is the absolute pits!" Yasmine groans from her post on the floor in front of the fridge. She's been relegated to the kitchen sink and trash can. I've got the toilet, and Kat's in the shower with the curtain drawn, crying into a bucket.

My mobile rings and I answer it with my eyes closed, expecting it to be my mum. She likes to check in on me on

Sunday nights, but instead of Mum's chipper accent, I hear a familiar masculine voice that sends me into a panic.

"Candace? You there?"

LOGAN!

"Who is it?! The hospital?!" Yasmine shouts. "Tell them to send round an ambulance."

"Three ambulances!" Kat adds.

"What are your roommates shouting about?"

"Oh! Err…"

I try to muster up enough energy to sit up and talk to him like a proper human being, but I can't do it. After losing the contents of my stomach and probably 95% of my body weight down the toilet, I am bone-weary and weak. I close my eyes and drop back down to the floor. My mobile sits on my chest, on speakerphone, so I don't have to use my arm muscles trying to hold it against my ear.

"Oh, it's nothing. They think we're dying."

"And are you?"

"Maybe."

"You do sound like death."

"It's because of Yaz," I say, massaging my temples. "She's poisoned me with dumpster fish."

"It was supposed to be good! It had loads of good reviews on Yelp!" she argues.

"No, YAZ!" Kat shouts back brusquely. "The *other* restaurant had good reviews. *Yours* had *no* reviews, remember?!"

"Oh shit," Logan cuts in. "You guys had bad fish?"

"Loads of it. It was just so cheap, and once you got over the sewer smell, it wasn't so bad."

"Oh stop. *Stop talking about it*," Yasmine says, audibly gagging on her words.

"And now you all have food poisoning," he posits.

"Bingo."

"I'll come over and bring sustenance."

"You can't!" I moan.

"Then you come here and I'll nurse you back to health."

"I couldn't walk two feet, let alone make it all the way to your flat."

"Send me your address and I'll be there in a second."

"No! You can't—"

I'm cut off by Kat reaching out of the shower to yank my mobile off my chest. She's the one who gives him our address, thus it's her fault he shows up twenty minutes later and walks right in without even so much as knocking. None of us has moved positions. What's the point? There's nothing I could do to improve my appearance at this rate. And besides, I couldn't summon the energy even if I wanted to.

His shadow falls over my supine body, and I blink one eye open. He's there in jeans and a white t-shirt with a cool forest green jacket layered on top. His hair looks freshly washed and his skin glows with a healthy, warm tan.

"Hey champ," he quips, looking down at me.

"Even upside down you're bloody gorgeous."

He grins and reaches over to set a bag on the bathroom vanity.

"Don't look at me too closely," I warn. "And don't breathe through your nose or you might pass out."

The amount of bodily waste that has passed through our plumbing system in the last four hours is alarming, to say the least.

He bends down and brushes my sweaty hair off my forehead, assuring me, "It's nothing compared to our locker room after a game. Don't worry."

"Do you have to be so nice all the time?"

He frowns. "I'm not that nice."

I think I understand his reaction. Nice is his cute. He doesn't want to be called nice just like I don't want to be called cute. It irks him, and that only makes him seem even nicer.

"I brought some electrolyte drinks and broth. I figured you guys wouldn't be able to stomach anything solid."

"That sounds lovely. Would you mind just uncapping a drink and waterfalling it straight into my mouth?" I tip my chin up and part my lips.

He suppresses a smile. "You can't sit up?"

"I'm not sure. I haven't tried."

Kat yanks back the shower curtain, and Logan jumps in surprise. Oh right—he didn't realize she was in there.

Unbothered, she makes a *Give it here* motion with her hand. "Here, pass one over and I'll give it a go."

Over the next half hour, Logan gets us all situated with our drinks. He doesn't have to—he should be off having people tend to *him*—but he helps Yasmine to her bed and Kat to the sofa, and then he comes back into my room to see me sitting on the edge of my twin mattress, my head in my hands.

"I've just left a message for the school to get a sub for tomorrow. I'm disappointed because I hoped I'd get the chance to go talk to my headmistress about…well…*you*."

I look up to see him frown like he's as disappointed as I am by the turn of events. "You think you'll still be sick in the morning?"

I peer up at him as he strolls closer.

"Who knows, but even if I'm not, I'll be dead knackered. No way I'll be chasing after toddlers in this state."

"Right. Here, lie back."

I do as he says as I'm in no position to put up a fight. He tugs back my covers, and I lay my head on my pillow. He lifts the duvet up and over me and then he stands. My hand shoots out to grab his wrist, to keep him near me.

"You aren't going to rush off, are you?"

He rubs the back of his neck then pulls out his mobile and shakes his head. "I can stay for a little while."

"Maybe just until I nod off? I haven't had a proper tending-to like this in ages. It's quite nice, you know?"

He smiles and sets his mobile down on my nightstand then puts his wallet down beside it. After, he sits down on the edge of my bed and turns to look at me.

We don't say anything for a little while. There's a silence that feels heavy and powerful, and I'm scared if I pop it with a needle by opening my mouth, everything I think about him will tumble right out into the open.

His mobile buzzes on the nightstand, but he ignores it. I smile and prod his thigh with the tip of my finger.

"All right, Nurse Matthews, tell me something about yourself."

His brows furrow in confusion. "What do you want to know?"

"What are your parents like? Your mum? Is she really pretty? Must be to have made a lad like you."

I swear he sort of goes rosy on his cheeks as he looks away.

"There's not much to say. I grew up in Florida. My dad has an orange orchard, and my mom teaches."

"She's a teacher as well? Like me?"

"Yeah. She teaches physics, up at the high school. She studied aerospace engineering in school though."

"Bloody hell. She sounds brilliant. I haven't got the head for maths or science. It's why I stick with the youngsters.

Best to let them think I'm smarter than them, though I swear there are a few who could outpace me in a round of *Jeopardy*."

He laughs like he doesn't quite believe me (he should), and then I continue on, "How'd your mum end up teaching then?"

He shrugs. "She just sort of fell into it. She had a job working for NASA. She wanted to go to space and was even accepted into their astronaut training program and everything, but then one of her friends introduced her to my dad."

"She gave it all up for him?"

He aims a lopsided grin at me. "Well, it's not like she was about to leave for Mars the very next day or anything, but yeah, they dated for three weeks then he proposed. Said he wouldn't be able to live without her if she went up into space."

"I think I'm crying."

I sniff to prove it.

He laughs and shakes his head. "They've been married twenty-six years."

"What a story. *Sheesh*. My parents met at a bar then a few months later, my mum got knocked up with me and they sort of both agreed, *Well, we might as well give it a go, right?* Never had a proper wedding or anything, just exchanged rings and went round to my gran's for some tea and cakes afterward."

"Do you think they regret it? Getting married just because your mom was pregnant with you?"

I think of the way my mum dotes on my dad, the way he's always teasing her and making her groan in annoyance and swear she's had it up to here with him, though we all know she secretly loves it.

I can't help but smile. "No, I don't think so. They're happy in their own way, even if it's not quite in the perfect fairytale sense, you know?"

He nods. "Do you have any siblings?"

"Just me. The parents love to joke that I was all they could put up with. Very wild child, so to say. I argue that they're just laying it on, but I've seen photos and I do look rather *untamed* most of the time. Sort of big-eyed and round-cheeked and quite rambunctious. What about you?"

"Just a sister. You know, Briggs' mom. She lives in the city too."

I smack my forehead. "Duh. Of course you've got a sister. Stella, right? That's Briggs' mom? I think I've only met her the one time right after winter break."

"Yeah, I don't see her much either. She and Bobby, her husband…they're…well, we don't really speak a lot."

"Did you have a falling out?"

"No. They're just busy with work, and I'm busy too, I guess. I don't know. I think they could probably pay more attention to Briggs, but maybe that's just me being judgmental. I don't know what it's like to be a parent."

No, he's spot on. Briggs is such a tender child, and I know how little time he gets with his parents. I'm glad Logan sees that too.

He shrugs and pushes up off my bed then.

"I'm going to go pour you some of that broth if you can stand it. It'll make you feel a lot better if you can keep it down."

"Oh, all right. I'll try to stomach it for you."

The moment he walks out of the room, my body seems to remember how crappy it feels. With him in here, distracting me, it's like my food poisoning took the back seat. Now my stomach rolls and reminds me how awful I feel. I turn on my side as his mobile buzzes again.

The screen illuminates, and I'm more than a little curious to see who's bothering him so late on a Sunday evening. I know it's wrong to go around poking into people's private lives, but well, I'm already facing that way and it would be more inconvenient for me *not* to look. I see the preview of an incoming email pop up, along with all the notifications he's missed sitting right underneath it.

From: BWright@WrightAgency.com
Subject: Charity Golf Game - THEY WANT YOU!

Logan, I've attached the invitation from Tiger's team. They're desperate to have you. Let me know how we can—

And then it cuts off.
Below it, another email.

From: HillaryKing@KingPR.com
Subject: SI Interview Request

Jeff is requesting a follow-up interview for the feature we did before the Super Bowl. They're suggesting—

Then below that, a text.

DARIUS: Training bumped to 6:30 AM tomorrow. Did you see the email Coach sent? I'll swing by and pick you up on the way.

Next, there's a final email header.

I can't see a preview of that email because it's fallen off the screen, and it's not like I can reach out and scroll to read it. It's one thing to look and another to actively snoop.

My stomach hurts twice as much as it did before I looked at his mobile. It's not like I just read a bunch of texts from ladies begging for a lay or anything like that, but sometimes it's easy for me to forget who Logan is. I met him at preschool pick-up. To me, he's just a normal bloke with an exceptionally defined rear end. But that's not really the truth, is it? Logan's a proper celebrity with a schedule that reflects it. I don't think I can quite imagine just how busy he is on any given day, and not just in the way I am, flitting from one job to the next, meeting my flatmates for a drink.

Logan is managing a successful career, and on top of all that, he's in my flat right now heating me up some broth out of the kindness of his heart.

Suddenly, I feel terrible for adding to his stress, for being one more thing he has to manage in a day. I immediately sit up on my bed, ignoring the wave of nausea that threatens to overtake me, and put on a real cheesy grin when Logan walks back into my room carrying a small mug of broth.

"You know what? It's kind of a miracle—I feel loads better."

He tilts his head in confusion. "Are you sure? You don't look better."

"Oh, *ha*." I force a laugh. "Thanks for the compliment. It's my English skin—always a bit flushed." I reach out for the broth, set it on my nightstand, and then take his wallet and mobile in hand so I can pass them back to him. "But really, you don't have to do all this, the broth and the drinks and the putting up with my flatmates. I bet Kat really took advantage of you when you put her up on the sofa."

He takes his things and puts them in the back pocket of his jeans. "Well, she did try to grab my butt when I gave her a blanket."

I groan and cover my eyes with my hand. "See? Can't take us lot anywhere. We're positively feral."

"It's really not that big of a deal. I'm happy to help."

I split my fingers in front of my eyes and look up at him. My heart lurches in my chest and I feel a foreign, yet somehow familiar feeling creeping in like a vine. It's the predecessor to the four-letter word every poet knows by heart. It's not love, per se, because that's mad, but I definitely *like* Logan more than I should. The man standing in my room with his heavenly hair and to-die-for face and, most of all, his golden heart—he'd so easily do me in. No one need bother trying to fill the gap after he's gone. There'd be no point. I'll just turn into an old maid, adopt a few cats, and develop an addiction to the Home Shopping Network, just like Mum. How depressing.

But who cares? Who cares about the *after* because I so desperately want the *now*—badly enough that I'll march into the headmistress's office first thing on Tuesday morning and lay all the facts out there. Hell, I might even camp out there Monday night, right in front of her door so she'll have to shove me aside if she wants to get in, all to ensure I get to talk to her as soon as humanly possible.

"Okay, well if you need anything, just call me," Logan says, stepping closer.

"Sure thing. Thank you for coming round. You were brilliant." I drop my hands to my duvet cover, letting my gaze follow.

He hovers near me for a moment, and I don't dare look up at him. I see his solid shadow cast across my bed, and it moves an inch toward me. I think he might bend down to touch me, maybe drop a kiss to my hair or something equally as divine, but then he tips back on his heels and turns to leave.

My bedroom door shuts behind him.

Kat shouts farewell to him, and then the apartment door opens and closes.

Logan is gone.

And he's damn well taken my heart with him. How rude.

Then I glance over at my bedside table again, noticing for the first time a small folded piece of paper. I reach out for it and laugh once I see it's a check written out to me from Logan to cover the cost of my couture dress. I study his handwriting, smiling at his aggressive penmanship.

Then I tuck the check against my chest like it's a love letter and fall asleep that way.

What an utter dweeb, *I know.*

I'm dragging by the end of training on Monday morning. Every muscle inside me aches, and I know from a quick glance around the field that my teammates all feel the same. A few of them are splayed out on the turf, too exhausted to move. I make it to the bench on the sidelines and sit down with a heavy groan, prompting a few athletic trainers to rush over to tend to me. I accept a water bottle filled with Gatorade and offer a quick thanks when one of them drops a cold towel around my neck.

Even though the NFL season only spans a few months out of the year, this is a full-time job. During the season, I'm dealing with muscle strain, long travel days, and injuries. The off-season comes with its own set of obstacles too, namely longer practices and harder drills. Our coaches know we can take the beating because we don't have to perform in an actual game. This is the time to get in shape, and every one of our coaching staff agrees we should be working our asses off. It doesn't matter that we won the Super Bowl earlier this year. We'll have a target on our backs come fall, thirty-one teams who want to strip us of our #1 title. But for me, that's not all. I also have to contend with a roster full of backup quarterbacks on my own team eager to take my place if I so much as flinch.

I shoot more Gatorade into my mouth then use the cold towel to wipe sweat from my brow.

Just because our morning training session is over doesn't mean I have the rest of the day to myself. I've got a meeting with the quarterback coach after lunch to go over game footage from last season, and then I have a few press interviews. The reporters and photographers are across the field now, relegated to a press box, but I see their pens wagging and their shutters snapping away. They're hoping to grab a photo of me where I look especially tired so they can morph it into a story about how I'm losing my edge. I twisted my ankle earlier today, and instead of giving in to the urge to limp off the field, I had to grin and bear it, knowing they'd play up the injury as something more serious than it is.

I hate press, but it's a necessary evil in this sport.

I have sponsorships and endorsement deals that are based around my public image. Acting like a dick to reporters might feel good in the moment, but it wouldn't be worth it in the long run.

Doc, our head trainer—an orthopedist with thirty years of experience in sports medicine—kneels down in front of me and asks to examine my ankle.

"I don't think it's bad," I tell him as he unties my cleat, tugs off my sock, and starts to work through a few mobility exercises. He dorsiflexes and plantarflexes my foot, rotating it and asking me when and if I experience any pain in my ankle. I have a pretty high threshold for pain. In this sport, you have to. There's no other way to survive a three-hundred-pound lineman pounding me into the turf if one of my guards fails to defend me in the pocket. Fortunately, though, that doesn't happen all that often.

Doc rotates my ankle again and it tweaks a bit, but nothing like I've experienced in the past with broken bones. Nothing, and I mean *nothing* can compare to when I broke my clavicle during a game back in high school.

"It's fine," I assure him. "I'll sit in the ice bath after this. It should be good to go for tomorrow."

He nods and stands, relaying notes to the assistant standing beside him and carrying a small laptop. They keep careful track of all my injuries, and I get it. I'm a commodity, something they've paid top dollar to acquire and something they'd like to ensure stays fit for the next decade. Sure, they might care about me as a person *somewhat*, but more than anything, they care about my body and the way it will perform on the field come next season.

Darius finds me on the bench after Doc leaves to assess another player.

"Guess we'll have to take you behind the barn and shoot you," he jokes, nodding at my foot.

"It's nothing. They're just being overly cautious."

He laughs and glares over at the reporters. "I bet the top story on *SportsCenter* later is about your damn ankle."

I laugh and shake it off. I don't watch that crap, so I don't really care.

"Anyway, what happened Saturday? It looked like you and Candace were getting pretty cozy in the pool."

I half-laugh, half-grunt in response.

"What? She rejected you?" He grins as he shakes his head in disbelief. "Damn, you win the Super Bowl and you could get any girl you want, and you happen to go for the

113

only one in Manhattan who turns you down? That's some shit luck."

The idea of her turning me down chafes my ego. "She didn't turn me down. She told me we can't be together because it's against the rules. I guess since she's my nephew's teacher, we can't date or she'll be fired."

Darius makes a face like that's the most fucked-up thing he's ever heard.

"These damn private schools...I swear, man."

I look away, thinking back on last night. Showing up to Candace's apartment was like a scene out of a comedy movie: her lying on the floor in her bathroom, blonde hair spilling out around her head, her baby hairs stuck to her temple with sweat. She looked so sick and yet somehow still so goddamn beautiful. It's the smile; she's always smiling.

I inwardly groan as I dig the palm of my right hand into my eye. *Do I seriously have it this bad for the girl already?*

"So what are you going to do? Leave it? Find someone else? You know we have that Feeding America gala this weekend. I'm taking Liz, and I know Melody's planning on going too. We could just all go together."

Fuck no.

"I'd rather not. Melody and I aren't going to happen."

"Suit yourself." He shrugs. "Would have been nice, dating friends. And you can't tell me you don't think she's hot."

Yeah, sure, on paper—but what does that matter when I can't seem to get a tiny British girl out of my head?

"I'll ask Candace to go with me," I say, standing up so I can head inside to take an ice bath.

"I thought you said she was off limits. Are you going to get the girl fired?"

Maybe.

If it comes to that…

After spending the entirety of Monday in a vegetative state on my couch, I feel much better on Tuesday, keen to head into work. I get up early and dress in clothes slightly nicer than what I usually wear to teach toddlers: smart black jacket, sleek ponytail, a swipe of lipstick. I call out farewells to Yasmine and Kat then set off to grab another round of coffee to bribe Mrs. Halliday and Laura. I can't keep doing this. My bank account is screaming at me, but I can't just walk in there empty-handed, asking for favors.

I'm too busy thinking over whether or not to bring them scones as well and nearly crash right into a man with a huge camera hanging down round his neck in front of my building.

"Oof! Sorry. Didn't even see you there," I say, sidestepping out of his way on the sidewalk as he blinks in surprise.

He makes some sort of noncommittal response and then I'm off, walking down the street toward my subway stop.

I'm only half a block away from my building when I glance across the street and see another photographer standing there, though this time he's got his camera poised in front of his eye and he's snapping away, aiming his lens right at me, or at least in my general direction. *Odd.* I turn over my shoulder, wondering what he's taking a picture of. The building behind me is quite derelict and not something I'd usually stop to admire with its crumbly bricks and rusted iron bars covering the windows. It's not exactly Kensington Palace, but then again, I'm no artist. Maybe he sees beauty there that I'm blind to.

"Sorry for blocking your shot!" I shout, scurrying along to get out of his way.

He probably stood there all morning trying to get just the right light for his photo and then I strolled along and mucked it all up.

The subway is crowded as usual, so I huddle in a corner, standing and holding on to a leather strap hanging from the ceiling so I don't go barreling forward into my neighbor when we take a harsh turn.

An older man dressed in a business suit is standing near me, though instead of holding on to a strap for dear life, he's just casually reading the newspaper. What a proper New Yorker. He's quite good at surfing along the subway line while he turns the pages and continues reading. The front page of the paper catches my eye. He's reading the sports section of the *Times*, and there's a huge photo of Logan taking up the top half of the page. He's sitting on a bench in his football gear while a man kneels at his feet, tending to an injury from the looks of it. The headline reads: *LOGAN MATTHEWS' CAREER-ENDING INJURY*.

I gasp and cover my mouth with my hand, drawing the attention of the businessman.

He follows my gaze, folds down the top half of the newspaper to see the photo I'm looking at, and then laughs.

"Don't worry. They love to sensationalize everything. From the sound of it, he barely hurt his ankle yesterday during a practice."

"Oh thank god. Poor Logan."

The man looks at me like I'm quite queer, and I suppose he must think I'm some kind of superfan or something. What a laugh it would be to tell him that Logan and I are actually friends. *More* than friends, maybe, depending on this meeting I'm about to have.

I tug out my mobile while I'm walking from my subway stop to the café, and I type out a text to Logan.

CANDACE: Just saw you in the newspaper! Hope your ankle is all right! XO

But I stop myself before I send it, not wanting to bother him. Judging from how his mobile looked on Sunday night, it probably gets blown up all day, and I don't want to add on to that. Not to mention, if I saw him in the newspaper, that means loads of other people saw it too and are now probably reaching out as well.

With a sigh, I pocket my mobile and push open the door, focusing on the task at hand.

It'll be a delicate matter, dealing with Mrs. Halliday. In the last few months since I took my post at The Day School, I haven't broken any staff rules, so I haven't had very many dealings with her. Just brief hellos and goodbyes in the hallway, quick chats whenever she pokes her head into my classroom—that sort of thing.

When I show up at her office with the lattes and scones in hand, I'm embarrassed to find I'm quite nervous, hands shaking and everything.

I ask Laura if she's in, and this time I've lucked out. No dental appointments to contend with.

"Come in, Candace! I'm free," Mrs. Halliday bellows through the open door to her office before Laura can answer me.

After passing one drink and scone off to Laura, I walk in with Mrs. Halliday's treats outstretched in front of me. She beams when I offer them to her.

"For me? You shouldn't have!" She smiles before accepting her drink and scone gladly. Then she takes a sip of the latte. "Mmm, it's extra sweet. Now *this* is a good bribe."

I nearly croak. BRIBE?! Is it that obvious?

"I had them add some vanilla," I respond in an awkward high-pitched voice, trying to throw her off my scent.

"Just the way I like it," she says, taking another sip before setting it down. She's a nice woman, really. Her appearance is rather round and matronly and she chooses clothes with the most horrid fabrics, but her smile is genuine when she glances across her table at me as I take a seat in a chair facing her. "So now tell me what you need."

I fidget nervously, surprised by her direct question.

"Can't I just bring my favorite boss a coffee every now and then?" I tease, embarrassed to find that I've broken out in a cold sweat.

She leans back in her chair and narrows her cool gray eyes on me. "Sure you can, but I've been around the block quite a few times and I know the drill. So what is it? Toddlers driving you insane? Want some help in the afternoons?"

I hurry to correct her. "No! No, that's not it at all. I think I'm faring quite nicely in the 3s room, actually.

It's…umm…" I twiddle my fingers, trying to get my words in the proper order. "It's a question to do with the rules in our employee handbook, actually."

She groans like it's the last thing she wanted to hear. "Don't expect me to know that thing backward and forward—it was written before my tenure here. Just come out with it and tell me what you're so worried about then I'll see if I can ease your mind."

I didn't expect to cut to the chase this quickly. I thought we'd do a bit of back and forth about the weather and school lunches and whatever was on the telly last night. I was going to feign a love for *The Bachelor* in case she's a big fan.

She's still waiting for me to speak, her gaze gently goading me to get on with it.

"Okay, so it has to do with the part about no fraternizing with the parents."

"Oh god, who did you sleep with?"

My eyes bug out of my head and my hands shoot out to stop her thoughts. "No one! I swear it!"

We just did a bit of humping in a pool. *Oh dear.*

"Okay…"

"It's…um…okay…one of my students has this uncle."

"Logan Matthews, yes. The NFL player. That's something you'll just have to get used to. At a prestigious school like this, we have quite a few parents and relatives who are famous in one way or another. Hell, some of our students are probably famous in their own right as well."

"Sure, but it's not his fame I'm worried about. It's about whether or not it'd be okay if he and I dated?"

Without missing a beat, she replies, "Oh, I'm afraid you'd be fired. Yes, gone immediately."

OH MY GOD.

I immediately panic. My heart starts to gallop like it wants to race right out of my chest. Fired. Axed. Gone. *NO!*

"Surely there's some way to—"

Then she bursts out laughing, really having a go, slapping her hand on her desk and everything. When I don't immediately realize what's happening, she only starts laughing harder, having to wipe tears from her eyes. "Oh god, I'm kidding! Can you imagine?! A student's uncle being off limits? And what about a friend of a friend? And that man down the block there? No, I choose to assume you teachers know what's best, and I trust your judgment."

"So it isn't against the rules? But wait—isn't that why the teacher who was in the 3s class before me was fired? She was sleeping with the father of one of our students, I thought."

Mrs. Halliday finally stops laughing, and her face screws up like I've really confused her. "Tara? Is that what you think happened?" She snorts. "God no. Tara was fired because she was stealing school supplies from the multipurpose closet and reselling them online for a profit. She had a whole system going, probably made a small fortune before we caught on to the fact that all of our paper clips had gone missing."

"*You're kidding.*"

"No, you'd be surprised. Paper clips sell for a pretty penny if you can get your hands on enough of them."

What?

"No. That's…" I shake my head adamantly. "I mean, I really thought she'd had an affair and been axed for it."

Mrs. Halliday shrugs and reaches out for her latte once again. "Well that's school gossip for you. Can never be too sure about anything people say around here. Everyone loves a good story."

Right. Well then.

I lean back in my seat, breathing in this new information. It seems too good to be true, so just to be sure, I decide to ask once more.

"So then it's okay if I pursue something with Logan?"

I say it real slow like I want to be sure she hears every syllable.

Her face turns serious then, her eyes narrowing. "It's not against school rules, though as your advisor, I'd caution you to tread lightly when it comes to dating someone in the public eye."

I think she keeps on going after that—warning me about what I'm getting myself into—

but I don't hear a bloody word. My brain has turned into a musical complete with dancing people twirling around light posts. She might be bestowing some real words of wisdom upon me, but all I hear is, *Yes, go! Screw his brains out! You won't be fired!*

When we're done, I see myself out of her office and get to work in my classroom straight away.

I'm extra patient with all the little kiddos, not even minding one bit when one of the boys wees on my shoe. See if I care! You can wee wherever you want! This day is so glorious nothing even matters!

I want to tell Logan about the news, of course, but then it doesn't seem like something I should spout out over text. Besides, it's a bit keen to just go right up to a guy and say he's basically got free rein. *Do with me what you will! I'm yours for the taking, big boy!*

And not to mention, since he's totally and completely out of my league as it is, I probably should feign some kind of cool-girl persona. Make him think I've got other lads lined up to fill his spot, that sort of thing. God, especially after he saw me all pukey on Sunday night. Blech. Not my best look.

Since I decide not to tell Logan straight away, I settle for shooting off a text to Yasmine and Kat.

They respond as I assumed they would.

KAT: ACE! Now you can bonk his brains out.

She caps it off with a row of eggplant and peach emojis. Real classy.

Yasmine responds a little later and has lots of advice for me.

YASMINE: Don't just throw yourself at him now that you're allowed to date him. Make him work for it. Maybe go for a blow job first? Or just do a hand job? We can discuss later.

YASMINE: Oh, and thank GOD you waxed last week.

CANDACE: HA! Get over it! It's just hair! And mine happens to be lovely, even down there.

YASMINE: Please stop. I'm already planning to call round to find a shrink who can hypnotize me and help wipe my memory. Only way I'll manage to get to sleep at night…

After I get home from school, I sit down on the sofa, place my mobile on the coffee table, and stare at it. It was one thing to avoid calling Logan all day—when I was busy chasing after tots—but it's another to stave off the urge now that I'm here…lonely…thinking of him and wishing he were here.

I reach out to pick it up but then stop myself, forcing my body back against the sofa cushions. I turn on the telly, flip through a few channels, decide every show is boring, and turn it back off. I look around the flat, wondering if I should clean it up a bit. Eh, not worth it. Kat will only wreck it again.

Then, my mobile rings.

It's Logan.

How did he know?! Did I slip into a hypnotic state for a bit and accidentally call him? Did I text him?!

Or maybe he's as anxious to hear from me as I am to hear from him?!

It rings twice. Then a third time, and I feel all kinds of nervous, fidgeting on the sofa like I'm a toddler in need of a bathroom break.

Finally, my hand shoots out and I answer it on a whim. The call connects and my breath gets caught in my chest as Logan speaks.

"Hey Candace."

His voice sends goosebumps down my arms.

I smile. "Hi."

"Did you talk to your boss?"

My smile widens. So he's been anxious about the meeting too. He wants to know if I'm off limits. *Why does that make me feel so special?*

"Is that all you care about? I thought we could do some chitchat first. You can ask me how my day was," I tease.

"How was your day?" he asks, tone perfunctory.

"Oh, not bad. Started out with some finger painting. Then outdoor play, and I got a bit of color on my cheeks because I forgot my sun hat. In the afternoon, I had to wash some wee off my shoes—"

"*Candace.*"

His voice sounds threatening, and I like it. I've never gone for the soft boys, the ones who let you walk all over them.

"Now I want to hear about your day," I say, prolonging his agony. I like this. Taunting him is fun, and maybe I've got a little evil streak because I don't plan on stopping any time soon.

"I can't recall much of it. I've been distracted."

Interesting.

Then he says, all commandingly, "Come over. We can talk about everything here."

"That sounds awfully bossy of you," I chide.

"Come over or I'll come there, though I saw your room, and that bed…it's not big enough."

For what?! Jesus. Warn a girl.

I walk into the kitchen, open our fridge, and bend down to stick my head inside for some relief. It smells a bit like moldy socks, but the cool air is nice on my heated face.

"I guess I could come round for a bit?"

There's no hesitation before he responds, "I'll send my driver."

I roll my eyes. "Oh no need. I've got a retinue of my own. Loads of them just waiting down by the curb eager to do my bidding. *Oh, please, Candace! Let me drive you! No, me!*"

"He'll be there in ten minutes."

I eek out a high-pitched "Oh Lordy!" and hang up on him so I can dash into my room and get ready.

What does one wear to seduce and ensnare a professional footballer? A dress? A nightie? Sexy knickers? *No* knickers?

Kat and Yasmine aren't home, which is probably for the best. They'd only war with me about what outfit to wear, and I think I've settled on something quite nice: a short black dress with sheer black stockings underneath. My checkered coat will have to do because it's all I own.

When I'm finishing up in the bathroom, refreshing my hair and makeup, I get a text on my mobile from the driver alerting me that he's downstairs.

Right then. Off to Oz, I suppose. I lock up the flat and hop-skip down the stairs, waving eagerly to neighbors, who only give me brief grunts in response.

The driver is this well-dressed lad about my dad's age, all done up in a black suit. His hat is very shiny, and he gives me a huge grin when I introduce myself then he tells me he's called Pat. I don't think he was expecting I'd shake his hand, but what was I supposed to do? Just ignore him?

We ride toward Logan's, me in the front seat beside Pat. He said I could get in the back, but that felt a bit odd, and this way I can fiddle with his radio.

"Do you like pop, or would you rather I find something a bit more mellow?"

He shoots me a sideways glance, chuckles, and then shakes his head. "Whatever you like is fine."

He's got a great New York accent, one of those you can tell he's cultivated since birth.

I pick his brain as we drive, asking where he'd go if he wanted a proper sandwich, pizza, a burger…basically I only care about food.

He's telling me all these great places and I'm loading them into a note on my mobile when a motorist comes out of nowhere, turns into our lane from another street, and nearly sideswipes us. Pat lays on the horn, real angry, and I do him a favor and roll down my window so I can add my own two cents.

"Oy! Watch it, buddy!" I say, sounding real menacing, and Pat gives me an approving nod as I roll my window back up.

"You're good people," he says as we slow down in front of Logan's building.

"Ditto. I feel like I've got a new friend." I beam then tuck away my mobile. "I'll try out a few of these restaurants soon and report back."

He tips his head, I give him a proper salute in farewell, and then I turn to head inside.

I'm not sure how all this works. For the party, there was a man prepared with a long list of approved guests. Now, there's a doorman who sees me coming from a few yards away, immediately straightens his posture, and moves to hold the door open for me with a sweeping gesture.

"Ms. Williams, right this way."

Whoa. Hello, royal treatment.

I'm so gobsmacked that he knows who I am, I don't even think to thank him for holding the door for me. It feels so unbelievably rude. I make a note to be double nice to him the next go-round as another attendant points me in the direction of the central bank of lifts.

Inside one of them, there's yet another man in the building's crisp navy uniform, and when he sees me, he nods and swipes his keycard over an invisible panel. On command, the lift rises and takes us up toward the penthouse floor.

"Thank you."

"No problem."

"Having a good day?"

"Can't complain, miss," he replies shyly, offering me a small smile before we arrive at Logan's flat.

Like the last time I was here, the lift sweeps open to the small antechamber that leads to Logan's front door. As I head toward it, my mobile vibrates again, and I realize I missed a text from Logan a few minutes ago.

LOGAN: I'll be back soon. Got held up.

LOGAN: Go in and get settled. There's food in the fridge if you're hungry.

Oh, this is heaven. Even better than expected. My stomach's been in knots for the last half hour in anticipation of seeing Logan, but knowing he's not in the flat makes it so much easier to stroll in past the unlocked door.

It's dead silent inside, and all the lights are off. I hover in the foyer, kick off my ballet flats, and sort of do a bit of bobbing and peering down deserted hallways to check there are no ghosts about to pop out and scare me.

"Anyone home?! *Yoohoo!* If you're going to leap out at me, at least give me a heads-up so I don't soak my knickers!"

When no one from the other side responds, I get comfortable. I flip on lights and stroll through rooms, making a mental map as I go. Powder room, living room, bar, guest room, gym, sauna, kitchen, butler's pantry, *real* pantry, another bathroom, another bedroom, a tunnel to China—just kidding on that last bit, but wow this place is huge. It might as well take up a whole city block.

I retrace my steps and try to make it back to the kitchen, but then I somehow find myself in a whole other wing with its own set of bedrooms and bathrooms, and I sort of go into a bit of a panic run because my brain immediately assumes I'll lose myself in this labyrinth forever and eventually starve. *Dear god no. Any other death, please!*

Eventually, I do find my way back to the kitchen (after I've gone sweaty), and I immediately scour the cabinets for a loaf of bread so I can leave a trail of crumbs for myself if I go off wandering again à la Hansel and Gretel.

This, of course, leads me to finding a veritable cache of snack foods: crisps, crackers, popcorn, biscuits, nuts, cereal. It's endless. I think I'm close to tears, but maybe it's because only moments ago I assumed I'd never eat again.

I've just popped the lid on some Pringles when Logan strolls into the kitchen and catches me red-handed.

My cheeks are so flushed you could fry an egg on them.

"Oh, I do hope you were serious about the 'making yourself at home' bit," I say, scanning guiltily across the junk food I'd already begun to pull from the shelves. It nearly covers his kitchen island, and now I realize I might have gotten carried away.

Logan doesn't move from the doorway, at least not at first. He hovers there, looking at his kitchen then looking at me. The edge of his mouth tips up into a smile, and then he laughs and strolls in to dump his bag on the island (on the edge, where there are still a few centimeters of free space). He doesn't stop walking until he's right in front of me, taking the Pringles tin from my hands and dropping it on the counter beside me.

I get a heavy whiff of his spiced body wash as his hands come to my hips and he pivots us, walking me backward until my back hits the edge of the island.

"You've just showered," I blurt out.

"Yeah. I had a late workout today. I called in the middle of it."

130

That sends my brain spiraling with glorious images of him lifting heavy objects while sweat drips down his bare abs.

"Tell me about it?"

His dark brow quirks. "What do you want to know?"

"I'm trying to create a proper fantasy, but I don't know what all you did. A bit of running? Did you lift some of those huge tires? Tell me everything," I tease while my eyes flutter closed.

He laughs under his breath then leans in to press a kiss to my cheek. With my eyes closed, it feels even more intimate, and I don't stop myself from resting my palms flat against his hard chest.

He tightens his hold on my hips and I stay perfectly still, wondering what will happen next. Will we sweep all this junk food aside and go at it right here in his kitchen? *How sinful!*

But when Logan's mouth doesn't immediately descend on mine, I open my eyes to find him studying me with a smile.

"So you spoke to your boss?" he asks, letting his gaze fall to my mouth.

I wet my bottom lip and his eyes narrow.

Oh…interesting.

"Yes. This morning."

"And?"

"Well…it's not against the rules per se to engage in…well…err, I don't think I should call it dating yet, right? A bit presumptive of me."

"You're allowed to date me and you won't be fired?"

"Ye—"

The S sound gets stolen by his lips as they crash down onto mine.

131

I'm so dead shocked I sort of flinch in fear until my brain can put two and two together and I realize I'm being kissed, *properly kissed*, by Logan Matthews!

He's ace at it, by the way.

His mouth moves on mine and his lips are gentle at first, not too forceful or overly keen like some lads. At first, it's like he's testing the waters, making sure I'm okay with what he's doing. I fist my hands in his shirt in case he tries to pull back. *Not an option.* Then he steps toward me to deepen the kiss, and the countertop bites into my lower back.

Oh, *bliss*.

I think I must say that aloud because he pulls back half a centimeter to chuckle, but I don't let him go any farther. I kiss him again—harder. I wrap my arms around his neck and bring our bodies flush together. It's not so easy with his height, so I rise up onto my tippy toes. That's apparently still not good enough for him because he hoists me up by the hips and plops me on the edge of the island.

My arse crunches half a bag of crisps, and now I'm laughing too hard to be kissed properly.

He groans in annoyance and grasps my chin in his hands to hold me still.

His eyes lock with mine and *oof*, his brown eyes are like a punch to the gut. The last of my laughter dies a swift death.

"Spread your legs," he says, all confident, causing my insides to liquify instantly.

I do as he says then he steps between them, nestling us together like a lock and key. My dress slides up high on my thighs, revealing more of my sheer black stockings.

"Better," he says, leaning down to press a chaste kiss to the edge of my mouth.

I try to turn to land my mouth on his lips—suddenly desperate to kiss him again—but he doesn't let me. His hands hold me perfectly still as his mouth drops down to my neck. He kisses there, just at the base of my chin where my pulse seems closest to my skin. He can feel it, I bet, hammering away as his lips move a little lower and touch my skin again. He breathes me in and my thighs want to clench together, but since he's standing between them, they tighten around him instead. He likes that; I can tell because he rolls his hips against me, giving me a little taste of everything that could be if we took things a bit further.

When his mouth gets to the collar of my dress, he pulls back and looks down at me.

I'm breathing hard. It's sort of embarrassing, but he's not paying a bit of attention. His gaze is on my thighs as he pushes the material of my dress up higher until it's right at my waist. My sheer stockings reveal a hint of my skimpy black panties. They're nearly indecent and I'm almost tempted to yank my dress down to cover them up once again, but then Logan reaches down to trace a line along the hem. The pad of his finger runs over my stockings so the material is yet another thing used to tease me as he continues, over one thigh, down between them, and then back up.

"Black is an interesting color on you," he says, and his voice sounds different than I'm used to.

A little scary, if I'm honest.

"Oh?"

"You with your ballet flats and your blonde hair and your freckles on your nose. I would have expected you to wear pink or white."

"I like black," I say, trying not to fidget under his gaze.

His eyes flit up to mine, and he grins like a villain who's bested his nemesis.

"I do too."

Then with a groan, he pushes off the counter, swipes a hand through his hair, and yanks the fridge open.

I'm so bereft in his absence that I nearly tip off the side of the island before catching myself.

"Where've you gone?" I ask, aware that my bottom lip is jutting out a bit.

I thought we were onto something. I thought he was feeling everything I was.

"To get ahold of my sanity," he says, reaching in to grab a package of lunch meat. "I haven't eaten since lunch, and I planned to ask if you were hungry. I was going to make you dinner."

He retrieves more sandwich supplies then carries them over to the island to set them down beside me after he shoves aside some snack food bags. When his gaze falls between my open thighs, I slam them shut again.

His eyes narrow as he sucks in a deep breath and refocuses on the task at hand.

"So we're going to eat dinner?" I squeak.

"Yes. I'm going to make you a sandwich."

"So *chic*."

The glare he shoots me warns me that he'd like to punish me for my impertinence. *Oh! Please do!*

"You could just drape some ham on me and eat it off?" I suggest, liking this game we're playing where he pretends to be serious and I persuade him otherwise.

He squeezes his eyes shut then casts his gaze heavenward as if looking for some divine help with dealing with me.

"Just stay put right where you are, will you?"

"Sure thing," I say, chipper as a Girl Scout.

I stay up on the counter, helping him construct sandwiches for us to eat. We load them up with cheese and avocado and tomato and lettuce. By the time we're done, his is so massive I doubt he'll be able to fit it into his mouth at one time.

"Let's go to the table," he says, helping me down from the island, taking my hand in his, and leading me across the room.

Everything in his flat is well-designed. The whole place is a mixture of traditional furniture and lighter, more modern details. Someone definitely did it all for him, which is fine. I bet he doesn't have much room in his schedule to worry about interior design.

"I really like your flat. I did get a little lost earlier, I will admit, but I found my way back to the kitchen soon enough."

"Thanks. It's… It works."

He doesn't sound all that enthused.

"You don't like it?"

"I'm a little embarrassed by it, to be honest. I didn't grow up in this world. I told you my dad has that orange orchard. That's where we lived, which meant we all had chores to do around the house and yard. It was a nice life, don't get me wrong, but we didn't have any of this," he says, sweeping his hand around the room.

"I see. Well, I grew up with about forty butlers, so I'm quite used to the pampered life. No doing my own dishes or laundry," I tell him with a wink. "Truly though, it's great. You've accomplished quite a bit from the looks of it. You should be proud."

He nods and chews a bite of his sandwich. I do the same, wondering why it doesn't feel more awkward to be alone with him like this. We haven't gone on a proper date. We haven't even really gotten to know each other, but then he's already seen me puking up my guts and there was that business in the pool on Saturday…

"So…um…I was wondering," I begin, after finishing up my bite. "Do you see lots of girls?"

He tilts his head, wondering what information I'm after.

"I mean, like, dating-wise."

My gaze is pinned on my plate.

"Candace."

"Hmm?"

"No, I'm not dating anyone else. Are you?"

A laugh spills out of me before I can help it. Oh right, he's meant to think I'm cool. "No, erm…not at the moment."

"Good. Then we should talk about this. Getting involved with me isn't as easy as you might think."

CANDACE
11

"How so? Have you got a weird proclivity or something? A fetish with bondage and trapeze equipment?"

He looks positively confused, so I laugh like I wasn't being 100% serious. I should probably lay off the taboo books.

"No, I mean, I'm a public figure, and that comes with consequences."

I wave away his concern. "Come on. It's nothing I can't handle."

A bit of press? No big deal.

He sets down his sandwich and frowns. "I don't think you understand what's going to start happening if we spend more time together."

"I do though—you'll get totally infatuated with me, and I'll have to bat you away with a stick."

"Be serious."

"I can't be. It's physically impossible."

He releases a soft laugh and shakes his head, apparently not interested in pushing the subject. "Well…I guess we'll see then. This weekend I'm going to a Feeding America gala. I was planning on going alone unless you want to come with me."

My eyes widen in shock. "As your date?"

"Yes, though we won't be able to arrive together."

"What? Why?"

"Because the press will have a field day, and I'm not quite ready for that."

"Oh…okay. Sure. You know more about this world than I do. I'll just follow your lead."

He says his assistant will get me the details and I nod like that's a sentence I hear all the time, though really it makes my stomach twist into a knot.

I like Logan, but it's this version of him that I know, the down-to-earth handsome bloke who makes me a sandwich, not the real version of him, the proper celebrity with loads of fans and assistants and drivers.

A tiny part of me wonders if I really know what I'm doing, getting involved with him like this, but I shut the door on that thought immediately, not wanting to go down that road and let worries about the future ruin our fun for now. Besides, he's probably making it out to be worse than it is.

"Are you done?" he says, standing and rounding the table. He's cleared off every speck of food on his plate, but I've only eaten about half of my sandwich. I can't be bothered to finish the rest.

"Yes, but let me wrap it up and take it home. I'll have it for lunch tomorrow."

"Home? Are you leaving already?"

I shrug. "I probably should. I have an early morning tomorrow at The Day School and then I've got a shift at

District tomorrow night. I'm on the schedule for Saturday too, but since you want me to go with you to that gala, I'll have to see if someone can switch with me so I can work Friday instead."

"Right, well, just stay for a little bit longer. It feels like you just got here," he says, dropping our plates on the island to deal with later and then disappearing into his pantry, only to reappear a moment later with a bottle of red wine. I watch him uncork it and grab two glasses. *Twist my arm, why don't you?*

"Okay. I'll stay just for a bit. But you know, it's not as if I've just arrived. I've been here for a while. I got here before you and did a little snooping around."

He peers up at me with an arched brow. "Find anything good?"

"Just your stash of itty-bitty condoms. I didn't know they made them so small."

A normal bloke would probably get real defensive, but the grin Logan aims my way tells me he's not bothered by my joke in the least. Why? Because it couldn't be further from the truth.

I gulp down a heaping mouthful of wine after he passes me my glass, and I distract myself by strolling into the living room and walking over to a large window with an expansive view of Manhattan.

The city skyline is dark with ominous black clouds bulging overhead. Off in the distance, a bolt of lightning pierces through the blackness, and I scrunch my nose, already anticipating how soaked I'll get on the journey home. Bugger.

"It's supposed to pour," Logan says, strolling into the room and looking at the weather forecast on his mobile. "You can't leave until it's cleared up."

139

"It's not like I'll be walking. Surely Pat could give me a ride if I asked him nicely enough?"

"I don't want either of you out on the wet streets. Driving in the city is crazy enough as it is."

"Oh I see how it's going to be." I twist around to face him. "Quite controlling, are you? Used to getting your own way?"

His eyes narrow on me. "You'll leave after it stops raining."

As if on cue, thunder rumbles outside, and I shrug, not quite willing to put up a fight. I like my company and I like my wine; it can't hurt to linger a *little* while longer.

Logan walks toward one of his long sofas and sits down, stretching his tall frame out so he looks positively royal sitting there, all confident and at ease. He has one arm slung over the back of the sofa and one ankle resting on his other knee so he's aimed in my direction.

I stay standing near the window as I sip my wine, looking at him from top to bottom. I try to find any imperfections I've missed in the previous times we've been together. Unsurprisingly, I come up short.

"Tell me why you're not taken," I blurt, suddenly feeling mad with curiosity.

How's it possible he's available? What dark secrets is he hiding?

His brows furrow in thought, and he glances down at his glass. "It's not from lack of female companionship."

"Oh. Ohhh, I *see*. Have you slept with every girl in Manhattan then?"

His dark eyes slice up to me and I zip my lips.

"I've had girlfriends, Candace. But no, I don't think I play the field—not like a lot of my other teammates do."

"So, it's not because you're a player. Hmm...so then what is it?"

"I could ask you the same thing, you know?" He juts his chin toward me. "How is it possible that *you're* single?"

I choke on my wine and have a hard time clearing my throat. Eventually, I manage it, but he's not going to let me off the hook. He's still sitting there, calm and composed, waiting for my reply.

I shrug and try to play off his question while I pace back and forth in front of the window. "Oh, who knows? Maybe I haven't been able to find a guy who's worth bothering with. I have a busy schedule, and the last few blokes I've been with seemed to enjoy playing games more than they enjoyed being with me. It was always a struggle to figure out who was going to text who first. Who was going to make the first move? Who was stringing the other along? It gets old."

I look away before he answers. "I feel the same way, except my games involve slightly higher stakes. Ever since I started to shine on the football field, I've had to wonder what women really want from me. Some like the limelight. Some like the notoriety of dating someone they feel is important. I doubt I've had a woman love me for me in a very long time."

His words sit heavy in my chest, and I peer over at him with a frown.

"Total idiots, the whole lot of them."

He smiles and shrugs, refocusing his attention on his wine glass. "On top of all that, I don't have all the time in the world to devote to relationships. It's not worth it to try to reconfigure my schedule for someone I'm not really interested in."

"Oh."

He seems to have left off the part that's most important.

That he's willing to do that for me means he *is* interested in me. Very much so.

He nods his chin toward me. "Are you all the way over there for a reason?"

I look down at my stockinged feet on the smooth wood floor and wiggle my toes. I'm as far from him as I can be without having my back pinned to the windows.

"Yes. A few reasons, actually."

His brow quirks, asking me to provide them.

"Well first, I don't trust myself with red wine on that fancy sofa."

"I don't care about the sofa."

I gulp.

"And also…" I let my finger drag around the rim of my glass, deciding to be painfully honest since we've both agreed we're tired of games. "I wouldn't mind continuing what we were doing in the kitchen, but I like this talking too, getting to know you and all that. So maybe keeping myself across the room is a good idea."

"I can keep my hands to myself if you come and sit by me."

Bollocks. That's on par with a lion sitting right beside a nice juicy steak and swearing it's a vegetarian. I can practically see him licking his chops.

He must sense my doubt because he pats the cushion beside him. "I'll prove it."

Oh, I'll just bet.

I make a big show of crossing the room toward him, holding my wine gently so it doesn't splash over the rim and onto the rug. Then I perch delicately on the edge of the sofa cushion beside him. It's not close enough for his liking, apparently, because he laughs and tugs me back, closer to him. My dress gets hiked up a little bit, but I'm too scared to adjust it because I think it'll draw his attention and then this whole farce will end.

"Relax," he insists, and I puff out a breath of air as if to say, *Not bloody likely!*

I suppose I have to try at least. I reach my feet out to attempt to prop them up on the coffee table, but it's too far away. My toes wiggle in my stockings, and he laughs and leans forward to drag it closer then props his feet up beside mine. There. Now we're sitting side by side, not touching, not really, but desperately wanting to. It's obvious. It's in the air somehow, permeating the space between us. I swear the atmosphere is crackling like there's lightning in here, not just out there in the storm.

It's then that I notice how hard the rain is coming down now. It's taunting me, as if to say, *Candace, you aren't going anywhere*, which means Logan is feeling mighty confident.

He moves his wine to his opposite hand and sets his free hand right between us, palm up. I stare down at it like it might bite me.

He waggles his fingers tauntingly, and I can't help but laugh.

Still, I don't give in to the urge to touch him. Instead, I gulp my wine and then ask him, "Just how long do you plan on keeping me here? What if it rains all night?"

"Let's just call it then. I think you should stay. It's easier. You can sleep here then Pat can drive you to your apartment in the morning so you can get your things before work."

"Sleep here? Ha! You're rather sure of yourself. A ham sandwich and one glass of wine and now suddenly it's knickers off for a sleepover?"

143

He smiles, a cocky little grin that does my head in. "I'll sleep out here." He points to the sofa cushion. "You can have my bed."

I roll my eyes. "No one will sleep on the sofa. There're fifty-some odd beds in this place. I'll just take a guest room...*if* I stay."

"*When* you stay."

"I'll need to phone my flatmates. They're probably worried about me."

He pushes off the sofa, walks into the kitchen, and strolls back out with my mobile from my purse. He hands it to me as he sits back down, a few inches closer to me this time.

Right. Well. He's quite pushy, isn't he?

I phone Yasmine because she generally has her mobile on her more than Kat does. She answers quickly and there's a good bit of moaning in the background, so much so that I'm worried I've caught her in the middle of a shagging session with some bloke.

"What is it?" she huffs, annoyed. "I've just found the best porn and you're ruining the best part. The lad's got her sort of hoisted off the ground and—"

Logan hears this, of course, because we're sitting so close together. Color blooms down my chest, and I clear my throat to quickly cut her off.

"Right! Well, maybe pause it so you can hear me over all the...noise. I'm only phoning to let you know I'm staying round at Logan's tonight."

"You two are banging already? Have you totally forgotten what I said about playing hard to get?"

Logan pretends to be focused on his wine, though by the cheeky smile he's wearing, I know he's heard every word. Best to cut this convo short, I see. "Right well, ta-ta for now! See you in the morning!"

Then I hang up, toss my mobile on the empty cushion to my left, and drop my head back against the sofa, staring up at the ceiling.

"Remind me to toss them out and find new flatmates first thing tomorrow morning. I swear they'll do my head in."

"I like them."

I let my head roll to the side so I can face him. He picks his arm up so he can drop it on the back of the couch behind me, and then he brushes aside some of my hair so he doesn't accidentally tug it. He does it so reverently I can't help myself from leaning over and kissing him again. It was only meant to be a quick peck, but he won't let me go now that I've initiated it. Our mouths taste like wine, and he needs no prodding to take the kiss further. His mouth slants over mine, deepening the kiss. My mouth opens and his tongue touches mine, eliciting a soft moan from me. I've vaguely aware of him setting his wine glass on the coffee table then reaching for mine as well as we kiss and reach for each other. Once that's done, his hands are on my hips, shifting me so I can sit on top of him. I love how big he feels underneath me, how much space his body takes up. I've been with some blokes who're skinny little things, so thin I'm worried I'll hurt them if I'm too aggressive. Logan can handle anything I want to do. He can take my full weight, and in fact, it's like he relishes the feel of me on top of him, straddling his hips, kissing him senseless. His hands tangle in my hair, keeping me on him, and I kiss him until my lips feel like they might bruise.

Thunder booms overhead and I jump back in shock, breaking away from him.

My eyes flicker open and lock with his, and we go absolutely silent, listening to the rain and the sound of our

145

hearts thump-thumping in our ears. I can taste him on me, or maybe it's the wine, but either way it's a heady sensation, feeling him underneath me even now while we aren't kissing. He's still got ahold of my hips, and I know if I tried to move, he wouldn't let me.

His eyes are so moody and dark I'd think he were angry if I didn't know better.

He's turned on.

Starved for more from the looks of it.

I wonder if I look the same, if my cheeks are flushed and my lips are as swollen as they feel.

I should get up and put a stopper on this madness, but instead I lean in gently and kiss him again. *Once more*, I tell myself, but it's the same as before. The moment our lips touch, it's like I'm uncorking a champagne bottle that's been shaken until the contents are ready to explode. He doesn't hesitate this time. He doesn't let me take the lead and stay sitting on top of him, calling the shots. He turns us and sets me down on the sofa so he can come up and over me. I'm pressed down onto the cushions and he gathers my wrists in his hands, holding them up over my head, locking me in place. His grip isn't so tight that I'm nervous, but it bites in a way that makes me feel captive and *free*. I haven't ever been with a guy who took the lead like this, who felt confident enough to pin me down and look down at me like he's contemplating what he'll do next. I can see all the dark thoughts imagined in his eyes.

Then his mouth descends on mine again and he's relentless, kissing and nipping as his knee starts to wedge between my legs. My dress is up at my waist and it shouldn't feel so bloody good to feel that pressure there from his thigh, but it's heaven and he knows it. He keeps his leg there and I press against him, squeezing my thighs and trying to relieve some of the heat building inside me. He lets me grind against him as he kisses me deeper.

My stockings are abrasive, especially combined with his denim-clad thigh. The friction is driving me mad and I worry I'll crumble at any moment, from nothing more than his thigh between my legs. I should be embarrassed, but deep down I realize he wants me like this, helpless, splitting apart at the seams, grinding and moving against anything that feels good. Right now, it's his muscled leg. It's not like I can try for anything more. He still has my hands locked up by my head, and his grip is as tight as ever. His mouth leaves mine and his lips fall to my ear. I shudder as his voice whispers that he wants me to come just like this, from his thigh.

My eyes nearly roll into the back of my head.

It's one thing to privately feel as though you're about to burst and another for a man to openly discuss it, to *demand* it.

Then his lips slip down to my neck and he conquers newfound territory. It's an area that's yearning to be touched, sensitive skin right above my collarbone. It's skin that usually doesn't get its due because guys always seem to be rushing to get to the more obvious parts of a woman's body.

There's also new pressure between my thighs: him, moving his up and down, a little preview of what's to come. I make a desperate sound, a plea, and he must understand because his leg splits my thighs farther, opening me up and leaving me no way to fend off the overwhelming feeling there, the need to implode.

I imagine myself as if I'm an onlooker, pinned beneath Logan's huge body, my dress in disarray, my hair fanned out around me. I imagine how pink my wrists have turned underneath his grip, how wet I look down there, and the image combined with his thigh is enough to send me careening over the edge. My muscles clench tight as pleasure racks through me and then I'm nothing but a loose sack of limbs, limp on the sofa, underneath Logan.

He pulls away from me, and I'm too scared to open my eyes, too afraid to name what we've just done. Feelings that felt sexy and empowering in the moment have left me raw and embarrassed. Did he really ask me to come or is he angry that I used him that way? Without giving him anything in return?

I suppose it's not too late to reciprocate; I feel his hard length against my leg. I know he's probably desperate for my hands to slide down into his jeans, to give him the same relief he's given me, but then he sits back, separates us, and uses my wrists to lift me into a sitting position. He keeps tugging until the momentum carries me forward, against his broad chest. I'm confused and wondering what he's after, until his arms wrap around me and he keeps me there, in a hug.

We don't say a word as he holds me, and my heart is a train, racing along the tracks, but then gradually starting to slow, syncing with his. At first, I'm on high alert, so bloody aware of his body pressed against mine. Every groove. Every muscle. Every breath. Then, the longer he keeps me pressed against him, his hand drawing slow circles on my lower back, the easier it is to slip off and let my mind rest.

We fuse together as I start to nod off, forgetting where I am and why it's so important to keep my guard up with a man like Logan.

Hours later, I wake up, alarmed because I don't immediately recognize my surroundings. I've lost track of where I am, why my sheets feel so soft, why my ceiling is so much higher than usual, why my twin bed seems to go on forever in both directions.

Then I register the feel of a warm body beside me, and I turn to see Logan asleep on his stomach. It's so dark, but my eyes have adjusted, so I can make out his naked back perfectly in the moonlight. My eyes skate down the hard planes of his shoulder blades and spine. The blanket is gathered at his hips, and I see his boxer briefs peeking out of the top. I'm still properly dressed, which I find charming considering he could have done whatever he wanted with me asleep like that.

The rain still pitter-patters outside, and I wonder what time it is. Judging by the groggy feeling in my head, I know it's likely still the middle of the night and I'll need to force myself back to sleep if I have any hope of surviving tomorrow without an IV drip of caffeine.

But now that I'm awake, my bladder is as well, and I know I won't be able to rest again until I use the loo.

Carefully, so I don't disturb Logan, I slip out of bed and tiptoe toward the bathroom door. The cold tile stings my toes even through my stockings, so I scurry quickly toward the water closet. Once I'm done in there, I wash my hands and look around for a bit of toothpaste. My breath is loathsome. I find Logan's red tube of Crest and use a dollop on my finger to scrub inside my mouth. It's not perfect, but at least my breath is minty when I'm done. After a quick rinse of my face to get the makeup off, I feel like a new woman as I head back into Logan's bedroom.

I've managed to do all my bathroom business with the lights out so I can still see properly as I creep toward the bed.

149

Logan hasn't stirred a bit. His big body is splayed out, taking up just about every inch he can manage. He might be the only person I know who *needs* a king-sized bed.

I stand off to the side and consider, briefly, not getting back into bed with him. I could go out into the living room and lie down on the sofa, or I could find a guest bedroom, or I could just leave and take a cab home, but I don't want to do any of those things, and the fact that Logan carried me to his room earlier proves he wants me here too. With that blissful thought, I slide back under the covers and lay my head on the pillow. I'm so aware of him beside me, but we're not touching, and that feels like such a colossal waste, so I sort of scoot my body closer to his and gently lift his heavy arm so it goes up and over me. He responds immediately, pulling me close and tucking me up against his side. His weight is lovely, and I lie there for ages, awake and smiling like a fool.

"Ms. Candace…*Ms. Candace!*"

"What?"

"The paint is spilling!"

I look down to see I've overfilled a little cup of pink paint so it's oozing over the sides and onto the counter. "Oh. Bugger!"

The kids snicker because I've said a bad word, but I'm too busy to care. I run round my classroom, grabbing napkins and water to clean up the mess. I should have realized painting was a bad idea.

I've been off all day, moony and distracted. I keep thinking about this morning and what it was like to start my day off at Logan's flat, the milky coffee and little yogurt parfait with loads of berries and oats. He was up way before me, already showered and dressed for a meeting with his agent. He was done up in slacks and a button-down with an expensive watch on his wrist. It was a totally different look, and one that caught me off guard. When he strolled into the kitchen looking like that, I lost track of what I was meant to be doing (spooning yogurt into my mouth) so that a bit of my parfait slid off my spoon and splatted onto the table.

"Morning," he said, going round the island to fetch himself more coffee.

"Oh! Morning!"

When he turned his back to me, I tried desperately to straighten my appearance in the hopes that he wouldn't notice how disheveled I looked.

"Pat will be ready to drive you to your apartment in fifteen minutes. That should give you plenty of time to make it to work, right?"

What did words like "time" and "work" have to do with anything when Logan was strolling around his kitchen looking like that?

He looked at me over his shoulder when I didn't reply, so then I rushed out a half mumbled, "Oh sure! Yes! That's fine."

"And you work tonight?"

I stifled a groan. "Yes, and maybe the next two nights too."

"Really?"

I looked down at my parfait, more than a little bummed. I was already on the schedule for tonight, and I knew I needed to swap with someone so I could work Friday instead of Saturday. The thing is, with Logan inviting me to that gala, it means I need to buy a dress. I don't just have "fancy dress" funds sitting idle in my bank account, so I figured I'd need to pick up another shift Thursday night too to help cover the cost. I felt awkward explaining that to Logan, though, seeing as how I could have probably hawked the breakfast table I was eating at and been able to pay my rent for half a year.

"Yeah, just busy season and all," I said, keeping the truth close to the vest.

He furrowed his brows but didn't argue as he carried his coffee toward the table to sit near me.

"How did you sleep?"

I blushed a little. "Good. And you?"

"Better once you got back in bed and latched onto me."

"*What?!* I only did a little cuddle. You were the one to drag me underneath you. Could barely breathe, really…"

Drat. I'd assumed he was asleep when I did all that. I guess not.

We chatted for a bit after that, about everything that was on his schedule for the day and the plans I had for my 3s class. Then he had to dash off to his meeting and I decided to leave with him, so we rode in the lift together, him holding my hand, and then he kissed me right before the doors swept open and we walked out into the lobby.

I was not at all prepared for the loads of paparazzi out on the sidewalk, snapping away.

In fact, I froze at first, thinking for a second they were there for someone else before they started shouting Logan's name.

Logan totally ignored them and moved toward Pat's waiting SUV quickly, but I couldn't take it. It was bloody early in the morning and we were only trying to hop in the SUV and get to work. How dare they hound us like that? Maybe they thought he didn't care, but I sure did, and I decided to tell them.

"Can't you lot clear out? I think it's quite rude for you all to gather here like this. Don't you have something better to do? There's a nice café just a block over. They've got these cream pastries and nice foamy lattes. If I were you, I'd—"

Logan had to get in front of me then and cut me off from their view. Their cameras continued to snap away, but I didn't care one bit.

"All right, c'mon," he said, backing me up toward the car. "They're not going to leave."

"They might if you ask them to!"

Then I peered around his broad chest to see if they were scattering like cockroaches—as I expected they would be—but Logan was right. My words hadn't affected them in the least! If anything, they only snapped photos with *more* zeal, shouting Logan's name and asking for mine.

I groaned with anger as Logan loaded me into the back seat of the vehicle.

Pat was on my side, of course, cursing the paps right along with me as we pulled away from the curb, but Logan was only smiling and shaking his head, unperturbed by the insanity.

"Next time maybe I'll give them a real piece of my mind," I threatened.

"Oh yeah?" he teased. "I thought that's what you just did."

"What? That was *mild*! Next time I might just tell them all to sod off."

"They'd love that. It'd give them more to report in the magazines."

"Magazines!" I cracked up then. "You've lost it if you think I'm going to be in any magazines."

There's no way I'm important enough to be featured in any magazine anywhere, but Logan's words are still haunting me. The whole day I've wondered if maybe I'll become important by association, just by hanging around him. What would they even call me in the captions beneath the photos? *Logan's lady friend? Logan's loony acquaintance? Some wild woman on the street?* There's no way they'd think we're together. It's mad even to me, and I'm the one who had him on top of me last night!

I'm actually relieved to have my shift at District in the evening because it keeps me ultra-busy, running round and grabbing drink orders. Wednesdays are nowhere near as packed as weekend nights, but we've still got a big enough crowd that I'm on my feet constantly.

Roger loads up another tray with drinks for me and I'm off, unloading them onto my assigned tables and carrying away empties I gather deftly.

One of my tables is really chatty, a load of blokes who look like they've only just started their twenties. They've still got some baby fat on their cheeks and haven't quite figured out that less is more when it comes to hair product.

"Hey, my friend is wondering if you're single," one of them says to me, nodding his head to another guy at the table who's gone totally red in the face. When I smile nicely at him, he looks down, probably wishing he could disappear altogether.

"Well you can tell your *friend* that I think he's quite nice-looking, but I'm not in the market for anything at the moment."

They all laugh and carry on while I walk away with their empty beer bottles.

Roger's heard it all go down and he smiles when I post up against the bar, taking a load off for a moment.

"Aren't you going to take him up on his offer?"

I scrunch my nose. "I don't go for younger men, unfortunately. He looks like he's barely gone through puberty."

"Right. So then it doesn't have anything to do with Logan Matthews?"

155

Good going, Roger. I'd nearly gone three *whole* seconds without thinking of him and now you've ruined it.

I feign total innocence. "I have no idea what you're talking about."

But of course, Roger was here the night Logan came in with his friends and left me his number along with that ridiculous "tip". He knows *something* is going on with Logan and me.

"So you aren't dating him?"

"We're just friends," I reply like some well-trained diplomat.

"Friends? Not likely." He nods his head behind him, to the absolutely ridiculous bouquet of flowers sitting on the back counter of the bar.

"What in the hell are those?"

"Roses, if I'm not mistaken."

The bouquet is bigger than my head! Bigger than the coffee table in my flat! I'll have to just set the vase on the floor and have Kat and Yasmine walk around it. There're enough roses to fill an English garden, all of them blood red and dripping with intent. There's no note nestled in the blooms, which seems even more romantic. It's like Logan knows *I* know who they're from and that's all that matters.

Of course, I wonder how the hell I'll manage to tote them home at the end of my shift. It'll make my subway commute quite a calamity, but then I shouldn't have worried. Pat is waiting out in front of District when I leave, looking down at his mobile until he sees me walking (or rather stumbling) out on the sidewalk, struggling with the bouquet, and he hops out of the black SUV to help me.

"Pat! What are you doing here?!"

I assume, at first, that it's a total coincidence. I'm sure he must have just been in the neighborhood on business, but then he announces, "I'm driving you home."

He says it like it's the most obvious thing in the world. Of course Pat would drive me home from work. How silly of me to assume I'd have to hop on the subway like every other New Yorker!

He takes the massive arrangement from me and sets it in the back seat of the SUV. Once it's buckled into place, he opens the front passenger door for me, continuing our tradition.

"You all set?" he asks as I hop in.

"Sure, but you really didn't need to sit out here and wait for me like this. I'll bet you were bloody bored."

He holds up his mobile, and there's some kind of sports game on it. It's too small for me to make out what it is though.

"I was watching an old World Series game. You know you can watch just about anything you want on YouTube these days?" He sounds like he thinks it's the best invention since sliced bread. "World Series game seven from the 80s—bam! Right at your fingertips."

I grin. "You'll have to tell me more about it on the way home."

We chat so much the drive flies by, and before I know it, I'm carrying that massive bouquet of flowers up the rickety stairs toward my flat. I unlock the door and try to be quiet as I arrange the vase on the TV stand. I know Yasmine and Kat are both asleep; I envy them. It's late, and I've got to be up early for work at The Day School. I half-groan just thinking about it, but I know I'll be fine. I've done the late night/early morning routine loads of times before and survived, so there's no point in feeling sorry for myself now.

Using the dull light filtering in from the street, I unload my tips from the pocket of my District uniform and count out the bills, slightly disappointed with how few there are. Some nights are like that. Here's hoping tomorrow and Friday are better.

I wonder for one quick second if it's worth all the trouble—extra hours on my feet, carting drinks around—and then I catch sight of the huge roses, big and fat and lovely, and I know I'd work a thousand shifts to be able to go to that gala with Logan.

I text him Thursday morning when I get to school, before my students have arrived, to thank him for the flowers and for having Pat come round to get me.

LOGAN: Glad you liked them. I told the florist I had a girl I really wanted to impress…

CANDACE: Well they did a good job! They must have used every rose in the tri-state area for the bouquet. I'll have a whole swarm of bees in my flat later if I don't keep the window latched.

LOGAN: Ha. What are you doing tonight?

Ugh! I wish I could reply with *Oh nothing much, just coming round to your flat to do a bit of humping*, but I absolutely *have* to work. My bank account is filled with tumbleweeds and I can't be expected to buy myself a new fancy-shmancy dress, *and* pay rent, *and* cover the rest of my bills, *and* send money back home to Mum if I don't work my arse off.

CANDACE: Another shift at District, I'm afraid. And before you ask, I'll be there tomorrow night too, remember? I know, boooo. What a lousy schedule! What will you be doing? Lounging about?

LOGAN: I'm actually on Fallon tonight.

CANDACE: You mean like…Jimmy Fallon? The show?

Then I remember the email on his phone from over the weekend.

LOGAN: Yeah, and I have a few spare tickets. I was going to see if you and your roommates wanted to come.

I do about a thousand curses in my head, a whole long string of them that would make a sailor blush if he heard them said aloud.

CANDACE: That sounds brilliant! All this time I've been in New York, and I've never made it round to any of those live tapings. I suppose I'll be a nice friend and see if Yasmine and Kat want to go without me…

LOGAN: I'll have the tickets dropped off at your place just in case. Wish you could come, but at least I'll see you Saturday, right?

CANDACE: Yes! I'm counting the seconds.

Oh god. Is that too much? Have I come off too desperate? If only you could erase texts *after* they've been sent.

LOGAN: Me too. There're some details my assistant can email over to you, just about the location and timing, I think. Send me your email address.

I've just finished giving it to him when I hear the front door of the school open and tiny voices fill the hall outside my classroom. No more flirty sexts! Time to shape the nation's youth!

My assistant, Rosie, has been talking to me for the better part of thirty minutes. I'm amazed at how little air she seems to need compared to the rest of us; in fact, I'm more convinced now than ever that she's part cyborg. I'm studying her, trying to see if there's a battery pack or charging port hidden somewhere on her body, but even if there were, I'd never find it. She wears a lot of layers: black shirt, black blazer, poofy wrap thing that's looped twice around her neck. She has an earpiece on, a phone attached to her hip, a clipboard, and a tablet.

She doesn't look up at me as she continues speaking.

"They have the list of topics that are off the table, and it should be an easy interview. Jimmy will throw you a few softballs. Just ease up and don't fidget too much in the chair."

"Right."

"Tomorrow, you have training in the morning, and then Brett wants to meet with you in the early afternoon to go over the new contract from Nike."

"No can do," I reply, just to see if she'll flinch.

She doesn't even skip a beat.

"Then at 3:00, you have to be across town to shoot that Gatorade campaign. They're putting you on all the bottles of the Cool Blue flavor."

I screw up my face just thinking about how cheesy it'll look. "Sounds horrible. Who would want to buy a drink with my face on it?"

She levels me with a bored glare. "According to their market research, every male in America, aged 5 to 65."

"Right."

"Then you have a Tom Ford fitting for the gala."

"Can't they just use my past measurements and go from there?"

"Don't test me. Their offices have been hounding me for weeks. I've had to swear to get you there in person because they want a custom fit."

I sigh. "Fuck me."

"Yes, well, this is your life. Get used to it."

No kidding.

When I was a kid, I dreamed about becoming a professional athlete. I had visions of playing in packed stadiums, throwing touchdowns to the roar of surging crowds, winning Super Bowls, having a cool house and as many golden retrievers as I wanted. I never thought about everything else that's involved with the job. I'm essentially a one-man small business, and the better I play on the field, the busier I am off of it.

"You're scheduled on the carpet at the gala at 8:32, by the way."

"Can't promise I'll be exactly on time. You know how it is, traffic and all."

"Are you arriving with Darius and Liz?"

"Yeah, and I've been thinking about having Candace come with me."

She frowns; her internal hard drive must be short-circuiting. "Have you told me about Candace?"

"Yes. The girl I just started seeing? The teacher?"

She nods then whips out her tablet, fingers firing away. "That's right. You gave me her info earlier. I have her ticket for the gala and I can email it to her along with the other information: when to arrive, dress code, all that. She'll have to get there early, around 7:00 probably."

"Why can't she just come with me?"

Rosie sighs as if she doesn't have the energy to go over this with me. "You know why."

"She could walk ahead of me on the carpet."

"Right. Okay. And then you and I will have a media storm on our hands trying to contain the resulting attention if you show up to an event with a woman. No. I'm sorry. She needs to arrive early and be far away from you when those cameras start flashing."

I don't reply, and she's forced to continue, "Unless you're ready to bring her into the spotlight, go public, and expose her like that. It's up to you."

I think of the paparazzi at my apartment yesterday morning and shake my head. "No, this is fine. For now."

"Good. I think that's for the best. Now, sit tight. I'll have hair and makeup come in. You have about forty minutes until you're on air. Review those questions I gave you and try to come up with answers that will make good sound bites."

"Or I could just speak from the heart?"

She doesn't even bother replying to that, already flying out the door.

I'm sitting in my dressing room at *The Tonight Show*. It's an honor to be here for the fourth time and I should be happy that I'm relevant enough to get invitations to shows like this, but I just can't seem to muster up the energy I need. I know it's because Candace couldn't come tonight. I was hoping she'd be here, in the crowd. It's not like I could really acknowledge her even if she were here, but maybe I could have found a way to shoot her a little wave or a smile.

I think of her working at District, probably flying around like a pixie.

I think of the men there, no doubt hitting on her.

It makes my stomach tighten in annoyance.

Jealousy doesn't sit well with me, probably because it's been a while since I've felt it. I try to imagine the last few women I've dated going out with someone new, and I dig deep for some feeling, just to try to prove to myself that Candace isn't as special as I'm making her out to be. I picture Melody with another guy and feel the opposite of jealous. I'm apathetic—bored, even. Then I picture Candace smiling, just fucking *smiling* at another guy, and my fists clench. *Real healthy, Logan.* Jesus. I force myself to relax then drag a hand through my hair.

My phone vibrates with a new text, and I tug it out of my pocket.

CANDACE: Hey Lo! (Isn't that hilarious? I've just cracked myself up with that nickname. If you say it out loud in my accent, it sounds like I'm saying hey-llo, like hello. Funny, right? No?) Well...anyway...break a leg tonight! You'll do great! I'm going to ask the bartenders to pull it up on the telly for me, though I can't make any promises. If there's any sort of sporting game on tonight, everyone will moan at me to switch the channel! PS Kat and Yasmine are going to be there in the audience. I've told them to shout very loud and really cause a ruckus when you walk out so you know we're all rooting for you. XO, C

I'm smiling for what feels like the first time all day as I type out a quick reply.

LOGAN: I like the nickname. I'll be sure to listen for your roommates, though I wish you were in the audience too.

I'm expecting her to reply, so I'm looking down at my phone, waiting for a new text to pop up when there's a knock on my door and people start to flood into my dressing room for hair and makeup.

"We have forty minutes until airtime. I need everyone to focus," a producer shouts, grabbing everyone's attention, including mine.

If Candace texts me again, I don't have time to notice.

"Oh my god, I'm going to stand out like a sore thumb," I moan, turning in the mirror to check the back of the dress I'm trying on. There's a huge hole just under my left arm where the fabric has split at the seam, and even without that, the dress itself is still two sizes too big for me.

"Right. Well. This isn't exactly the winner, is it?" Kat says, scrunching her nose in distaste. "Just take it off and we'll keep looking."

We've been at it all day though, running round town, rummaging through resale shops for dresses that fit into the parameters Logan's assistant sent over via email. I've got them memorized by heart. I'm meant to wear a "formal evening gown *or* dressy cocktail dress *or* dressy separates, paired with an elegant wrap, brooch, or themed jewelry."

I haven't even found a dress, let alone a brooch! I'm doomed.

"Maybe we ought to search for some 'dressy separates'?" Kat suggests with a lopsided smile.

"Oh right, because I'll just bet this shop has got loads of trendy tuxedos for women!"

She shrugs. "They might."

Then I hear footsteps pounding out in the hall connecting the dressing rooms and Yasmine breathing hard on the other side of the flimsy door. Her fists pound for us to let her in, and when we do, I see her eyes have gone really wide like she's got a brilliant idea. In her arms is a silver shimmery dress comprising less material than what I'd use to cover one of my arms, let alone my whole body.

"Okay, I know"—*huff huff*—"what you're thinking."—*huff huff*—"It might be horrible. Or it might be—"

"Wonderful!" Kat squeals. "That fabric is so glam. You'll look like a disco ball!"

Just what every girl wants.

I wish I were at Bloomingdale's picking from a slew of gorgeous gowns, but the issue lies in the fact that I've got absolutely no money to spare on this dress even after covering all those shifts at District this week. I managed to land tables who were absolute shite tippers, so here I am, searching through secondhand racks and praying I'll find a dress for about fifteen bucks that will look like it's worth fifteen *hundred*.

Yasmine hands the dress over to Kat, who holds it up for me to inspect. There are loads of flimsy straps, and it's all kinds of twisted.

"Where's the top part? I can't make it out."

"Just take off that monstrosity you're wearing and we'll figure it out," Yasmine says, squinting her eyes at the dress I've got on like it's offensive to her. "I found this new dress in the bargain racks, way down at the end as if it'd been totally forgotten, but then I looked at the tag and it's VALENTINO! TRULY! And even more perfect, I think it'll have a tie in the back so we can get it cinched really tight and it'll look like it's your exact size."

All in all, it takes us about half an hour to get me into the damn thing. It's really confusing what with all the thin straps going this way and that across my back. It's a slinky material that clings to my skin and exposes way more than I'm comfortable with. There's a deep V-neck in front, a slit up my left thigh, and basically no back to speak of.

"Oh my god. I cannot wear this," I say after Kat and Yasmine have tied me into it so it's hugging my figure tightly.

It's divine, truly, something I'd never allow myself to wear in normal life. At The Day School, it's all day dresses and trainers. At District, I've got that black uniform and my work apron. This little number is for some confident model traipsing around St. Barts while every hunk in a ten-meter radius salivates over her.

"You'll have to go braless," Kat says with a shrug. "Your breasts are perky though, so it's no big deal."

"Oh great, thanks. Maybe speak up—I'm not sure the people one block over have heard you talking about my breasts."

"And your knickers will have to be tiny," Yasmine adds. "No pulling out the huge cotton ones like you normally wear—the same ones my gran uses. Not with that slit up the thigh."

I look at my reflection and instantly redden. It's a lot of dress. Or rather...*not* a lot of dress. It's obscene, right? I couldn't be caught dead in this in public! Mum would have a heart attack!

"It's great, Yaz. You did a good job, but we'll have to keep looking. I can't wear this to the gala. I'm not nearly chic enough to pull it off."

"Bollocks! You're making it out to be racier than it is. I bet every female there will be dressed sexy. This dress is fancy *and* tasteful and, more importantly, within our budget."

Kat chimes in now. "Besides, it's not as if we've got the time to keep looking. We have to get back to the flat if you want us to help with your hair and makeup. Didn't Logan's assistant say you had to get there by 7:00 PM?"

Oh jeez. My pulse is pounding. I hate this. I was hoping to find some simple gown that fit well enough to let me blend in with the crowd tonight, something black and sensible. This dress, however, ensures I won't be blending in at all. My stomach twists into a knot, but it doesn't even matter because my mates are already collecting our things and helping me get out of the dress so we can take it to the counter and buy it.

I haven't even fully agreed to wear it, but the wheels are already in motion. We head back so I can shower and take my time lathering on lotion everywhere so my skin glows. Then I slip into a robe and sit down in the living room so Kat and Yasmine can work their magic on me.

Kat does my hair while Yasmine applies my makeup. Yasmine is bloody brilliant with a makeup brush, way better than I could ever hope to be. She says she used to spend hours applying shadows to her eyes back in school instead of doing any proper studying, and it's paid off.

"I think because your dress has got a sort of vintage vibe, I'm going to straighten your hair so it's sleek and shiny and then leave it down. Then we can pin it behind your ear so it's not in your face the whole night."

Thank god it'll be down; maybe it'll help conceal how racy the back of the dress is.

I'm too nervous to bother checking my mobile while they get me ready. I know Logan texted me earlier, reminding me that I'll have to get there before him. I hate the idea of being there when he's not. Who am I going to talk to? Where will I stand? Off in the corner? With the bartenders? Argh. It sends my heart racing all over again just to think about it. I wish we could just go together, but I guess I understand. Don't want the press going crazy, I suppose. *It's fine*, I assure myself all over again.

I have to hand it to Yasmine and Kat. By the time they're finished with me, I blink at my reflection in disbelief. I look like a proper Bond girl what with my shimmery dress and my heels and my fancy makeup. More importantly, I *feel* like a Bond girl. I turn in a circle to inspect and admire the way the straps crisscross over my back. I like the dress now more than I did in the shop. I think with my hair and makeup done, it seems more realistic that I could pull it off.

After I grab my clutch and load it full of the essentials (snacks mainly), they make me pose for loads of pictures out in the living room, like they're my two mums sending me off to a school dance.

"Don't slouch! Hold your head up and make sure to walk in like you bloody well belong there!" Yasmine reminds me as they direct me toward the door of the flat.

"And send us loads of pics if you can! Remember what kind of food they serve! And all the celebrities you see!" Kat shouts out as I start to head slowly down the stairs, careful not to trip and fall and ruin all their hard work.

I breathe a sigh of relief when I see Pat down at the curb waiting for me. When he sees me, he gives me an over-the-top reaction, clapping his hands against his cheeks as if he can't believe how nice I look.

"You're the most beautiful gal in New York City!"

171

I roll my eyes teasingly. "Now now, don't go filling my head up with compliments. I'll need to remember who I am come midnight when my carriage turns back into a pumpkin."

He laughs and shakes his head, and we hop into the car together.

There's terrible traffic on the street around Gotham Hall. I tell Pat he can drop me a ways off and I can just walk the rest, but he says he doesn't mind.

"You're early anyway, right? Looks like there isn't anyone on the red carpet yet."

I gulp. Did I read Rosie's email wrong? Was I supposed to arrive later? No. I check again. She said 7:00 and it's only 7:01. I'm on time and have no choice but to open my door when Pat pulls up to the curb.

"Any chance I can convince you to come in with me?" I plead, looking back at him as I hover halfway out of the car.

He gives me a lopsided smile, like he pities me. "Would if I could. Bet there's going to be some good food in there."

"You could be my date," I tease, and he laughs.

"Your date will be here soon. You're gonna knock his socks off. Have fun, kiddo."

"Right. Okay. I'll see you later! Thanks for the lift!"

I step out onto the curb and fix my dress so the slit is centered on my left thigh and not my crotch (lovely). Then, instead of making a move for the front entrance, I watch as Pat drives away and makes room for the next car to pull up. My gut twists as I watch him leave, like he's my security blanket and, without him, I've got nothing.

A group of people hop out of the car that just pulled up, laughing and chatting as they pass me by. I feel lonely as I follow behind them, letting them lead me in the right direction. There are loads of media already lined up on either side of the red carpet, but they don't bother looking our way. It must be clear that all the normal people are arriving early and skipping the red carpet, so there's no need to turn around and snap photos of us.

I slip right behind them then wait my turn at the side entrance. A group of people dressed in black with headsets on and tablets in their hands asks each guest for their ID before they're allowed past. I'm shaky with nerves as I pass mine over.

"Hopefully my name's on your list! I was only added this week, I think," I stammer, though she's paying me no attention.

"Williams, Candace. You can go in."

Then she hands me back my ID and looks behind me toward the next person.

Right, well, I've breached the defenses rather easily!

The joke makes me smile to myself as I join the small crowd of people heading inside Gotham Hall. The building is huge, but it's easy enough to follow the carpet-lined passage toward a huge set of double doors, which are open so people can flood into the main event space. The gala is housed inside a huge round room covered with a dome made up of ornate stained-glass. Wowzers, it's quite a venue, all tinted blue with snazzy lighting so everyone looks their absolute best. There're loads of attendants hovering around in tuxedos, ready with trays of canapés and flutes of champagne. I grab one and take a heavy sip, smiling with delight as the bubbles fill my mouth.

"Delicious," I say, smiling at the waiter.

He grins back and I think he's about to say something, but then another guest catches his attention and asks for two flutes of her own.

I drift around the perimeter of the space, taking in the crowd. Since it's still early, not many people are here yet. I sort of hate it because it makes it harder to blend in. I look for someone else standing off by themselves, like me, but it seems like everyone else belongs more than I do. I try not to stop walking for long, aware that if I do, I'll really look like a sad sap. I sip my champagne and try to take my time looking around the room at the stained glass and the night sky showing through it.

It's lovely, really, and I'm trying hard to admire it and forget about how self-conscious I feel when I sense someone stop near me.

It's the waiter from earlier, a young guy about my age with floppy blond hair and a huge smile.

"Nice party, huh?"

I laugh and nod. "Very *fahn-cy*," I drawl.

His grin widens. "Yeah. Never been at an event like this."

"Neither have I," I admit, feeling better having gotten the confession off my chest.

He nods and volunteers, "I don't usually work these things, to be honest. I'm a grad student over at NYU and needed some spare cash." He shrugs. "Thought it'd be fun."

"That's great. You'll probably make great tips." Then I hold up my hand in warning. "Not from me, mind you. I'm one of the poor ones. You'll have to spot the guests whose purses and trousers are sagging from all the cash they've got loaded in them."

He laughs and shakes his head. "It's cool. Tips aren't really necessary. They're paying us pretty well."

"Really? That's good. I sort of wish I were working the event with you. I think I'd feel loads more comfortable."

His gaze falls on my lips, as if he's finally caught on to my accent. "You're British?"

I shrug. "Guilty."

"Cool. I like the accent. It's…" His gaze sort of falls down my dress for a moment, and I think the word "cute" dies on his lips. "It's cool. I like it."

I blush like a bloody buffoon and take another sip of my champagne.

"You should finish that quickly so I can hand you a new one. That way it looks like I'm supposed to be hanging around you."

"Ha. What a ploy! I'll be tipsy if I go too fast. Kind of a lightweight."

His brow quirks. "Yeah? All right, then I'll go easy on you."

He's definitely doing some proper flirting, and it feels so odd considering I'm waiting for Logan to arrive. It's not like I want to lead this guy on, but it feels nice to not be standing totally alone.

"Ah hell. That's my boss waving her hand, telling me to circulate. You stay put. I'll be back soon."

I laugh and promise him I won't be far. It's not like I've got anywhere to go.

The minutes drag while I stand alone, damn near close to twiddling my thumbs. I check my mobile and see a text from Logan. My heart skips a beat.

LOGAN: Be there soon. Leaving my apartment now.

Thank GOD.

I might leap on him when he arrives.

My waiter friend comes back a few minutes later with a tray of food. Little crab cakes preloaded on spoons and crackers with something lovely and savory heaped on top. I take one of each, and then another, and then tease him that he'll have to leave or I'll finish off the whole tray by myself.

"That's okay. As long as I come back with it empty, they won't care."

I grin and take another sip of champagne.

I ask him about what he's studying at NYU, and he asks me how long I've been in the States. I try to give him my full attention, but truthfully, my gaze keeps leaping back to the entrance of the room, waiting for Logan to pass through the doors.

A real crowd is starting to gather now, and I've seen more than one notable person walk in: the mayor of New York City, Billie Eilish, Lester Holt. The crowd is quite diverse, and I'm giddy from how many celebrities are circulating the room now. One actress from *Modern Family*, the one who plays the older sister, even compliments my dress as she walks by me! Ace! I can't wait to tell Yasmine and Kat. They'll die!

Then I finally spot Logan at the entrance, and my heart sort of collapses in on itself. Maybe it's the fact that I've waited so long for him to arrive. Maybe it's how kind he's been this week, sending the flowers and having Pat come round to District to drive me home every night. Maybe it's the way he looks. He walks in with a crowd around him, donning a sharp black tuxedo. His hair is combed back, real formal and sexy. My hands instantly go clammy and I lose the ability to do much of anything except stare.

My waiter friend notices. He follows my gaze and laughs in disbelief.

"Logan Matthews is here. That's so fucking cool. I should try to sneak his autograph without my boss seeing."

I force out a tight laugh and try not to pass out.

176

It takes me too long to register that I recognize the people he's walking in with. There's Darius and Liz, and Melody too. I wasn't expecting to see her tonight, but duh, of course she'd attend. She belongs here way more than I do. She's right beside Logan, tugging on his arm to get his attention, and they chat for a moment. I try not to let it bother me. They're friends, of course; he's known her longer than he's known me.

He'll find me soon enough, I assure myself, wondering what I should do. Run across the place and fling myself at him? Play it cool and sort of wave if he looks in my direction? It's totally hopeless—there's no way he'll spot me in the crowd now. He has the advantage. He's tall and...well, famous. Everyone sort of either gives him a wide berth or rushes in to get closer. He draws a crowd, and I frown, looking down at my nearly empty champagne.

"Have you got another flute I could top mine off with?" I suddenly regret not getting utterly toasted while I waited for him to arrive. Some liquid courage would be quite nice right about now.

"Sure thing," the waiter says, taking my flute so he can go swap it out for another. "Oh shit, he's headed this way."

"What?!"

I turn, and it's true. Oh Lordy. Logan has somehow spotted me amidst the masses, and he's cutting through the crowd to get to me.

My new friend turns to me, more than a little confused. "Do you *know* him?"

I try to feign surprise. "Oh. Well...*yes*? A bit?"

What am I supposed to say?! *You know what? I happened to have humped his thigh just the other day, if you can believe it, and then I cuddled with him in his huge bed all night. It was absolute bliss.*

177

"Candace," Logan says from a few feet away.

I glance over and wave like we're two mates meeting on the street. "Fancy seeing you here."

His eyes narrow and then he glances at my new friend standing beside me.

"Logan," I start. "Err…this is…sorry, didn't get your name?"

"Max."

"Right, this is Max. He's been so nice and kept me company while I was waiting for you. I think he'd like an autograph."

"That'd be awesome, but like, no pressure. I'll probably get in trouble for asking."

"Nonsense!" I grab a cocktail napkin and hold out my hand for the pen Max has in his apron pocket. He fumbles for it then hands it over with shaky fingers. "I'm asking for the autograph, not you. See? Here Logan, sign right here."

He does, and then I hand the napkin to the waiter, who immediately stares at it like I've just handed him a solid gold bar.

"Thanks, man. This is so cool!"

"No problem," Logan says, stepping toward me. "Candace, can I talk to you for a second? Alone?"

"Oh. Um…" I look around us, wondering where exactly we could go to be alone. Already I see people starting to whisper about Logan. It'll only be a matter of seconds before we're surrounded again.

But Logan knows what he's doing. He steps closer and turns me so he can rest his hand on the small of my back, directing me to a side door just to my left. It leads back out into the hall surrounding the main room, and since it's so far from the main entrance, it's deserted.

I think he'll stop propelling me forward now that we're out here alone, but he keeps right on prodding me along until he yanks open a door he seems to find satisfactory. It opens into an auxiliary storage room filled with linen and folded tables and spare chairs. The lights are out, but he flips a switch and we're coated in dull yellow light.

Then he pushes me inside before him.

"What—what in the world?! Why've you gone and stuffed us into a broom closet?"

CANDACE
15

"Because there were hundreds of people in that room and it probably wasn't a good idea to greet you the way I want to. Not while they all watch."

My eyes go wide as he steps near me, crowding my space.

"Right, well, say your hello and then we can—"

He lifts his hand to the base of my chin and tilts it up with his pointer finger. I go absolutely silent as he stares down at me, taking his time as his gaze drops from my face, lower, over my dress, eating me up.

"You look stunning," he says, his eyes still on the shimmery silver fabric covering my body.

"Th-thanks. Kat and Yasmine convinced me to wear this. I thought it was a bit *much*."

"Oh, it definitely is."

My lip trembles. "You don't like it?"

His dark eyes whip back up to my face. "I didn't say that."

Then he takes a step closer and his hips touch mine. My body softens instantly, like I've been waiting days for the moment I'd feel him against me like this. Clearly, he's been anxiously waiting for this too, because he's not acting decent at all. Dragging me in here, pinning me up against the wall—the nerve!

"Are you going to kiss me?" I whisper as his head starts to descend.

Instead of answering me, his lips capture mine.

It's like I've just been struck by a bolt of lightning, all that electricity zapping through me as he kisses me harder. I drop my clutch on the floor so my hands can slide up to the lapels of his tuxedo jacket, and I hold on to him there as I rise up onto my toes. My high heels don't do enough, not since he's so bloody tall.

His hands find my hips and then he skims them back and around, touching my bare skin underneath the thin straps holding my dress in place. His touch is fire, and I respond like a pyromaniac, wanting to set us both aflame.

I grip his lapels harder as his hands slide across my skin and press against my lower back, bringing me against him. Our bodies are flush and hot and the longer we kiss, the less I can think straight. He's too good at this, dismantling me so that I'm nothing more than my baser needs. His kiss is the only lifeblood I need. He sustains me with it, not letting up even when I start to feel lightheaded.

His hands lead me further toward darkness as he slides back around to my front, then lower, between my legs, up and inside the slit that keeps the two parts of my dress together. I'm staring down the barrel of the gun as his fingers slide over my panties. And then his finger is on the trigger.

Wet. The word rattles me as he brushes me there. Again.

I shiver and push him away, hard.

I blink my eyes open, and I know this idea I just concocted is wild. I know…but well, this dress is giving me quite a lot of courage, and the last time we fooled around, I was the lucky one. It's only fair that this time it should be him. I want to drive him mad. I want to provide him with an image that racks through his brain the rest of the evening, so I ignore him when he protests the fact that I've broken off our kiss. He even steps closer and tries to grip my chin and seal his mouth on mine again, but I tut like he's being naughty then lock eyes with him as I start to get down on my knees. My chin slips from his fingers and his eyes go molten. He knows what I'm after, and there's no going back now. A woman only kneels down in front of a man for one reason, and it's not to surrender. It's to wage war.

"Candace," he murmurs breathlessly, his voice heavy with lust as my hands glide down his tuxedo-clad thighs.

The cold concrete bites into my knees as I settle in place, but what's a little discomfort compared to the look on Logan's face right now? I'm not even touching him, not yet, and already I've won. Poor guy.

"You look really handsome tonight," I say, my hands drifting up higher, toward the noticeable bulge in his trousers. I skim around it like a tease, and he hisses in a sharp breath as my fingers fall on the black button. I shift it out of the hole then reach for the zipper. It slides down with no effort at all, and then his trousers slip down his toned hips enough that I can reach my hands inside and start tugging down his boxer briefs.

My mouth waters as my fingers brush over his hard length.

This is so, *so* wrong.

We're at a gala! We're in a *supply closet* at a *gala*!

But there's no stopping me, not when I look up and see the way Logan is staring down at me, like I'm not quite real, like this is all a dream. It gives me the courage to close my hand around him and start to slide it up then pump back down, harder and faster, again and again.

He groans deep and low, and I know he's going mad. I lean in close to brush my lips over his hardness and then his hand falls on my hair, tangling in the strands. Just like that, he's mine, utterly lost in my mouth as I take him deeper.

My lips tighten around him and my hand keeps pumping and Logan's eyes flutter closed then blink open quickly, as if he doesn't want to miss a single moment of what I'm doing to him. Our gazes connect and there's a transfer of emotion, like he's trying to tell me something, but I can't make out exactly what it is. I'm too scared to let the full weight of it sink into me. So, I use my mouth and my tongue and my lips and let my body do all the talking.

He whispers my name and then his hips start to pump forward, harder, taking back a little control. I ease up and let him, and now the tables have turned. He's using me now, and all the uncomfortable sensations come flooding in: my aching jaw, the cold concrete, the burning desire to suck in a deep breath of air. I'm almost at my tipping point, close to tapping out—but then his hand soothes my hair and my eyes find his again and I see the emotion there. The adoration and the *need*, pure and simple. He's so close so I dig a little deeper, ignoring the ache, and choose to stay down on my knees in this closet, letting him use my mouth, knowing he loves it, knowing ultimately, I'm responsible for that look on his face right now. Then, finally, when I'm desperate for air, he jerks forward and his body shakes with uncontrolled surges as he finishes. Shattered. Done. So am I.

We stay silent, gulping in breaths. It's like we've both been stuck under water for too long and we're trying to recover, attempting to piece ourselves back together. My heart starts to calm, but I still feel like a wreck when he helps me stand.

The high has burned off, and now I'm left feeling like I can't possibly go back out in public without everyone realizing what we've just done.

For some insane reason, tears burn the edges of my eyes, and maybe it's just the fact that all my emotions seem to be living right on the surface lately, or maybe it's the feeling of wrongdoing falling heavy on my shoulders.

Logan settles me back on my feet and hugs me close, wrapping his arms around me so I'm totally sheltered from the world. We don't say a word for a long time as he holds me. I breathe in his cologne and try to pretend we're completely alone, in a vacuum of our own making.

But then a jazz band starts to play out in the main hall, and even in our supply closet, we hear it.

Logan pulls back and holds me at arm's length.

I arch a brow at him, and his solemn expression starts to lessen. He shakes me back and forth, trying to tease a smile out of me, and eventually, I relent. Then, he tugs a handkerchief from his front pocket and passes it over to me. I use it to dab at the corners of my eyes then fold it over to wipe around my mouth.

"I could use a shower."

"I think there's a bathroom just around the corner."

I groan. "Do I look like I've just given a blow job?"

He laughs and shakes his head. "You look as sexy as you did when I first dragged you in here."

"You're biased. You've just had a lovely time, so nothing quite matters. Be truthful—do I look like a mess?"

185

He tugs me toward him and kisses my hair. "I promise you look fine, but I'll lead you to the bathroom so you can see for yourself."

Then he picks up my clutch and passes it over so I can tuck it under my arm, and we start to head for the door. He opens it and pokes his head out. I laugh at how ridiculous he looks, like he's on some sort of reconnaissance mission. A regular secret agent.

"The coast is clear," he tells me, taking my hand and pulling me out after him. We close the door and walk out into the hall, and just like that, we're two normal people attending the gala once again.

My cheeks go red, though, just knowing I look a fright. I see the door for the loos up ahead and practically bolt for it.

"I'll be in there! Don't bother waiting for me—I'll probably be a while."

"All right, I'll go get us drinks."

I wink then push through the door. It's blessedly empty and cold, but I don't bother looking at my reflection yet. It'll only depress me. I do my business in the stall and rearrange my dress so it sits where it's meant to. Then I walk out to the sink, take a deep breath, and lift my gaze.

Oof.

My lipstick is smeared round my mouth. I look like I belong in a striped circus tent, and the damage doesn't end there. My hair is standing on end in a few places, from where Logan was gripping me to keep me where he wanted. He really did a number on me. My cheeks are flushed and my eyes are a bit glassy.

Fragile. I look fragile.

I groan and grab a load of paper towels to carefully dab off my smeared lipstick, without ruining even more of my makeup. Then I toss them and start to finger-comb my hair. It's sort of useless, but it's all I've got. I'm still going at it when the door opens and Melody strolls in. She sees me and jumps in shock.

"I know you!"

I smile. "Oh, err…hello there. Yeah, I'm Candace."

She narrows her eyes in thought as if trying to place me, and then she smiles. "Right! Candace. You were the waitress at that bar we went to the other night."

"Right-o," I say with a little shrug of my shoulders. "District. And you're one of Logan's friends."

"Well, more than friends." Then she sort of claps a hand over her mouth and rolls her eyes. "Forget I said that. God, being with someone in the public eye is so complicated."

"What do you mean?" I ask, voice weak.

"It can be so tricky dealing with our public image. It's one way behind closed doors"—she waggles her eyebrows suggestively—"and another way in the public. You have to play it cool all the time."

I can feel the color start to drain from my face. I'm a pale ghost as she steps closer and takes a spot at the sink beside mine. She starts to fuss with her appearance, but there's no need. She's flawless.

"What are the odds I'd bump into you like this? Here of all places." She laughs as our eyes meet in the mirror. "Are you involved with Feeding America?"

I shake my head quickly. "No, actually."

"Oh, so you must have come as someone's date? Who is it? I might know them. This town is smaller than you think," she says, giving me a big smile.

And worse, the smile seems genuine.

And if she's being genuine…

She's still waiting for me to respond to her question. I blink and try to come up with something. It's not like I can tell her I was waiting here for Logan, not after what she's claimed, so I give her a real truth.

"Myself. I came by myself."

"Oh? Good for you! This cause is so important to me, so I'm always happy to see a packed event. I bet we'll raise a lot of money tonight."

"Yeah…I hope so."

"Did you manage to avoid the red carpet on your way in?" she asks with a little groan, as if red carpets are the bane of her existence.

"Just about. I came early."

She sets her clutch on the counter and opens it so she can reach in for her mobile.

"I wish I had thought to do the same, but with Logan, there's no way to avoid it. Let me look—I bet they've already started posting pictures." Then she laughs at what she sees on her screen. "God, those photographers work fast!"

She turns the mobile so I can see what she's looking at. It's a photo on Twitter, an image of her standing beside Logan as they both smile for the cameras. The room goes hazy as my eyes focus in on an image I wish weren't real: Melody and Logan side by side on the red carpet, her hand resting possessively on his shoulder. She looks completely gorgeous.

My first instinct is to assume it's an old photo—I want it to be old or fake or *something*—

but then rationality sets in. Gotham Hall is in the background, behind them. Melody is wearing the dress she's got on right now. Logan is wearing the exact tuxedo he had on as I slid down to my knees to give him a blow job a few minutes ago.

I feel sick, truly. My stomach rolls, and nausea threatens the back of my throat. Melody looks at me like she's deeply concerned as I pull myself together in an effort to keep my embarrassment to a minimum. I have no idea what's going on, but I know I don't like it.

"Are you okay?" she asks, reaching her hand out to touch my arm.

I flinch away then grimace at how awkward I'm being. I force myself to glance up at her face, and I ask her a question I'm dying to know the answer to. "Are you and Logan dating?"

The edge of her mouth rises then and she rolls her eyes. "You know how it is. We haven't gone public. We're not officially *anything*, at least not on paper. He'd deny it if you asked him because he's so ridiculously private about his life. He doesn't want it getting out to the press."

He'd deny it if you asked him.

"But you're his date tonight?" I prod, trying to pin down the truth.

She looks thoroughly confused, as if I've got a few screws loose. "Are you sure you're all right? Should I call someone for help? You look kind of sick all of a sudden."

I glance at my reflection and sure enough, she's right.

"Bad, um...champagne, I guess. I'm just going to get some fresh air. I'll see you out there, yeah?"

And then I grab my clutch and rush out of the bathroom like my life depends on it.

Out in the hall, I try to force myself to calm down. I can't breathe, not properly anyway. I press my hand against my chest and wonder if these are the initial signs of a heart

189

attack, but no, I realize—these are the initial signs of betrayal.

I consider leaving right then and there. The side hall rounds toward the front of the building, and I could be out on the curb in a few minutes, free from this hell—but I have to talk to Logan. I have to get his side and be mature about this, even though Melody seemed honest and sweet. Even though she had that photo of them arriving together. Even though they look like they'd make the most perfect couple...I have to hear it from Logan's lips.

I force myself back into the main hall, and it takes me bloody ages to find him. Now that the gala has really gotten underway, the walkways are thick with bodies and I'm annoyed that no one's sitting in their seats yet. They're milling about trying to talk to anyone and everyone they can get their hands on. They want to schmooze and network and do whatever the hell else it is rich people do at galas other than donating to the cause at hand.

An event photographer steps close and snaps a photo of the group beside me, the flash momentarily blinding me.

Bloody brilliant!

I push past him and toss back an apology afterward, and then finally, I spot Logan talking with Darius and a few other guys. They're standing in a thick group, talking and laughing, and suddenly there's a lead weight in my stomach, keeping me from going over to him.

It's the last thing I want to do, confront this issue. I want to run for the hills and lick my wounds in private, but I have to know what wounds I've got. I'm still utterly confused about what's actually going on. Did he really arrive here with her? After telling me I had to come early? What the hell is going on?

With trepidation, I make my way toward him. He doesn't see me even when I'm right on them because I'm so much shorter than the rest of the group. I bet they're all professional athletes, the lot of them.

I tap him on his shoulder, and when he turns around to face me, his eyes light up with excitement.

"There you are," he says with a smile, though he doesn't reach out to touch me and now I'm not sure why. Is it because he doesn't want Melody to see? "I was going to get us drinks and I got sidetracked by these guys."

"Could we speak for a minute?" I ask with a shaky voice, aware that his friends are all looking over at me with curious expressions. Some of them probably remember me as the girl in the pool at his party. How embarrassing. I'll bet they're wondering what I'm doing here, and I can't blame them. After all, I'm doing the same.

Logan frowns and turns to lead me away from the group. "Sure. What's going on?"

I wait until we're out of earshot of his friends before turning to him and coming right out with it. "Um, this is sort of awkward. But, well…did you come here tonight with Melody?"

His smile immediately falls and his dark brows furrow. "Crap. I meant to warn you about that. Listen, out on the red carpet, Darius and Liz arrived with Melody. We took pictures as a group and then Darius and Liz stepped away. I was about to step away as well, but Melody put her hand on my shoulder and I didn't want to cause a scene or anything, so I stood there for a second before walking away. They only took that one photo before I moved away from her."

Oh okay. So she arrived with his friends, and they had to take photos as a group. And then when Melody wanted to take a photo with him, he didn't want to embarrass her, so that's how this all happened. What a perfectly reasonable explanation. I should feel loads better.

I don't.

"But then why does she think you two are dating?"

He rears back as if utterly confused.

"*Dating?*"

I point in the direction I just came from. "I just ran into her in the loo. She showed me the red carpet photo and mentioned you were a couple but said you would deny it because you don't want it getting out. I just... Please be honest with me. Am I being played here? Am I the fool?"

"No. Listen." He reaches out to touch me, but I jerk back.

I don't want to be touched right now. I really don't.

I look around me, at all the faces in the crowd of people who seem to know exactly what I've just done and who I am.

Everything suddenly feels tilted out of proportion, like I'm looking at the world through a funhouse mirror. The lights, the music, the crowd—everything is *off*. I hate it all and I want out. Right now.

"Candace—"

"What the fuck am I doing? Oh my god. What am I doing?" I've lost my grip, truly. I can't stop myself from mumbling. "I just gave you..." I slap my hand over my mouth. "Oh my god. I'm going to be sick."

I turn away from him and rush toward the front exit of the hall.

"Candace, stop."

I can't. Doesn't he see? I'm the gross one, the loser. He arrived on the red carpet with Melody, and even if it was an accident (*Was it?!*), the whole internet is probably aflame with how gorgeous they are together, and then here I am...the other woman. The one in the supply closet!

I feel so disgusted with myself, like I'd peel my skin off if I could. I want to run out of this room, but I don't let myself. I only walk quickly, aware of Logan calling my name, but I don't bother to stop. It feels like none of this is real, like I might wake up tomorrow and find it's all been a horrible nightmare.

Logan only catches me because on my way out, I realize I haven't donated yet. I might not have much to spare, but the people who benefit from this charity have even less than I do. I yank open my clutch, grab what little cash I have, and stuff it in a donation box near the door. Logan grabs ahold of my arm just as I'm walking away, and he tugs me to a stop.

"Please don't leave," he says in a quiet voice near my ear. He's trying to keep us from causing a scene.

"Logan." I turn around to stare up at him with pleading eyes. "Let me go. I truly can't be in this room. I feel like I might throw up or embarrass myself even more. I'm not mad at you, I promise!"

And it's true. I'm not. I'm just confused. I want to leave this room and leave this dramatic life Logan leads. I want to get some space from the events of the last twenty minutes so I can put the pieces together in a way that makes sense. I can't do that here.

I try to get free of his grip, but he doesn't let me.

"I want no part of this strange love triangle you've got going on with Melody."

"There is no love triangle. I'm not seeing her," he insists, his voice hard and clear as he leans in close to me. He really wants me to hear what he has to say. "I swear to you, I'm not. I have no idea what she said to you, but the fact is, she and I have only gone out in a group *twice*. The last time was the night I saw you at District. Nothing has happened since

193

then. Darius and Liz invited her here tonight. She's not my date. *You* are."

Then, because maybe he feels like I still don't believe him, he leans in and kisses me with the whole room watching.

I'm so caught off guard I don't flinch back right away. We kiss, and I let him try to lure me back to our blissful bubble. My concerns start to creep back into the shadows, but just before they're gone completely, I break away from Logan and end the kiss.

No. I don't want this. I need to clear my head.

"Come back to the table?" he asks after I turn my face away from him.

I frown, feeling horrible for having to disappoint him. "I truly can't."

Honestly, this night has been a total disaster, and even though I think Logan is telling the truth, I can't just walk back into the thick of things and act as if nothing has happened. I need a breather and some space. I need a moment to reset and collect my thoughts.

"I'm going home."

His whole body sort of sags as if he's never been more disappointed.

"I can't go with you. I have to stay and take my reserved spot at the table or it'll look horrible. I've committed to being here for the charity."

My eyes go wide. "Of course! I understand. I wouldn't expect you to leave with me anyway. I'll go and we can regroup tomorrow or something? After we've had some time to cool off?"

He nods, and I'm not going to lie, it's extremely awkward to sort of shuffle a step back and break his hold on me. It's not a breakup, but it feels an awful lot like one. He looks at me like I'm tearing his heart out, and I probably don't look much better myself.

I force my body to turn and leave. It's for the best.

Out in the hall, it's quiet and empty. Everyone is inside there, with the band and the crowd and the noise of it all.

The city street is just what I need, packed with real people and their real problems. No one seems to care at all about me as I reenter it. The photographers have all gone home. Workers are dismantling the red carpet, and I pass by them unnoticed. I know I could call Pat and have him come round to get me, but it doesn't feel right to ask him to do that. Besides, he's not my employee. I can't just ask him to drive me around for free. He's on Logan's payroll.

Instead, I start to walk. I'm highly aware of what I'm wearing and how little protection this dress provides me, so I eventually bite the bullet and flag down a cab. It makes my stomach hurt to spend money on things like this. I can't even look as the ticking dollars start to accumulate as the driver heads back toward my flat.

We don't talk, and I feel bad for being such a lousy customer. He probably thinks I'm always this rude, but well, I guess we're all allowed to have a bad day every now and then. When we arrive, I thank him for the trip and try not to groan as I swipe my card and pay for the fare.

It's too much. All of it.

Maybe I'm just not equipped to be in Logan's life this way. Maybe I haven't got the makeup to deal with women like Melody. After all, I couldn't even smell her bullshit in the loo. I thought she was really being truthful, but now that I've had a bit of time to mull it over, I know I believe Logan. He was all over me at his party, in the pool, and Melody was there. If they were really dating, she would have flipped when she saw him with me.

No. I realize now that she was playing a game—a game she's much better at than I am.

I sigh as I take the stairs up to the flat, and I've already braced myself for what Kat and Yasmine will say when I open the door.

Kat sits up on the sofa in surprise when I stroll in. "You're home early! Is everything all right?"

The answer is a long one, and I don't bother starting to reply until after they've helped me out of my dress and I've had a nice long shower. I don my comfiest pajamas and walk back out into the living room with damp hair and a bare face. I feel loads better already.

"Spill," Yasmine insists, and I do. I tell them every detail, from the supply closet onward, and they listen with wide eyes until the very end.

"So what are you going to do? Even though I think Logan was being honest, it doesn't change the fact that things have gotten bloody complicated. Are you going to walk away and try to find a less difficult relationship? Maybe with a normal bloke?"

I shake my head and stand up to grab a snack. I was meant to eat supper at the gala, and well…that didn't happen, so I'm bloody starving.

"Let's not go down that road right now. I don't have the head space for it, to be honest."

"All right, fine. Let's just forget it all for tonight, shall we?" Kat says, patting the cushion beside her after I grab a bag of popcorn. "And if you want, you can come round to a cleaning job with me in the morning."

She's offering because I complained about the cab fare home.

"Thanks, I'll definitely join you. Can't believe I spent all that money on that silly dress, even if it was from a resale shop. Maybe I can get them to buy it back."

Later, after we're nearly done with the movie, Logan rings my mobile.

I consider answering it, and then I think better of it. It's late and I still haven't quite worked out what I'll say to him when we speak next.

He doesn't phone again or text, and I go to bed with a pit in my stomach. Nothing feels quite right, and I think maybe I've really gone and mucked everything up.

The whole point of me not walking the red carpet with Logan was so we could keep our relationship private and under the media's radar, but the moment he kissed me in Gotham Hall, our illusion of privacy was shattered.

I've officially been thrust into the limelight whether I like it or not, and I find that out the hard way: by waking up the next morning to a million texts on my mobile from people shouting at me in all caps.

YOU ARE ALL OVER TWITTER!
GIRL! You're famous!! WTH???

Hi there! It's Amy Nichols! I'm a friend of Kat's. We did that summer holiday together years back? Anyway, I was wondering if you'd fancy coming on my podcast so we could chat about your relationship with Logan Matthews?

"Kat! Wake up," I say, reaching for my pillow and tossing it across the room, at her head.

"What have you gone and done that for? I was having a lovely dream with a sexy bloke. He had this nice French accent...oof, it was good. Maybe I can close my eyes and get back to it—"

"KAT! Wake up. Really! This is huge. I'm all over the internet!"

"What d'ya mean?"

I type Logan's name into Twitter, and there are loads of photos of our kiss with all sorts of captions.

Mystery lady locks lips with New York's most eligible bachelor.

Logan's new girl revealed: Candace Williams, Manhattan preschool teacher.

After arriving to the Feeding America Gala last night with model Melody James on his arm, Logan seemed quite cozy with British teacher, Candace Williams.

Worse, there are also photos of the morning from a while back when I shouted at the paps in front of his flat! I look like a raving lunatic going at them with my finger wagging and my mean mug frowning at them in condemnation. I groan. Then my mobile rings and I sort of scream and scramble to answer it once I see it's only Mum.

"Candace! *Finally*, we've got you!" She turns away from the receiver to address my dad. "Honey, turn it down! I've finally managed to get Candace on and I can't even hear her over your program!"

"Blimey! All right! I've done it then! I've turned it down."

"Not down enough, Herald! It's still ear-splitting. I think they can hear our telly all the way up on Mars!"

I try to ease the tension headache forming near my right eye. "Mum. *Hey*. Good morning."

It's like she's only now realized I'm still on the phone. "Oh hi, dear. Did you manage to get some nice rest last night?"

"Oh, so-so."

"Good. I'm glad to hear it. I'm only phoning because…well…" Then she laughs. "Drat. I've gone and forgotten already!"

"The program!" my dad calls out.

"That's right! Dad swears he saw you on the telly this morning! It was on the news hour when they go over a bit of celebrity gossip. I don't pay all that much attention to it, though I do love when they show the royals. Who can resist that little Princess Charlotte?"

"*Mum.*"

"Right, anyway. They said *you* were dating someone! Who did they say she was seen with, Herald?"

"Some bloke called Logan!" Dad shouts back.

"Yes! Logan! Lovely name. He's a footballer from America. Very handsome. Anyway, that wasn't you, was it? Dad swears, but I think he just didn't have his glasses on and he saw a blonde girl who sort of looked like you."

I look over to Kat for some sort of guidance, but she only shrugs as if to say I'm on my own.

"I well…I'm not sure what story you're referring to…"

"Well, I think you'd know if you were dating someone as famous as him, honey!" My mum gets a real laugh out of this like I'm a total nutter.

"It's, well…um, okay, yes. We have been seeing each other, but it's new—"

Then she screams and drops the phone.

"Mum?"

There's only static from her end of the line now.

"I think she's gone and broken it."

Kat sits up. "That's probably for the best anyway, don't you think?"

"Right. Suppose so. I wasn't sure what I was going to tell them anyway."

"Of course. You still haven't made up your mind about what you're going to do, have you? Oh well, no time to dwell on it now. My alarm was due to go off any minute anyway. We haven't got long to get over to that job if you still want to come with. We can grab some coffee on the way if you want?"

$8 latte from the corner café? No can do.

"I'll make us some coffee here."

"Oh *fine*. Have it your way, though you never make it quite like they do at the trendy shops. After we're done at the job, we'll go for tea or something." She whips her blankets off and stands up to stretch. "I flat-out *refuse* to work on a Sunday morning and not have at least *something* to look forward to after I'm done."

She's right. It's not exactly the way I want to be spending my Sunday morning either, but that's our lot in life. We're not one of the lucky ones, the made-up ladies we pass

201

on the street, having a lazy boozy brunch with loads of coffee and mimosas and croissants and eggs and sausage. I nearly pass out from all the delicious smells as we walk by, and then I look down at my slice of toast with a bit of cheap-o butter smeared on it, and my nose shrivels on impulse.

Kat laughs and locks her elbow with mine. "Oh come on, don't go feeling sorry for yourself. The building's just up ahead, and the flat isn't too big. With the two of us working together, we should be able to finish it in under an hour."

She's wrong. The place is huge—at least eight bedrooms with loads of crap everywhere, and the family's made a real mess of it. I've been assigned the kids' rooms, and in one of them, I find three dirty nappies hidden in random spots: inside a cabinet, under the bed, tucked in with some socks. The last one's so rotten I gag as I rush it toward the rubbish bin in the kitchen.

"No no no! I can't stand people!" I shout out. "How in the world do they not notice that there's a ripe old nappy stinking up the place?! It practically smells like a farmyard in here!"

"Yeah? Well I've just cleared off about three weeks of nose hairs from the bathroom sink, so quit your bellyaching!" Kat shouts back to me.

We go on working through the morning, doing our best to make this place *semi*-livable again, and by the end, my legs and arms are killing me. We load up our cleaning supplies and our sacks full of trash so we can clear out. As we head for the lift, my mobile buzzes in my pocket, but I can't answer it. My hands are too full of the rubbish we've got to take down to the building's dumpsters. We tried cramming it in the shoot up on the fourth floor, but the bags are too full.

"Your mobile's going off again," Kat says from behind her mound of rubbish sacks. "I'll bet that's someone else asking you for a favor." She snorts. "I can't believe Amy asked you to go on her podcast! I haven't talked to her in like a decade!"

I groan. "I wish I could make it all go away."

"You can't though, you know. You're dating him now. It comes with the territory."

"Am I? Dating him?"

"What?" she says, sticking her head round the tower of rubbish. "You're going to let that little tiff last night ruin it for you? Or is it the mags doing your head in? Oh what a sad lot in life to have your lovely photo splashed across the internet!" She shakes her head as if she doesn't understand me. "Right, well, if you do break it off, be sure to send him my way, because he's bloody gorgeous and rich, and charming, too! And maybe I'd be willing to put up with a bit of press if it meant getting to squeeze that arse of his."

I laugh and knock my elbow against hers. "You're mad, you know that?"

"That's nothing new. Now come on, let's go toss this rubbish then grab a sandwich somewhere. I'm starved."

My mobile goes off a million times the rest of the day, but none of the texts or calls are from Logan. Most of them are from people I haven't seen since primary school. A few are from family back home, and one is from a news outlet asking if I'd sit for an interview! I hung up on them immediately, of course. What else was I supposed to do?!

Other than the call from last night, Logan has been dead silent. It's late evening as I'm sitting on our sofa, going at a frozen block of ice cream with a spoon, when I realize the ball is probably in my court. He phoned last night and I didn't answer; if I want to talk to him, I should probably make a move.

I pause in my ice cream endeavor and glance around. The flat's dead silent. Kat and Yasmine went out for groceries, and I'm all alone. It's kind of nice.

My eyes skim over the huge bouquet of roses Logan sent earlier in the week. I've been tending to them as if they're absolutely priceless: changing the water, cutting the stems, singing them a song or two. They say you're supposed to talk to plants and they really respond to love and affection…and oh hell, I've done it again. I'm avoiding the issue at hand.

Logan.

It's time for action!

I set down my ice cream and reach for my mobile, scrolling through contacts until I get to the Ls. His name is quite nice there, all masculine and strong. Logan Matthews. I would be Mrs. Candace Matthews. *Oh get a grip, will you?!*

I dial him before I wimp out, and it rings and rings like the universe wants me to suffer.

I eye the roses again. Then the ice cream. Then my stomach clenches in a real painful way, and then finally, the call connects.

"Hey."

That's all he says, and he doesn't sound too keen to hear from me either, at least I don't think he does.

"Hi."

The line goes dead silent for a minute, so much so that I pull the mobile away from my ear to check that the call hasn't dropped.

"Logan?"

"I'm here."

204

"Oh right. That's…good."

No response.

Oh dear.

"Are you okay? Are you knackered or something? Have I caught you at a bad time?"

He sighs, and I can practically see him sag in defeat. I wonder where he is. What he's doing. What he's wearing. Then I roll my eyes and force myself to stay on task.

"No, it's fine. I'm just going over my schedule for the week. Nothing important."

"Sounds lovely. I'm doing the same, actually."

"Oh yeah?"

"Yes. We're both quite busy, I'll have you know. The queen's asked me round for dinner tomorrow, so I'll have to pop over to England for that. And then I've got squash with the Obamas on Tuesday, though I might have to cancel because Beyoncé wants to see me as well, and no one turns her down."

He laughs like he can't quite help it, and then he says my name.

It's so bloody lovely to hear him say it that I go limp on the couch, staring up at the ceiling, wishing we were together.

"Truthfully, I've been wondering why you haven't called or texted me all day," he admits. "Especially when you didn't answer my call last night. I didn't like how we left things at the gala."

"Right. That's my fault. It had all gotten to be a bit much, you know? The whole conniving woman cornering me in the loo bit…I'm not quite used to all that."

"Yeah. Sadly, I think it comes with the territory."

He sounds hopeless, and I hum, feeling sorry for him all of a sudden. I haven't stopped long enough to look at the situation from his perspective, but it's been a bloody awful turn of events for him. He was probably excited to have me attend the gala with him and I was excited too…until Melody ruined it. Instead of piecing myself together and staying there at his side, I ran off and have been MIA for the better part of twenty-four hours.

"I've behaved like a total idiot, I think," I blurt. "Please don't be mad at me."

"I'm not. I'm frustrated. This isn't anything new. The things you're feeling are the same things I've dealt with for almost a decade, and I feel bad dragging you into it."

"Don't feel bad," I rush out. "I can't stand it. You're too handsome to be moping about."

"I'm not moping."

His voice doesn't convince me. I know we still have a lot to discuss, logistics and all that boring nonsense, but I want to lift his spirits and have a pretty good idea of how to do it.

"Tell me, are you really over there scheduling your week? *La-de-da.* You can do that any time. Why don't we have a bit of fun? Something to put you in a better mood."

"Fun?"

I suppose I'll have to spell it out for him then. P-H-O-N-E S-E-X.

"Yes, well seeing as it's already late and we've both got early mornings…" My voice is heavy with suggestion. No subtlety here. "I can't come round to you, but maybe we could do a bit of…*y'know*…"

"Aren't your roommates there?"

"They've gone, *finally.* I'm all alone, and I'm wearing…" I look down. "Right. Well, not exactly lingerie, unfortunately. I do like to be comfy when I'm home."

He laughs. "Tell me. I want to know anyway."

"It's a huge 'I heart NYC' t-shirt with a chocolate stain near the middle, and underneath I've got my shorts on. They've got little sheep jumping about. Oh, maybe I shouldn't have said that. Could you forget it and I'll start again with something a little more sexy?"

"No. You're always sexy."

His voice has gone all raspy, and I have to bite my bottom lip to keep myself from losing it.

"Well, thank you…now tell me, what have you got on?"

"Black sweatpants."

"And?"

"And boxer briefs."

"Hmm…is this how people do it? They describe what they're wearing and then they sort of just lead into it? I'm not so good at this." He laughs, and I toss my head on the back of the sofa like I'm utterly hopeless. "Right, how 'bout this? Let's start over, and I'll make it really good." I drop my voice an octave to sound all phone-sex-operator-y. "Oh, Logan, *hello*. You've just caught me at a bad time. I'm totally nude, you see."

"Candace—"

His voice sounds amused, and that is not what I'm going for. He can laugh at me any time. This is serious sex business.

"Oh, *no*. I'm so cold. I haven't got anything to put on. What will I do?"

I can barely make out his laughter, as if he's trying to stifle it with his hand. I double down on my efforts.

"Oh myyyy. My legs are so smooth and silky!"

"I can't take you seriously when you're like this."

"Like what? Naked and oh so sexy? I know, it's hard to handle. Now stop messing about and put your hand down your trousers. I'll do the same."

I lie back on the sofa and hoist my t-shirt up so it's just covering my breasts.

"Are you touching yourself?" he asks, more than a little curious.

"Well not yet. I'm trying to loosen the waistband on my shorts. It's like I've done a sailor's knot on them or something," I groan, wrestling with it. "It's hopeless."

Just then, the door to the flat flings open wide and Kat and Yasmine stroll in, their arms laden with grocery sacks. They spot me in my compromising position right away.

"Oh, come on, perv!" Yasmine groans, shielding her eyes. "Not on the sofa! We all sit there!"

"I wasn't doing anything!"

"Yes, you were!" she argues. "Why's your shirt all scrunched up like that? Were you going to have sex on the phone in our living room?"

"NO!"

Logan's really laughing now. He's never been so amused in all his life, I'll bet.

Kat, meanwhile, strolls right toward me and takes one look at the coffee table, her face crumbling in anguish.

"Candace! You cow! You've let a perfectly good pint of ice cream go to waste!"

I immediately hang up on Logan.

LOGAN
17

Though Candace and I didn't work everything out on Sunday night, at least there's some hope for us. I was worried after the gala that she'd been pushed to her breaking point. I know how hard this life can be, and I don't begrudge anyone for wanting to escape it. Even though I talked to Melody at Gotham Hall and she broke down and apologized for causing a rift between Candace and me, it doesn't mean it'll be smooth sailing ahead.

This way of life isn't for the faint of heart and I don't want to force Candace into it, but after our call—after she hung up on me and I sat on my couch laughing about it—I know she's worth fighting for. Her brand of crazy feels too unique to pass up.

My week starts the way they always do. Weights. Training. Interviews. Meeting with my financial planners. Meeting with my apartment manager. Meeting with my agent. Meeting with my marketing team. Meeting with my coaches. Sleep. Food. Repeat. Candace. Candace. Candace.

She's the silver lining in all the bullshit I trek through on a daily basis, and she doesn't even know it.

We live in the same city, but we might as well be in two different worlds.

With how busy we both are, we don't manage to see each other on Monday, Tuesday, or Wednesday. We do talk on the phone, though. After Sunday night, I can't resist calling her. Even if her roommates usually interrupt us, I still like hearing from her. It's easier to get her alone in the middle of the day when I call and catch her during her lunch breaks at school. She eats in her classroom while she puts me on speakerphone, and today, she's telling me about an art project she has planned for the kids in the afternoon.

"We're making slime!"

I frown, not quite understanding. "Slime?"

"Oh, it's this gross toy kids absolutely love. Like a sort of Play-Doh goo? But somehow worse? It drives me absolutely insane trying to clean it up, but they go wild for it. Plus, I can usually get them to act sweet for at least twenty minutes after we've done it. Er…okay, that's a stretch. At least *five* minutes. Five minutes of peace is worth the trouble, *believe* me."

"Take a picture of it so I can see what you're talking about."

"Will do!"

She has to rush off the phone before I do and I'm left missing her, which doesn't sit well with me. I distract myself by looking at Rosie's itinerary for my afternoon. She has my life broken down into fifteen-minute intervals all the way from now until 8:30 PM. Tomorrow, my day starts at 5:00 AM.

I know Candace doesn't have it any easier. She has a shift at District tonight, and I send a quick text to Pat to make sure he'll be there to drive her home when she's finished. He shoots back "10-4" and then Rosie arrives with a box full of empty Gatorade bottles.

As promised, my face is plastered all over them, and I don't even realize there are a few different versions until she tells me we have to give the team at Gatorade our final approval by the end of the day.

"Uh, right. Let's just go with that one then," I say, pointing to the one closest to me.

Rosie laughs as if I'm a complete idiot then walks to the door as if she knew there was about to be a knock. She tugs it open, and in they come: half a dozen people with huge presentation boards that list out the pros and cons for each image. *You see, in this one he's holding the football a little higher, more toward his face. His stance is more dominant, and his smile looks sincere.* I sit near the window, stare out at the New York skyline, and think about Candace.

The next day is Thursday, and I'm scheduled to pick up Briggs from school. I'm fucking giddy as the afternoon flies by. I'm at The Day School earlier than planned—*too early*—so instead of going in, I pace out on the sidewalk, trying to come up with a way to tell Candace I've missed her so damn much over the last few days that won't scare her off.

I tug my hand through my hair and look up to see a woman approaching the school. She's either a mom or a nanny; it's impossible to tell. Her brown hair is tugged up tight in a bun, and she's wearing slim-fitting athletic clothes.

"Are you here for pick-up?" she asks me with a huge smile.

"Yeah."

"Great! We can go in together."

Awesome. I didn't want to be the first person to arrive, but if she goes in front of me, I'll technically be the second.

"You're Logan Matthews, right?" she asks as we head inside. "I know it's probably so annoying to be recognized everywhere, but well"—she shrugs—"the moms here love to talk."

"Oh." I force out a laugh. "Yeah."

I never have a good response for when people ask me who I am. It feels too blunt and rude to just say yes, so I reach my hand out. "And you are?"

She blushes and accepts my hand. "Erin Carson. Margaux's mom!"

Margaux, right. Briggs has told me the names of the kids in his class, but there are a lot of them and I can't seem to keep up.

"Margaux and Briggs absolutely *adore* each other. We need to get them together for a playdate soon!"

I shrug and offer a lopsided smile. "That's not really my jurisdiction. I'm just the uncle. I bet you could coordinate something with Stella or Bobby though."

She scrunches her brows. "Who?"

"Right." I forget my sister rarely makes it up to this school. I doubt any of the parents know her. "Never mind, just coordinate it with Briggs' nanny. She's usually the one to pick him up."

We reach Candace's classroom, and the top half of the Dutch door is open so we can see in over the bottom half. Candace is sitting on a colorful rug, reading to the kids. They sit in a semicircle, fanned around her, listening intently while she finishes a page. It's a cute scene and I wouldn't think anything of it, *except* for the fact that she's completely wrapped herself up in toilet paper.

"When an Egyptian king died, his body was made into a mummy in a complicated process that took *70 days*!"

212

"70 days?!" one of the kids shouts, as if it's the longest amount of time he's ever heard.

"Doesn't that seem like forever? It is quite a long process. But listen," she returns to reading, "mummies have lasted *thousands* of years and continue to fascinate us today."

"I want to be a mummy!" Briggs declares, jumping to his feet.

"Me too!" A girl jumps up to stand beside him.

"I don't blame you. I do look quite cool, don't I?" Candace says, standing to spin in a circle.

Some of her toilet paper ensemble falls to the floor, but there's still a ton left behind. The kids must have spent half the day spinning her into it. She even has it tucked up around her face and covering her hair.

I smile when she looks over and spots Erin and me standing at the door.

"Oh! Drat. It's pick-up time! All right everyone, let's pick up our reading pillows and toss them in a pile over here near the wall. And then Margaux and Briggs, come on, let's get your lunch sacks."

She has a hard time walking across the room with the toilet paper wrapped around her legs.

Briggs comes running over to the door, peering up at me. "Uncle Logan, I'm going to be a mummy like Ms. Candace!"

"Cool, bud."

"Can you wrap me up in toilet paper when we get to your house?"

"Sure thing," I say, reaching down to ruffle his hair.

"Here you go," Candace says, coming over with lunchboxes for Margaux and Briggs. "Everything should be in there. I've washed out the containers already. Erin, Margaux ate all of her couscous and veggies for lunch, but

213

she didn't go down for a nap today. She insisted she didn't need one so I let her read quietly with a few books—"

"What?" Erin groans and cuts her off. "You know how much that throws off our entire day. Now she's going to be cranky for the whole afternoon." She reaches out to snatch the lunchbox from Candace and then looks to *me* as if I'm going to back her up on this. What the fuck?

Candace's smile falls. "I know. I did *try* to have her lie down, but she must have been too energized. She did rest for a bit when I rubbed her back."

"You *see*—that's just it! You coddle her, so it's no surprise she doesn't want to go to sleep. At home, we turn out the lights and shut the door. She goes to sleep just fine."

"Hey, I think you should maybe ease up a bit."

Erin's eyes slice to me like I'm Public Enemy No. 1 now. "Are you kidding me? Now I'm getting advice from *you*?"

"Mommy, Ms. Candace did tell me to lie down—"

Erin yanks the door open and grabs Margaux's hand tightly. "I don't want to hear it. You have Mandarin lessons this afternoon *and* piano. How are you going to concentrate now? Hmm?"

They wander off down the hall as Erin continues berating her young daughter, and I feel sorry for the kid.

I shake my head in disbelief as I look back to Candace. "That was…"

I'm at a loss for words.

Candace only shrugs and tries to play it off. "Unfortunately, quite common. Welcome to parenting on the Upper East Side."

"Jesus. Mandarin? She's what, *three*?"

"Oh, that's how it goes. Every child here is learning at least one other language, some of them two. Mika can speak nearly perfect French. It's lovely."

She smiles then, forcing it, but I can tell Erin really rattled her. It's not a surprise. No one should speak to another human like that.

"Margaux's mommy is so mean. Ms. Candace is nice! She rubs my back when I can't fall asleep too!" Briggs says, going over to wrap his arm around Candace's leg. It's difficult with all the toilet paper, but Candace leans down to embrace him.

"And don't you worry, I'll keep doing it."

"Good. Don't listen to that mean lady," he tells her emphatically.

"I agree," I say, aiming an apologetic smile her way. "Briggs, how about you and I ask Ms. Candace if she wants to come to dinner with us?"

"Like a date?!" he exclaims, his eyes going wide. "I've always wanted to go on a date!"

I laugh. "What do you know about dates?"

"A lot!" he claims. "I know all about them! First you have to ask out the person you like." He turns to Candace. "That's you. Then if the person says yes, you have to get a babysitter, and you can't just go in your regular clothes. You have to be very fancy and nice if you want to go on a date."

"Wow. You do know a lot about it," I add, and he grins proudly.

"And then after the babysitter comes, you can leave and eat oysters and drink campaign."

"Drink what?" I ask, wondering if I heard him right.

"Campaign! Like the stuff grown-ups put in those cups that Mom says I can't touch or I'll get in trouble."

"I think you mean champagne," Candace says gently.

He stomps his foot in annoyance. "That's what I said!"

"Right, well, that sounds very lovely. I'd love to join you," Candace says, a blush forming on the tops of her cheeks. She's looking down at Briggs instead of me, and I wonder if it's due to nerves.

She explains she still has to finish with pick-up and then clean up her classroom. I ask her when she'll be done, and we promise to meet her out in front of the school then.

When we leave, Briggs insists we have to go get really dressed up while we wait for Candace to finish. There's a kids' clothing store on our walk home, and it's a good excuse to duck away from the photographers out on the street.

Briggs marches right up to the clerk behind the counter and speaks with very enunciated words. "Excuse me, I am going on a date. I need to be fancy. Like a prince."

The shopkeeper looks to me for confirmation, and I nod in agreement.

"Of course, right this way. I think I have just the thing for you," he says to Briggs, talking to him like he's his most loyal customer.

Briggs follows after the man until we make it to the back corner of the shop where there are outfits for kids to wear to weddings, little suits and dresses.

Briggs surveys them for one second then points his finger up to the top. "That one. It's perfect."

"Briggs, that's a tuxedo."

Why do they even sell tuxedos for kids?

"Right. It's what princes wear in the movies. I want that one."

It doesn't stop there either. Once he has his tuxedo, apparently *I* need one to.

"I thought *you* were the prince," I tell him as we continue our walk back to my apartment, now with a huge shopping bag in tow.

"I am, but so are you," he says exasperatedly. "We have to *both* wear tuxedos. And I promise I won't look more handsome than you, so don't be sad."

Right. *That's* what I was worried about.

218

I'm still worked up about the way Erin shouted at me in front of Logan. It's the plight of a preschool teacher working in a place like The Day School. I try my hardest. I wrap myself up in tissue and read a book about mummies and really feel like I'm going the extra mile to be a good teacher, and then BAM, a parent like Erin waltzes in and has a go at me.

I'm not very good at taking criticism even when it's the constructive sort. I wish I could stop going over her words in my head, but they're in there good and cemented and they've got me wondering if I tried hard enough to get Margaux to take a nap earlier, if I should have been stricter and really forced the issue. No. It's useless. In this line of work, you're damned if you do, damned if you don't. On another day, Erin would have shouted at me if I *had* forced Margaux to have a lie-down.

I'm sitting out on the steps with a stomach that's quite grumbly and annoyed with me and a brain that can't seem to get over the terrible end to my workday when Pat's SUV pulls up to the curb.

Briggs and Logan climb out from the back, and a laugh bursts out of me before I can help it.

It's not that it's funny what they've done. It's just so wonderfully *cute*!

Briggs is dressed in a tiny black tuxedo! I didn't even know they made tuxedos so small! And his lovely brown curls are all tucked back and real glossy like he's got some hair gel on them. In his hands, there's a bouquet of sunflowers.

Behind him, Logan stands with his hands in his pockets and a sort of nervous smile playing on his lips. He's dressed up too, just like he was for the gala, all black and debonair and drop-dead gorgeous. He doesn't have flowers; he's let Briggs have them all, but well…what does he need flowers for? *He's* the gift, isn't he?

I sort of wobble as I push to stand, a cacophony of butterflies fluttering loose in my stomach.

"Ms. Candace! I mean, *Princess* Candace! Your carriage is here!" Briggs says, sweeping his arm back to the SUV.

"Wow, how did I get so lucky? *Two* princes?"

"Don't worry, I'm just the chaperone," Logan teases as I step toward them. "But we better hurry and get off the street or the photographers will find us. I saw a few a while back."

"Well then, let's set off!" I say, hurrying toward the vehicle. I get in first, followed by Briggs, and then Logan. We fill the back seat, and Pat's up front with a friendly smile and a nod in greeting.

We buckle up then Briggs passes over my sunflowers.

"Those are for you. I picked them special myself."

"Wow. They're lovely."

"Do you like yellow?" He sounds deeply concerned, like maybe he's worried he made the wrong choice.

"Absolutely. One of the best colors there is. It always reminds me of sunshine."

Briggs grins and looks over to Logan to give him a little thumbs-up, like they've really pulled off quite a wonderful surprise.

Logan glances over at me over top of Briggs' head. I mouth a thank you, and then he reaches back over the edge of Briggs' car seat to touch my shoulder. It's the first time we've touched in days—since the gala—and I'm starved for more. We didn't even get a proper hug out on the street.

"We're going to eat at a very fancy place," Briggs says, jarring me out of the private moment with Logan. "The food is going to be dazzling."

My brows shoot up. "*Dazzling*, huh?"

"Yes, dazzling. Like in that book you read to us yesterday."

"Wow, I'm very excited."

We end up pulling off into an alley a few minutes later, and Pat must see my confusion because he offers, "Better if you two go in the back door. The restaurant knows to be discreet, and this way you all can eat like normal people."

I beam. "Brilliant! Ready, Briggs? We'll be like secret agents sneaking in the back!"

"I'm ready!" he says, taking my hand.

As promised, there's a hostess waiting just at the door, ready to usher us to a private table in a back room, which we have all to ourselves. Logan and Briggs have brought me to a lovely little Italian restaurant, not real posh and modern or anything, but I like it all the same. There are real ivy plants growing on the tables and those old-school red and white checkered tablecloths.

221

"This is my favorite restaurant," Logan tells me, leading me to my chair so he can tug it out for me to sit. "There's no better Italian food in the whole city. I swear."

"Oh good! I'm starved. Let's get loads of bread."

"Uncle Logan," Briggs says, clearing his throat. "Could you go sit over there?" He points to the door of the private room where there's another small table set for two. "Since this is a real date, Ms. Candace and me should be at our own table."

I use my napkin to smother a laugh as Logan rolls his eyes. "Okay there, Casanova. Cool your jets and I'll see if they have some chicken nuggets on the menu."

"And ketchup!" Briggs adds, having forgotten all about his request to sit alone with me.

Logan sits beside me, and Briggs takes the seat across from me.

When our waiter comes, Logan asks if I want some wine, and I nod my head greedily. "Whatever you think is best. I'm not picky at all."

"Let's just do the house red then. The bottle, please. And Briggs?"

"I'll take your finest purple. Juice, that is," he says, looking up at the waiter. "With a straw."

I bark out a laugh and Logan rubs his temple as if to say, *I can't handle this kid anymore.* "Briggs, how about we remember our manners and add on a please there at the end, bud?"

"Right. With a straw, *please*."

The waiter smiles and nods. "Right away, sir. I have a bottle of Welch's I think you'll really enjoy."

Then he winks at Logan and me and leaves the room.

222

"This is the most *dazzling* date I've ever been on," I say, and Briggs perks up in his seat. "Though I will say, I think you're a bit too young for me."

"I know, I know. It's really my uncle you like because he's so big and tall, right?" He sits up in his chair even more, as if trying to compensate for the fact that he's only three years old. "When I grow up, I'm going to be just like him."

Logan seems embarrassed by the attention, and instead of responding, he opens up the coloring page and a pack of crayons the waiter left for Briggs.

"Here you go. They have a maze on there I bet you can do with your eyes closed."

"With my eyes closed! You're so *silly*!"

The coloring page does occupy him, though, long enough for me to turn to Logan and aim a little smile his way. "I do like the look of this place. It's not at all where I thought you'd take me."

He nods as if understanding what I mean. "There are nicer places in the city. I mean, it's New York. There are probably a thousand places to eat that would take ten hours and come with a dozen courses, but I really like their lasagna here, and well…you can't beat Italian food."

I smile. "Agreed. So then I should get the lasagna?"

"We can share and get something else too?"

"Wow, what a nice gesture. I would have thought you'd be all, *Get your own food, lady.*"

"Well normally I would, but considering how much I like you…"

I beam.

"Doesn't it feel like it's been the longest week?" I ask, turning a bit in my chair so my knee knocks into his leg under the table. He reaches his hand down underneath the tablecloth to keep my leg there against him.

"I swear Monday had its own Monday, and don't get me started on Tuesday. I looked at the clock once and thought it was running backward."

I nod in agreement. "I think I've been rather annoying to Kat and Yasmine. They say I'm only allowed to bring you up once a day now. Any more than that and they've got permission to kick me out of the flat."

"That's fine. You can come stay with me."

"Oh really? Then maybe I'll sabotage myself on purpose. Maybe I should give them a ring now and go on and on about how nice you look in your tuxedo."

"No need. It's already settled. You'll spend the night at my place tonight."

"Oh I will? You haven't even asked me."

His brown eyes lock with mine, and my stomach tightens.

"Do you want me to ask?"

"Are you guys flirting?" Briggs asks, cutting in. "I can't tell what you two are talking about. Are you going to have a sleepover? Because if so, I want to come too."

My cheeks go beet red, but Logan's the one to save the moment. He leans over and compliments Briggs' coloring, and then Briggs goes right back to it as if forgetting his question altogether.

Logan smiles at me, and then the waiter arrives with our drinks and a lovely overflowing basket of warm breadsticks. I think I eat about half a dozen before our food arrives.

It's all so good I can't keep myself from moaning in bliss. The lasagna! The baked ziti! The fettuccini sauce! I could bathe in it.

"I want to eat here every day until I die," I proclaim once I'm too full to eat another bite.

"Me too," Briggs says, leaning back in his seat and patting his belly. "I finished all my chicken nuggets. Can I have some dessert now?"

"On the way home, maybe," Logan replies. "It's getting close to your bedtime."

We don't end up fulfilling that promise, because once we make it back to the car and buckle Briggs into his car seat, he's asleep within a few minutes of driving. It must be the lull of the city noise. He's a trueborn Manhattanite, and to him, it's probably the best lullaby there is.

We pull up in front of a nice-looking brownstone a few minutes later, and Logan carefully unbuckles Briggs so he can carry him inside.

"I'll be right back," he whispers before taking him into the house.

While he's gone, I help Pat undo the car seat so we can set it in the back of the SUV. Then he switches the radio to a sports game and we sit quietly, listening while we wait for Logan.

"I can put it on music if you'd like?" Pat offers.

"No. This is nice. I think I'm following along. Is this hockey?"

"Baseball."

Ah well. I tried.

A few minutes later, Logan appears on the doorstep of the house. Briggs' nanny is at the door, waving him off, and he nods to her before starting to tug off his bow tie. I still can't believe he put on the whole getup just to make Briggs happy. It makes me want to squeeze my arms around him and never let go. He's too good to be true, I think. At least that's how it feels.

He opens the back door and slides into the seat beside me. Now that the car seat is gone, I can push right up against him so we're thigh to thigh, finally close in a way we haven't been able to be all evening.

"Home?" Pat asks, glancing back in the rearview mirror.

"Please," Logan nods, pulling off his bow tie the rest of the way then laying it flat against his thigh. I reach out for it and feel the silky material in my hand. Then, like a weirdo, I bring it up and sniff it, knowing it'll smell like his cologne, and it does. My stomach squeezes tight and I smile as Logan looks over at me with narrowed eyes, assessing me. He seems to do that a lot, stare right at me like he's trying to pry back all my layers and see me at my very core. I want to tell him I haven't got any layers. What you see is what you get, but maybe he feels the same way about me that I do about him—too good to be true, perhaps. *Wouldn't that be nice.*

I have the urge to kiss him but don't want to make Pat feel uncomfortable, and I'm not so crazed and horny that I can't wait ten more minutes to have my chance when we're back at his place and all alone.

Instead of dropping us out front, Pat rounds the block to the back of Logan's building then drives down into a car park.

"From now on, we'll enter and exit here. Just to be safe," Logan tells me. When he sees my confusion, he adds, "Photographers aren't allowed in here. It's private property, so they won't get any more photos of you coming and going from my place."

Pat waves us off after we step out of the SUV. Logan grabs my hand and heads toward the back entrance of the building that leads straight into the lift, where he retrieves his wallet from his tuxedo pocket and swipes it along the panel underneath the buttons. We start to glide up toward the penthouse, and my mind immediately starts to wander toward nefarious goals.

"Do you reckon there are cameras in here?" I ask, glancing up at the corners of the rectangular box.

"I'm sure. This whole building is pretty secure. There are a lot of people who live here who value their privacy."

"So if we kissed...someone could be watching?"

He turns to look down at me, and I don't smile. I don't want him to think I'm kidding. I'm definitely *not*. He glances up at the ceiling for a moment as if thinking it over for himself, then he looks back down at me. There's a heat in his eyes now, this hunger that's plain as day.

He turns his body so he's facing me, and he takes a step forward.

I take a step back. It's instinct, and I keep doing it as he advances on me.

I'm the one who put this idea in his head, but now suddenly, I'm tempted to shout, *Chicken! Ha ha. What a lark, am I right?*

It's only because he can look so intimidating sometimes, especially when he hovers over me like this, his hand coming up to cradle the bottom of my face so he can tip my head up.

"What do you think they'll see?" he asks, letting his gaze drop to my mouth. "Me kissing you?"

Are we still going up? How many floors do we have to ascend?! Surely, we're in the clouds by now.

"Maybe they're waiting for it," he says, bending low so his lips hover right over my mouth. "Maybe they're wondering why I haven't done it already."

But he doesn't do it. That's just it! We aren't kissing. We're suffocating to death. There's no air in this lift and maybe I've sucked it all in with my big heaping nervous breaths. We'll die here, I think, right as the lift *dings!* and we're on Logan's floor.

227

He smiles like a deviant then steps back to walk out before me. I'm trailing after him, thinking of ways to do his head in like he's just done to me. He opens his door and reaches back to take my hand, and then we're inside. Alone. His place is dark and quiet, a backdrop to all the things I think we should do together. *Let's have sex in this foyer, right on this cold tile. And there, against that wall.* My head might hit that lovely picture, but who cares? It's probably only worth, oh, a couple *thousand*.

"Well, strip down then," I tease as he kicks off his shoes.

He looks back at me with a smile. "We aren't going to have sex, Candace."

My jaw drops. "Why wouldn't we?"

"Oh, I don't know—maybe because the last time we were intimate, you freaked out and ran off on me."

"Well that was bloody complicated! Or have you forgotten about your psycho ex-lover cornering me in the loo?"

"I haven't forgotten, which is why I think we should take things slow."

"SLOW?"

Oh now he's done it. This is going to be the end of me. I haven't had a proper lay in months—more than that, probably, if I actually tallied the days. I've been careful not to so I could preserve some sort of facade that I am, in fact, a sexual creature unable to be tamed. In reality, I might just be Ms. Candace the preschool teacher, good for making a bunch of slimy goo for children but not much else.

"What a sad turn of events! I suppose you're going to suggest we watch a movie or something?"

He shrugs. "We could."

I toss my hands up. "Oh bore! Well why don't you just get me a nun's habit and I'll slip that on. Have you got a chastity belt lying around here anywhere? Might as well put that on too."

He laughs and comes toward me, taking my purse from my shoulder and dropping it on the little table in his foyer. Then he comes back over and kneels down in front of me so he can help me take my shoes off. Meanwhile, I'm moaning on and on about how he's ruining my life.

"I don't think I'm ruining it."

"You *are*. This is actual real torture, the sort that makes people go mad."

"You're already *mad*, so we don't have a problem there."

"Oh, ha. You are one of the funniest blokes I've ever met. Remind me to put that in my diary alongside the entry where I write about how you won't sleep with me because you're worried I'm too fragile. *Dear Diary, me again, the loneliest girl in New York—the one who hasn't had a man between her legs in nearly a century.*"

"A century, huh?"

"Feels that way sometimes."

"Do you really keep a diary?"

"No! Can you *imagine*?! The entries would be crude, to say the least. I couldn't trust that they wouldn't fall into the wrong hands. Tomorrow, if I died and the police went round to my flat to round up my things, one of them would find that diary and think I'm the perviest perv he's ever met. He'd think, *Jeez, this poor girl. If only her boyfriend had given her a proper lay, she wouldn't have died in that horrific ice cream accident.*"

"Ice cream accident?"

"Yes. Kat once dragged me with her to a psychic, and the lady sort of hinted that I should stay away from soft serve. At least…I think that's what she said. Her accent was quite thick. Ever since then, I've been very careful around the stuff so as to prevent my death. What are you doing unbuttoning my jeans like that for?"

"I'm trying to get you out of them."

"Well you've already taken off my blouse, and I was joking about the nun's habit. I didn't think I needed to point that out, but well, I suppose men can be quite dim sometimes."

"Step out," he says, before tugging the denim material off my legs.

I'm standing in my knickers and my bra in his foyer, and he's already starting to undress himself. His tuxedo jacket goes first, strewn on the floor beside us. Then he goes after his cufflinks.

"Is this some kind of a cruel joke?" I ask, propping my hands on my hips. "Let me see the goods but not taste them sort of thing?"

"If you'd stop talking for five seconds, you would understand that I'm giving in. You're getting your way."

He unbuttons his shirt and lets it drop onto his jacket. His blessedly tan and toned chest is just *there*, right in front of me, like one of those neon signs on the Vegas strip. I'm a sad little gnat drawn right to it. My hands reach out and I smooth my palms over the rigid planes.

"You're going to do me?" I sound more than slightly amazed by the prospect.

"Could you not say it like that?"

"Oh right. Are we going to *make love*? I didn't realize you were such a romantic."

He laughs and shakes his head then he reaches down, no pretense, no proper warning, and kisses me full-on. His mouth is so good at getting what it wants. I shut right up and let him continue the kiss. My insides turn into jelly, and that's okay because Logan reaches out to grab hold of me and we do this perfectly synchronized move where he lifts and I wrap my legs around his waist. He's so bloody strong I don't even worry about him dropping me. I guess his career in football is good for something.

I wrap my arms around his neck and deepen the kiss, letting my tongue touch his. He moans into my mouth and his hands find my butt and he grips like he's angry with it— angry with me! This isn't my fault! He's the one with that body. What am I supposed to do, *not* jump his bones? Too late. My ankles hook behind his back, and I'm attached to him like a barnacle. He'll have to get an ice pick to scrape me off him.

He starts to move us into the living room. We bump into a wall and then a lamp. It crashes to the ground and I'm laughing, but he doesn't seem to care at all. Once we reach the sofa, he lets go of me, and I sort of fall with an audible *oomph*. He hovers over me like an animal who's just successfully brought his prey back to his lair. He peruses me from head to toe, taking in my chest and the delicate lace of my bra, down over my stomach and then lower, between my legs. My knickers are a bit askew thanks to his hands, but it's not like I have time to adjust them. He bends down, takes the straps between his fingers, and tugs.

Down they go, over my knees, and then they're at my ankles. Tug. Rip. *Gone*.

He takes my thighs in his big hands and he splits them apart. No asking. No eye contact or confirmation that I'm not dying a thousand deaths here. He just peels me apart and then he licks his lips.

I swear to GOD, I am done. The psychic was wrong—I do not die floating in a mound of ice cream; I die here. On

Logan's sofa. As his head descends between my legs and his lips touch me *there*.

I take my bottom lip between my teeth to keep from shouting out something horribly inappropriate, but he doesn't care in the least. There's no letting up, no coming up for air. His mouth stays there and his tongue turns circles, and just when I think, *Wow, so this is what Buddhism feels like. Hello, nirvana*, his hand slides up my thigh, between my legs, and he touches me. He turns his hand so his palm faces the ceiling, and then I watch with a barely contained moan as he presses his middle finger inside of me.

Tongue and finger. Finger and tongue. Is there a better combination in this entire world?!

After that, I must pass out for a moment, but when I gather my senses again, he's continuing to turn circles with his tongue and pump in and out of me with his finger, and I really only have myself to blame for this. I asked for this treatment, but maybe I would have held off if I'd known he'd be so bloody good at it! I'm not containing myself at all. I should be lying back, as if bored by his average bedroom skills, but instead my thighs try to grip him like an anaconda. My stomach is quivering. My hands are fisting the sofa cushions. Then I twine them in his hair.

I tell him he's good at this—too good. Instead of thanking me, he continues the endless torture. I am going to lose control of myself, and I warn him of this. Maybe he should know I'm seconds away from crying out? But he only pumps into me harder with his finger. Faster. And then his tongue touches me in the exact perfect spot and I detonate. I'm a bomb exploding into a thousand pieces, leaving shrapnel scattered across his flat, and he's with me, until the end, until my body stops shaking and I sink heavy into the sofa.

He hovers over me, his eyes molten and hot. I think to make a joke, some kind of thank you to him for doing that, but then my gaze drops between his legs and all my premeditated words pop and disappear.

Suddenly there is one thing I want more than anything in the world: to feel him inside me. To feel stretched by him. To feel his weight and pressure between my legs. I need it more than air.

I push to sit up and reach out for him, to touch him and wrap my hand around his hardness. His eyes flutter as soon as I grip him, and my smirk unfurls on its own. I doubt it will ever get old, me overpowering him, even for a moment. It's just everything he is and everything he stands for. He's this hulking guy with muscles of steel. He should be impenetrable, a brick wall, but I know his weakness, and I'm holding it in my small hand.

"Well then...should we continue?"

CANDACE
19

Instead of answering, he reaches down to wrap his hand around mine. He grips it and starts to pump faster, tightening my hand on his length. He's showing me what he wants me to do, and I'm nothing if not a star pupil. I learn quickly and tighten my grip, using both hands, because well—he is bloody tall and proportioned everywhere, if you catch my drift!

His head lolls back for a moment and then he leans forward, releasing my hands so he can bend down and unsnap the back of my bra. He doesn't get it the first time and I want to shout, *RIP IT! I DON'T CARE*, but then he's got it and he's tugging it off. I let go of him so the material can slip down my arms, and then he stares down at me in awe, taking me in. I'm sure I'm blushing all over, a real embarrassing red tinge. I imagine how I look in his eyes. I'm slender and petite. My breasts are perky, but they aren't the best in town by any means. Still, judging by the way he's looking at me, I think he quite likes them.

235

I reach out to grip him again, and then his hand reaches out to touch me. He drags the pad of his finger softly over my collarbone and then lower, curving around my left breast. Teasing me. That's fine—I'll tease him right back. I slow my pace, sliding my hands up and down his length in a rhythm that's no doubt pissing him off. His eyes flare with emotion as they lock with mine, and I smile. It's innocence personified, but he reads between the lines. His brows furrow and he reaches out to skim his hand over my breast. I arch into him, and he rewards me for it. He cups the weight in his hand, feeling it, and I think—not for the first time— that he's got lovely hands. They're big and calloused and confident, the hands of a man who takes what he wants.

I start to pump harder, faster. He responds in kind, thrusting his hips as he feels me up.

It only takes a few more times before he grunts low and deep, and then he's coming onto my hands, onto my chest. My jaw goes slack as I watch him.

It's…beautiful.

Is that odd? To think he looks beautiful right now? It's in the angular cut of his jaw and his manly features all locked in pleasure, the way his muscles clench and the absolute surrender of it all—him in my hands, all mine.

It takes him a moment to orient himself again, and he doesn't open his eyes right away. He releases a long exhalation, blinks one eye open. Then the other. He looks down at me with a lazy smile, and I grin up at him.

"You've really made a mess. I hope you're happy."

He laughs and shakes his head, looking around for something to help us clean up. There's nothing. A maid must have come round to clean his flat because there's not a single thing out of place in the room, except for…well, us.

"Don't move," he tells me before rushing down a side hall. He comes back carrying a towel, and instead of passing it over, he kneels down to clean me up himself. It's only the beginning. I'll still need a shower, but it's lovely to have him dote on me like that. When we're done, he wads the towel in one hand and reaches for me with the other.

"Come on. Let's shower."

"Oh, together?! Lovely. But you need to slow down! My legs are half as long as yours and you can't just drag me along after you."

It's true. I think he forgets how small I am compared to him. He takes one step and it covers half the length of the room! Meanwhile, I'm left scurrying in his wake.

He laughs and slows his gait exasperatingly. "Sorry. Habit."

We go down a hallway then turn a corner. He opens a door, and we're in his room. I was in here before, but not during the day when I was fully awake enough to appreciate it in all its glory. It's not like a room some lazy boy would do up if he had it his way. *Oh I'll just tack a sheet up against the window. That oughta do it.* No, his room is definitely decorated, and it's masculine. The bed is covered in white and gray linen. He's got lovely wooden side tables with twin hunter green lamps on each side. There's black and white abstract art on the wall and a plush rug covering the dark wood floors.

I'm amazed, really. His room is the size of my entire flat. I think my twin bed could fit over in that nook there just fine. He wouldn't even notice.

"Come on. Shower's in here."

"This is your bathroom?!" I sort of shout before I can get ahold of myself.

Last time I was in here, it was pitch black. Now I can see it's ridiculously nice. It's just so bloody big with lots of marble and mirrors and two sinks on opposite ends so that if he had a girl living here with him, she wouldn't have to deal with any of his whiskers—though even now, as I inspect what I assume is his side (it's the sink with a toothbrush by it), it's sparkling clean. Either he's the tidiest man in the entire world or he's got a bloody good maid, much better than Kat and I could ever do.

"It's nice. Yeah. Nothing like I had growing up. Don't worry—I haven't forgotten my humble beginnings."

He says this while walking away from me so he can turn on the shower, but all I hear is Charlie Brown teacher's *wah-wah-wah-wah* gibberish because I've caught sight of his arse in the mirror's reflection and HOLY BUTTOCKS, BATMAN! I could break a tooth on that thing.

He turns around to eye me in the mirror, and I frown. "I was having a lovely time staring at your derrière."

"Yeah, well, try to contain yourself," he teases, waving for me to join him in the shower.

"I can't. Truly. It's the best I've ever seen. I can't wait to tell Kat about it. She'll go mental."

"Do you have to?"

"Talk to my friends about your arse? Of course. Why would I keep that information to myself?"

At this, he groans and tucks me up under the shower stream so I get doused from head to toe. Then he pumps some soap into his hand and starts lathering me up. I try hard to get my mind out of the gutter, but his hands feel so good, and suddenly it's like we didn't do anything out on his sofa. I'm ready and raring to go again.

I think I must make a little noise or whimper when his hands slide down my thighs because his eyes shoot up to me.

"Sorry. I'll be quiet," I promise, miming turning a lock over my lips.

"Why?" he taunts with an arched brow. "I'd rather you weren't."

Then his hands slowly glide back up my legs and between my thighs and *Farewell, sanity! It was nice knowing you!*

The shower takes much longer than either of us probably originally intended. He gives me two orgasms while I lean against the shower wall like a heaping pile of useless bones, and then I return the favor by sliding down onto my knees. After that, we have to rinse off all over again. Showers can be quite dirty endeavors if you take them with the wrong (or *right*) person.

He cuts the water, and we step out. He wraps a towel around his waist then grabs another to wrap around me. It's not one of those annoyingly itty-bitty ones that only covers half of one arm. It's huge and white and fluffy, enveloping me from my shoulders down to my knees.

"You want to borrow some clothes?" he offers.

"Have you got an old t-shirt? A worn one I can steal in the morning?"

He walks into his closet and comes back out with a huge shirt that has his football team's logo on it. It's perfect.

"I want it back though," he warns as I slide it on.

"Aye-aye, captain."

We both know that's not going to happen.

"Have you got some knickers in there I could slip on too? Maybe pink ones?"

"I have boxers."

"So I'm just supposed to go commando all night?"

"I don't see the problem."

I roll my eyes. "Of course *you* wouldn't. *Men.*"

He smiles—or rather, *gloats*—and then he walks over to grab me a spare toothbrush wrapped in plastic that he has in his vanity drawer.

"Do you keep a bunch of these for when ladies come round?" I ask as I accept it.

"I asked Lois to get it when she went grocery shopping this week."

"Lois?"

"She does everything around here for me. Part housekeeper, part chef. She's great."

"Sounds like it. How long has she been with you?"

I'm keeping him talking so he won't notice how pleased I am that he's thought to buy me a toothbrush. Some girls want diamonds, but I think this is just as lovely. It's purple with a little plastic handle and soft bristles. It tells me Logan thought about me this week, thought about me enough to ask Lois to get me a toothbrush, enough to want me to sleep over.

We brush our teeth at the same time, him at his sink, me at the other, swirling circles in our mouths and trying not to make each other laugh. We spit then swish our mouths with water.

"I'm exhausted," I admit after I finish patting my mouth with a towel. "Can't believe tomorrow is Friday. I've got double duty at The Day School and District."

"Come over after? I can ride with Pat to pick you up when you're finished?"

"I wish I could. It's Kat's birthday on Saturday, and we've got big plans. She wants breakfast in bed then Yasmine and I are taking her out for a spa day. We're going to this place Yaz found downtown that's a little sketchy, but the treatments are really cheap, so there's that."

"What about Saturday night?"

I frown. "We're headed to some club Kat's been going on and on about. It's supposed to draw in loads of cute guys."

Logan arches a brow.

"Of course, I'll only be there as Kat's wingwoman," I tease.

He hums as if thinking something over, and then he steps toward me to gather me close. "Maybe I could come out to the club with a few of my teammates? That way it's not like I'm trying to steal you away all for myself?"

"Ohh! That could work! Kat does get easily distracted, and there was this guy at your party a few weeks ago that she really fancied. I'll ask her what he looked like so you can invite him."

I decide not to tell Kat about Logan inviting his friends until I know for sure he can secure the hunks. It'll be my surprise birthday present for her. I mean, if it works out, she'll really owe me one. For my birthday last year, she got me a gift certificate to some fast food chain called Arby's I'd never even heard of. There was $1.05 on the card.

Kat's birthday starts with Yasmine and me making breakfast while she lounges on the sofa, flipping through channels. She's wearing a paper crown on her head that I had the kids make her yesterday. It keeps sliding to the side, but she won't dare let it fall.

"Are you two done yet? I'm starved!"

"Almost!" I reply.

"Right, well don't burn the toast," she warns. "You know how I hate that. And I like my coffee extra milky. Toss in a bit and then when you think you've added too much, go ahead and add a bit more."

"Whatever you want, birthday bit—" Yasmine starts before I cut her off.

"*Yaz!*"

"What?" she hisses. "She's being a cow."

"I can hear you!" Kat shouts.

"Well it's her birthday," I say, defending Kat. "She's allowed to be a cow once a year."

I eat my words when I pass her the toast a minute later and she takes a bite before pointedly spitting it back out onto the plate.

Dead serious, she holds it up and says, "Too cold. Make it again."

Yasmine sort of leaps at her like she's ready to have a go. I have to play peacemaker.

"Kat, eat the toast or I'll fling it out the window" is the diplomatic response I settle on.

"Right, right. *Sheesh*," she says, taking another bite before continuing to talk with her mouth full. "You'd just think on her *birthday*, a girl could get a decent breakfast from her *best mates*."

She only gets worse as the day goes on. At the spa, she demands to go first for the facial and massage, and then she insists we do our nails too even though we've already racked up quite a bill. When Yasmine and I suggest a little deli round the corner for lunch, Kat declares we must go to a salad bar clear across town. It takes us ages to get there by subway, and when we arrive, the guy behind the counter tries to get my number. When I politely tell him no, he gets real snippy and all but barks the total at me. I think about leaving him a bad tip, but instead, I huff my way over to the salad bar to fill my plate with more food than I would normally get. That'll show him.

After lunch, we head back to the flat to rest before our big night out. I know I saw Logan on Thursday, but it feels like it's been ages since then and I don't know what I'll do if he ends up not showing up at the club tonight.

I text him in the late afternoon as we're all lazing about, watching *Legally Blonde*. It was funny the first time, but Kat makes us watch it so often I can recite every line word for word. *What, like it's hard?*

CANDACE: Still planning on coming tonight?

LOGAN: I have a late dinner I forgot about, but I can still come out after with the guys. Just let me know where you end up.

"Candace! This is the best part!" Kat says, taking my mobile out of my hand and chucking it clear across the sofa.

I do a deep breathing exercise to keep from decapitating her. "Kat. I'm truly going to kill you. Remind me to book a trip abroad next year for your birthday. *Without* you."

"Shhh! I'm missing it!"

Yasmine shoots me a glare that says, *I won't say a word if you go ahead and kill her.*

I contemplate it for a good long while, right up until Elle Woods' speech at her graduation, then it's time to get tarted up. It's still hours until the clubs will be packed, but we all love taking our time putting on our makeup, tossing every item of clothing we own out onto our beds then mixing and matching them to get a perfect combo.

We all end up going with a variant of the same look: short skirt, cute top, ridiculous heels. Kat and Yasmine talked me into this coordinating black mini skirt and cropped top. At least the top has got long sleeves, but that's where the modesty ends. It's clingy and soft, the jersey material hugging my figure and making me look loads sexier than I usually am on an average day. Yasmine plays up my eyes with a bit of dark shadow, and then Kat helps me with my hair so it has some wave to it.

I think we look absolutely fabulous when all's said and done.

When we're out on the curb, waiting for our Uber, a passing cyclist gives us a whistle and I squeal. "See?! We look lovely! Even that biker says so."

"He was about 75. Did you get a good look at him? He had no teeth."

"So what? Clearly he's got great taste!"

Our car pulls up and we all slide into the back seat, fiddling with our skirts. It's no real use; they barely cover our knickers. If I were our mothers, I'd be very angry at us for going out like this, but I guess that's the bonus of living across the pond—no one to tell us to cover up!

I text Logan which club we're headed to, but he doesn't text me back. I know it's because he's at his dinner, but it almost makes me a little nervous. I really want him to show. I want him to see me like this and eat his heart out. Wouldn't that be lovely? Especially after all the times he's seen me at The Day School, covered in tissue dressed up like a mummy or with a paintbrush stuck in my hair. It's only fair that he should see me like this too, right?

The club is closer to where Logan lives, up in a trendy part of town with a long queue circling round the corner.

For a moment, I think, *Ha! We don't need to wait in that—they'll take one look at us and* beg *us to come inside*, but then there are loads of pretty girls standing there, waiting to get in, and we aren't that special, are we?

We take our place at the back of the queue and fidget in the chilly air. It's getting on into spring, but New York has a way of sneaking winter in when you least expect it. I've got goosebumps everywhere and I'm shivering.

Kat groans at how slow the queue is moving, but I lift her spirits by promising to buy her a drink as soon as we get inside. A shot will warm us up, though it'll also be painfully expensive. In a place like this, I can only imagine what the drinks cost. *Water with lemon? That'll be $378.48.*

I'm already tallying up what I'm allowed to order: a shot for myself and Kat, and one drink. That's it. Anything else and I'll end up with a bill that'll give me a heart attack.

Yasmine pokes her head round the corner and assures us we'll be inside really soon.

The queue does start picking up then, and it only takes a little while until we're at the front. We hand over our IDs and the bouncer lets us in with a nod of his head. Suddenly, it feels like we've really arrived. I feel giddy with excitement. Maybe the queue's a smart move because it does feel like the place is really exclusive, all dark and moody with flashing lights and trendy furniture. There're different areas to sit: an outdoor garden with heating lamps near the back, an upstairs VIP area we don't even bother trying to get into, and a main dance floor. That's where we settle, trying to get drinks at the bar.

We agree on a Fireball shot and clink our glasses together before downing them in one go. The cinnamon-flavored whisky burns my throat, but I don't mind. It heats me from the inside out.

Yasmine slaps more money down onto the bar. "Another round please!"

"Yaz," I moan, not wanting her to feel like she has to fund the evening just because she's got more money than the rest of us. I can pay for myself if I just go easy.

"No! I don't want to hear it!" she says, covering her ears. "I've waited on Kat all day and she's been a real wanker. I need alcohol."

"*Hey!*"

"The least I can do is get us all properly toasted now, *her* most of all."

"Now, I truly can't find fault with that," Kat amends, accepting her second shot and passing me one as well.

"Why do I feel like this night isn't going to end well?"

"Nonsense! We're all so good at holding our alcohol!"

It's a barefaced lie. Wholly inaccurate. When Kat gets drunk, she gets real sobby. She always wants to have a good cry, hug us close, and moan on about how life is fleeting and we have to grasp it with both hands. Yasmine just gets so she's real horny. Once she's two sheets to the wind, she'll kiss anything—a boy, a girl, a broom.

"All right, let's just pace ourselves, yes?"

Kat ignores me and shouts, "HAPPY BIRTHDAY TO ME!"

And that's when the night takes a turn. Fireball is potent, and anyone who says otherwise is a total liar or a total drunkard. Three shots in, I'm feeling it. I know it's got a bit to do with my size and the fact that we had some wine back at the flat while we were getting ready, but I can't help it, I LOVE THIS SONG.

"WE HAVE TO DANCE!"

And we are dancing! Up on the DJ booth! I can't quite work out how we've made it from the bar to the booth, but we're up in here with the DJ and he's passing Kat his headset and she's putting it on then jumping up and down in time with the music. The lads in the crowd are eating it up, of course; she's quite well-endowed, so she's putting on a good show in her crop top. I'm laughing and I can't stop laughing no matter how hard I try.

All I care about is this song and how it sounds, like the music is living inside me. Yasmine turns me toward her and tries to go in for a snog, but I duck out of the way so she ends up kissing the DJ.

Let me tell you, he's not upset in the *least*!

Then I glance up in the crowd and, lo and behold, LOGAN! He's here, in the mad throng of people out on the dance floor, and he's brought his buds. Oh, this is *ace*.

"KAT! *Kat*!" I try to grab her attention over the music, but it takes ages. She doesn't listen until I pry the headphones off her ears and shout right against her head. "I've got you a wonderful birthday present!"

Her eyes light up with glee. "Oh, you have? What is it?"

She looks down as if expecting me to whip it out from behind my back. Instead, I turn her so she's facing the crowd, and then I point out to where Logan and his friends are standing.

It takes her a second to register what I'm pointing at. Then suddenly, she spins toward me, mouth gaping.

"THE FOOTBALLER!" Her eyes are bright with excitement. "You've brought him here!"

Without wasting a moment, she grabs my hand and I grab Yasmine's hand and we're running from the DJ booth. The crowd boos at our departure—like I said, Kat was really entertaining them—but what do we care?! We have lovely men waiting for us down below.

With Kat in the lead, threatening to tug my arm out of socket, we barrel through the crowd, leaving me shouting apologies in our wake. *Sorry about my friend! I've tried having her committed, but they won't take her!* We make it to the guys in no time. Blimey, they're all quite huge when they stand together like that. Three of them. One for each of us. Kat's man—the one she immediately steps toward—is lovely with brown skin, very short hair, and a big smile.

"Oh hello, you. Remember me?"

His smile widens. "I do, yeah. From Logan's party. I'm Jay."

"Hello, *Jay*. I'm Kat and it's my birthday."

"Happy birthday," he says, staring down at her with a mischievous smile.

I can't make out what she says next because she sort of whispers it in his ear, but then his eyes go wide, and well, there you have it. I've just given Kat the best birthday present she could have ever asked for.

Yasmine plays a little more hard to get with her man. She reaches her hand out to introduce herself and asks him his name too. He's called Marcus. He's got black hair down to his shoulders and some cool tattoos stretching up his arms. Yasmine has always gone for the bad boys, so I know she's only acting cool. Inside, she's screaming.

I finally glance over to Logan, and it's the first time I've really gotten to see him, standing there in his white shirt and jeans. He's had a haircut, and his brown locks are shorter now. It somehow makes him look sharper, not at all the sweet man I've become used to.

I find I'm shy all of a sudden, as if we hardly know each other.

He's studying my reaction to him, tipping his head to the side.

I cross my arm over my stomach so I can grip my other elbow.

"Hi you."

248

"Hey," he says, smiling.

He's not making it easy on me. He could step toward me and close the gap between us, but I get the feeling he's enjoying this, pinning my little mouse tail to the ground with his big cat paw.

"You look nice," I say.

He laughs and shakes his head, turning to his friends. "Come on, let's go up to the suite."

Logan glances over my shoulder and his eyes narrow, assessing the crowd. That's when I finally start to notice the whispers coming from around us. People have started gathering close, more than a little curious.

"Is that Logan Matthews?"

"Dude, I think it is. And that has to be Jay Cruthers with him."

"Didn't he win the Heisman at LSU?"

Curiosity morphs into courage.

"Hey! Logan! Can I get a picture?!"

"Marcus! Jay!"

It's definitely time we abandon the main floor and make for higher ground. Logan reaches out to gather me close, and then he pushes me ahead of him, his hand on the small of my back. I don't make out what he tells the others, but when I glance over my shoulder, they're following near us. We round the dance floor then head toward a roped-off staircase. The huge bouncer blocking it steps aside immediately once he sees Logan approaching. We start to go up and then once we're on the second-floor landing, Logan points to a door at the end of the hall.

It turns out he's somehow reserved a VIP suite that's totally separated from the rest of the club. We walk in and the room sprawls out in front of us. There's a main seating area with drinks and food already set out for us to enjoy. The vibe is even cooler in here than it is down in the rest of the club, not all black leather and tacky plastic lights. It's got paneled walls and lovely deep library chairs. A heavy chandelier hangs from the ceiling, casting a warm glow that competes with the moody club lighting seeping in from the far wall. Over there, the VIP suite has a sunken balcony that overlooks the first floor. I walk over to the edge and look over, and people start to go wild, thinking I'm someone cool. I sort of wave then immediately step back, nervous about all the attention. It's quite nice the way they've designed the space. Unless I'm right at the edge, no one from the first floor can see us. It's totally private up here.

The music from below drifts up, but it's muted so I can actually hear myself think for the first time all night. I turn back around to survey the group. Kat has convinced Jay to crack open a bottle of champagne, and the two of them don't even bother splitting it with the rest of us poor souls. They just take turns passing it back and forth between them while they sit on the couch, all locked eyes and pervy expressions. I swear Kat will pounce on him at any moment and then we'll all need therapy from having to see it. She's like a wildebeest sometimes, but from the look on Jay's face, he's not scared in the least.

Yasmine and Marcus are huddled together in another corner, talking low. He's twisting his arm, showing her one of his tattoos, and she reaches out to touch it, skimming her

252

finger along his skin. Well, I suppose they've hit it off as well.

Lucky how that's happened.

I gird my loins when I scan the area to look for Logan. He's in the middle of the room, sitting in a leather chair, watching me take everything in. It's like he's got it all figured out, like he's somehow in control of everything I do even though he's over there and I'm over here. I don't like it, the way my body seems to be on high alert, the way I've lost my grip on myself. I know if I go near him, it'll be game over. We'll be as bad as Kat and Jay...so instead, I distract myself.

I peruse my food options over at the buffet. They've got some shrimpy things on toasted flatbread, some chocolate cake bites, nuts, and loads of other finger foods. I don't eat anything; my stomach couldn't bear it. Instead, I move down the line to the drinks. There's quite a lot of liquor bottles up here. We could probably make any drink we wanted, but I've already reached my limit for the night so I move right along.

I tip back on my heels and turn around. Logan's still in his spot, making my knees go weak, so I turn away quickly. Well, right. Now that the food and drinks have been covered, guess I should take in the artwork on the walls. I get to one of the framed pieces and am having a good look at it when Logan's presence becomes painfully obvious behind me.

He's apparently had enough of waiting.

"What are you doing?"

"Appreciating art. I mean look at those colors! The movement! The subject matter!"

"Right. I think that's just the fire code information they have to post."

Oh. Well that does explain all the words.

"I wouldn't expect a brute like you to understand art."

He laughs and grabs my hand when I try to make a break for it.

"What are you doing?"

"Avoiding you. I thought that was obvious."

He frowns, and even *that* is cute. Ugh! Lord help me!

"Why?"

"Because, well…you…" I frown, trying to come up with some way to get my feelings across without totally scaring him off. "It's just a bit much, y'know. Do you feel it?"

I quirk a brow, trying for lighthearted, fun mate rather than girl falling hopelessly in love.

He steps closer and grasps my waist with both hands. My body gets hijacked right away. It's just the size of him, his huge grip on my middle. With him hovering over me, I'm cast in shadow, but so is he. I can only make out half his features, and it sends a little panicked thrill down my spine.

"Why do you think I'm here?" he asks, sincerely.

"Oh, for a laugh?"

"*Candace*."

"All right, fine. You wanted your lads to have a bit of fun. I'll bet Kat and Jay are ripping each other's clothes off as we speak."

"I'm not sure. They went out to the VIP bar."

Sure enough, when I duck around him to glance at the rest of the gang, everyone's gone. They've left us!

Logan keeps hold of my waist and starts walking us back to the chair he was sitting in. I let him, because…well, it gets exhausting trying to keep a distance. I've only got so much strength left in these weary bones, and if he's intent on having me sit down on his lap, who am I to argue?

"There's plenty of other seating," I tease.

He smiles and adjusts me so my knees go on either side of his hips.

Well, that's quite a wonderful position, I'd say. It's like he planned it perfectly.

"I don't know how I feel about this outfit," he says, glancing over me.

I'm tempted to cover up, but I force myself to keep my hands where they are, resting on his shoulders.

"Do you like it?"

"No." My bottom lip pouts and he shakes his head. "When I walked in and saw you up on the DJ booth, I felt pretty territorial. It's part of the reason I dragged you up here."

"Oh, don't want other lads having a look?"

"Not of my girlfriend, no."

That word is the sexiest thing I've ever heard come out of his mouth, so I lean in and kiss him quickly before pulling away.

Oh. He doesn't like that. His eyes narrow in disapproval and his grip tightens on my waist.

"It's just a skirt."

"Yeah?" he asks, moving his hands to gather the stretchy material and drag it up my thighs. "Maybe it's not so bad after all."

I can't look down. I'll pass out.

He adjusts me so I sit higher on his lap, and I feel him start to harden underneath me. It's like he can't help it, not with me on him like this.

"And the top?" I ask, wanting to continue our game.

His eyes flit up to my chest. "Is that what you're calling it? It's more like a bra with sleeves."

"Oh hardly. Half the girls downstairs are dressed even more skimpy than this!"

He hums from deep in his throat then reaches up to trace the V-neck of my top with one hand. He follows the way it

255

cuts low over my breasts. I didn't think it was so indecent, but then his hand skims over the sensitive skin there and I shiver.

He dips down to the center of my chest and follows the fabric up on the other side before hooking a finger into the edge and peeling the material back just a smidge, revealing more of my lace bra and cleavage.

I swallow and try not to fidget, letting him do what he pleases. I know he's the one in control, even if I'm the one on top.

The corner of his mouth perks up. "Yeah, I see your point. Maybe I do like this outfit."

He keeps touching me, adjusting my top on the other side too so more of the sheer parts of my bra are exposed.

"The others could come back at any moment," I whisper, trying to talk some sense into him. We can't just do this in the middle of a club! Even if we are in a private suite!

"I asked them not to."

I blink at his response, more than a little taken aback.

Then he leans forward and kisses his way around the edge of my bra. His lips touch my skin, and my eyes flutter closed as all my arguments dissipate into thin air. He traces delicately along each cup before tugging the thin material to the side completely. Lace scrapes over my breasts, and cool air hits my chest before his mouth follows.

"*Logan.*"

I breathe his name like he's my life force, and he continues on like that, teasing one breast then the other. My fingers grip into his shoulders, using him to anchor me.

It feels like we've gotten here so fast, me half-naked on his lap, but then again, it feels like it's been too long...too long since his hands have been on me like this, too long since his mouth has peeled apart my senses.

His tongue laps over the peak of each breast and then he pulls back to survey me. I know I'm pink and flushed, and I know he likes it. He rolls his hips so that I grind down on him, and then I lean forward to kiss him. Everything before has been a lead-in to this. Our mouths touch, and it's the last chance we have to gather our senses. Stop now or don't stop at all.

Neither one of us tries to move away.

He keeps a grip on my waist, rocking me back and forth across his hard length. With my skirt tugged up, it's only my knickers covering me, and I can feel him so well. The rigid outline is enough to send me over the edge, but we don't make it there. This is only a teaser, and he won't let me get too ahead of myself. Any time I work myself up and really start moving on him, grinding and kissing him harder, he slows us down.

Then he moves his mouth somewhere else. Down to my neck. Over my breasts. Back up to my mouth. I'm going insane. I am. I think I might cry from his wicked lips, but then his hand moves between my legs and hooks onto the edge of my panties so he can tug them aside and I fall back, breaking our kiss and setting my hands on either of his knees. I'm so exposed like this, but that's what I want. I want him to have all the access in the world as his finger slides into me. I clench around him, and the *sound* he makes…I could pray at the altar of Logan Matthews. Truly. I'm lost in him as he slides his finger out and then back in, his lovely long finger and the way it drives me mad.

Let's stay here forever.

Let's live in this dark room and we'll just continue on like this until we pass out from exhaustion. Then we'll wake up and eat from that buffet and start all over again. There's no world outside this room. Nothing.

I lock eyes with him then, and there's a plea in my gaze.

He knows what I'm after. It's been long enough, don't you think? Enough of the torture. Enough of the wondering what it'll feel like. We'll fit together. I know we will, and if we don't, I'll learn, change, become whatever it is he needs, because *I need him.*

"Hold on," he tells me, his voice a dark whisper compared to normal.

I do as I'm told, and he reaches down between us to unzip his jeans. It's hard for him to maneuver with me on top of him, so he doesn't tug them down all the way, just *enough.*

Enough for me to reach down and touch him, grip him in my hand and stroke up and down. I only stave off the inevitable for a few moments, a few passes of my hand up and down before I move back over him and let myself feel him between my legs. Logan's not wearing a condom yet but tells me he has one. He'll get it in a second, but I can't stop myself from rocking back and forth like this. He hisses as if in pain, but aren't we all?

The music down in the club switches to something more sensual and we're moving with it, kissing and rocking together. I shudder as he brushes across sensitive bare skin, and then, like he's angry with me for putting us here, he lifts me up so he can get his wallet out of the back of his jeans. He opens it and tells me to get the condom. I do as I'm told, ripping open the foil so he can do the rest. He sheaths himself and once that's done, it's like someone's shot a starting pistol.

We're fumbling together, positioning me over him. He takes his length in his hand and I lower my hips. I know it'll be a tight fit. I know it, but I'm still taken aback when I start to sink lower on him. I gasp and he gathers me against him so we're chest to chest.

"Go slow," he warns, and my muscles relax a bit, taking more of him inside me.

He murmurs a curse against the shell of my ear as I continue to move down onto him, taking him deeper. The hard muscles on his chest tighten as if he's holding himself back.

I know it's a tough position to start with. I should be on my back on a comfy bed, but this club and this chair is what we have and I'll be damned if we stop now.

It feels impossible to think we'll fit together and I let my teeth scrape against his neck, conveying my pain, but it's fleeting and the sharp bite burns away, replaced by delicious fullness.

We sit there for a moment, fused. He tugs my head back so he can look at me. His eyes flit back and forth between mine, his brown gaze trying to sear into me. He doesn't ask, but I know what he's after, and I lean forward to kiss him, telling him I'm okay. I'm *more* than okay.

Of course, there are feelings of wrongness—the fact that we're doing this with that door right there and the club at my back. I know he's asked everyone to stay away, but that doesn't mean they will. That knife edge of worry only adds to the moment, though. It feels terrifying and fleeting and wrong and I don't want him to stop once he starts to rock in and out of me. He holds me steady with one hand and tells me to lean back again so he can reach his hand down between my legs.

Oh yes.

His thumb swirls in combination with his thrusts. Every fleeting bout of pleasure from earlier comes rushing back so hard and fast that I come before I even realize it's starting. I squeeze around him and he continues to rub me, and then it's like the dam breaks. One orgasm isn't enough. It's the beginning. It's a tantalizing promise of what I can have if only we continue like this, pumping, thrusting, harder. He knows what I need and he does it, reaching up to play with one of my breasts as we rock together. I know he's close. I know he wants to come, but not before I do—again. I'm greedy, and he should know that now. Better he realizes exactly what he's getting into with this relationship. His thumb returns between my legs and his pace speeds up. We're lost, utterly. I'm probably screaming at the top of my lungs for all I know, but who cares? Nothing exists beyond these walls, remember? Just us.

His thumb swirls and swirls and my insides clench around him. I'm saying his name, letting him know how good it feels to come like this, alongside him, and then his mouth is covering mine, maybe to hush me up or maybe so he can pour his feelings into me.

"I can't believe we've done this."

They're the first words I say once the club atmosphere returns to the forefront of my mind like a tsunami. Oh god. We're *mad*!

Logan laughs and kisses my cheek. "It's fine. Here, let me help."

It's bloody awkward to sort of hobble off him and grab for a handful of cocktail napkins so I can help clean myself up. He tugs off the condom and ties it so he can stuff it into a bunch of napkins and dump it in the waste bin. Then I cover it with loads more napkins while my cheeks turn into Red Hots. He tucks himself back into his trousers and then I force him to give me all the cash out of his wallet.

"I was going to leave them a tip anyway."

"Yes, well, now they'll have to clean up after our little sex session, so fork it over. Everything you've got. Poor sods. I should go try to find a mop or something."

"We didn't make a mess. It's only the condom in the trash. Look, I'll tie off the bag so they won't even see it."

"Still! We're total heathens! We've just attacked each other!"

"You didn't mind it a second ago," he says with a cheeky smile that I love as much as I hate.

"*Mind* it? Of course not! You could have bent me over that buffet table over there and told me to fork shrimps into my mouth and I'd have done it, gladly. That's what you do to me. It's your fault, really."

"I think it's 50/50. I was only following your lead."

"My lead?! Not bloody likely!"

He's laughing and bending down to kiss my cheek. "Let's agree to disagree, yeah?"

"You only want that because you know I'm better at arguing."

I swear he sort of turns his gaze up to the ceiling as if he's had absolutely all he can handle from me. It's too bad. I'm his girlfriend now, so he'd better get used to it.

"Let's go to the bathroom and freshen up."

"You might want to…you know…"

He points down between my breasts.

Oh right! *Sheesh*, I'm still just hanging out there, open for business and all that.

I fix my top and skirt then force Logan to go out into the hall to confirm no one is out there before I scurry off to clean myself up. In the bathroom, I try to put myself back together so I feel utterly confident on my way back out to join the gang. My lips have a fresh coat of gloss and my hair is as good as ever. I feel great—properly laid, you know—so I'm sure I'm sporting a wonderful glow. Logan's found the gang at the VIP bar up on the second floor. I smile as I join them, and then Kat takes one look at me and loudly announces (so

261

everyone in the whole club can hear), "You've gone and had sex, you sly dog!"

"I think we should address the rumors," Rosie tells me during our meeting on Monday.

I bristle at the thought. "No. I don't discuss my private life with the press."

"Right, but if you don't discuss it, they end up printing whatever they want because you're not confirming or denying any of their articles and photos. The more you keep your relationship with Candace a secret, the more they're going to go after her."

I rub my temples, trying to ease the tension building there. It's been a long day, longer than most, like a whole week jam-packed into one day.

"Rosie, I'm not addressing it."

"Right. We'll discuss it another time."

Our meeting drones on. She's going over my schedule for the rest of the week and I'm listening, but I'm also checking my phone. Candace is going with Kat to clean a house after she finishes at The Day School. She said she'd call me when they were finished and maybe we could grab dinner. It's nearly 8:30 PM, though, and I'm not sure why she hasn't called.

Rosie leaves—correctly assessing that I don't have the attention span for work right now—and I go into my kitchen to make myself a sandwich.

It's been rough transitioning from the weekend back to real life. After we left the club on Saturday night, Candace came home with me. She slept in my bed, nestled against me, and then I made her breakfast Sunday morning. She ate just about anything I put on her plate, grinning up at me when she'd finished. After that, we tugged on hats and sunglasses, exited through the back entrance of my building, and went on a walk. It was nice for the first half hour, but then the press spotted us, so I called Pat and he came to get us so he could drive us back to my apartment. It wasn't all bad. Hiding out at my place all day meant we had a lot of time to ourselves. I put on a movie, which we mostly ignored in favor of having sex on my couch. God, just thinking about it makes my blood heat up. Candace is as crazy in bed as she is anywhere else, funny and passionate and sexy. I barely let her out of my clutches all day, but then she groaned and convinced me she had to go back to sleep at her place for the night. She needed to shower and do some lesson planning for the week. I relented, but now I regret it. I haven't seen her since last night.

I look at my phone again, but there's still nothing from her, no text or call.

I head back into the living room and flip on the TV. I never watch gossip shows, ever, but I had the news on earlier so I catch a glimpse of *Entertainment Tonight*. Candace is on the screen, laughing with Kat out on the sidewalk. The news story is about Candace—not about us and our relationship, but about her and her life and how a "regular" girl like her could have caught my attention.

They mention her job at The Day School and at District. Jesus fuck. They show a picture of her parents they must have pulled from her social media, and there's more: speculation about how we met, a tip from an anonymous source saying I'm not that into her and just wanted a distraction after my breakup with Melody.

I guess Rosie was right. I haven't confirmed anything, so they're saying whatever they want.

I turn off the TV and grab my phone to call Candace.

When she answers, she's out of breath. "Hey Lo."

The tension in my head eases a bit at the sound of her voice. "Hey, you said you'd call after you finished cleaning that house."

"I know—we haven't finished yet." Then she laughs. "It's been a wild day. There were photographers outside The Day School when I went in and they wouldn't leave, so my boss had to call the police to corral them all. I mean the kids couldn't even get in—can you imagine? Then, as I was leaving, I expected them to be cleared out, but they weren't. I had to hide out for a bit until Kat showed up with these ridiculous disguises, black wigs and huge sunglasses. Surprisingly, they worked, but we were late getting started at the house so we're still here."

"Crap. I'm sorry."

"What? No worries. I mean, it's different, yeah? Being in the spotlight like that."

"Yeah. It is. I just saw you on the TV, actually."

"Are you serious?" She sounds like it's too wild to believe.

"They were talking about your jobs and your parents. You need to make sure all your social media accounts are set

265

to private. They somehow got a photo of your mom and dad."

"Oh bugger. I didn't even think of that. I'm a total novice with all this."

"It's not your fault. This isn't exactly normal."

I feel horrible for dragging her into the fray like this, but it's inevitable. To bring her in closer, I'll only be exposing her more. There's no way around it.

"Right. Yeah. Logan, I've got to go. I need to finish up here and phone my mum. She'll probably have heard about everything on the news, and I still haven't really told her about us. I feel bad. I hope they're not worried or anything."

"Yeah, of course. I'll talk to you later."

"Right, phone you later."

And then there's a pregnant pause because neither of us hangs up. This is the part where if you loved someone, you'd say it. It's like we're both thinking it, and she even laughs, breaking the tension.

"Okay, well, bye then!"

She ends the call, and I sit on my couch staring down at my phone, wondering how on earth I can fix this.

I'm still getting used to the fact that I can't leave my flat on a whim. I can't go out on the sidewalk without someone shouting my name. I can't just pop into a café for a tea or coffee without people recognizing me. To have gone from total anonymity to veritable fame in a matter of a few weeks is doing a number on my head.

Mum and Dad can't stop phoning. They think it's all wonderful. The press is knocking on their door with questions, and my mum is inviting them into the house and showing them photos of me from my baby book. *There she is slinging around one of her dirty nappies. Poo went everywhere!* When my dad goes out to get the post, he waves and chats with the photographers, asking them if they need a cup of tea or to pop in to use the loo.

I've told them to cut it out, but that's nearly impossible. Telling two parents to stop gloating about their only daughter? Good luck with that.

Logan and I are still trying to learn how to navigate it. He's come up with a brilliant plan:

I should quit working at District, let him hire me a bodyguard, and oh yes, MOVE IN WITH HIM.

He told me all about it when I phoned him Wednesday night.

"I worry about you in that apartment. That building isn't secure at all."

"Isn't secure?! I've got at least *four* hardened Russian grannies between me and the first floor. They're as scary as they come. They shout at me if I bang up the stairs too loudly or if they think I've gotten too thin. One of them threatened a takeout man with an umbrella last week when he tried to bring Yaz and me some noodles. Believe me, *no one* is getting past them."

"*Candace*."

"Logan! What you're asking is insane. I can't move in with you! I barely know you!"

"You're deflecting. We know each other. *I know you.*"

"Yes, well, you know all the outer bits, don't you? But you don't know what I'd be like to live with. A real slob, I'm afraid. You'd hate it."

"Lois can help with that. Besides, I think you could learn to hang your clothes up in your closet instead of just throwing them on the floor."

I rolled my eyes. "You'd be surprised."

"I think you should consider it."

"Right, well, even if I did agree, good luck convincing Kat and Yasmine! I think they'd have my head if I tried to move out. We're a package deal, you know. I can't just abandon my friends."

The next day, I arrive back to the flat after work to find that Kat and Yasmine have gathered up all my clothes and dumped them in the living room in a huge pile.

"What in the world are you doing?!"

Kat glances up then from her spot on the sofa. "Oh look, Yaz, *Judas* is home."

Yasmine glares up at me with her arms crossed over her chest. "Who? I don't see anyone."

"Guys, what are you going on about—"

Kat shakes her head. "You're dead to us. Don't even look at me."

"KAT!"

She jumps to her feet, stepping over the mound of clothes in the middle of the room. They've really cleared out my closet, haven't they?

"So you're moving out, huh?" She starts circling around me like a seasoned interrogator. "Logan phoned me today, offered to cover your part of the rent. He told me he'd asked you to move in with him. Yaz! Grab a lighter—I'm burning all her bras."

I can't help but laugh, but that doesn't go over well.

"You're both in need of a mental check. Truly."

"She thinks she's too good for us now that she's got that lover boy of hers," Kat continues.

"I thought you and Jay were getting on well?" I prod.

"We are! But I'm not moving in with him and abandoning my best mates!"

"I think you're both overreacting. I haven't agreed to anything."

Yasmine rolls her eyes. "Oh sod off. There's no way you're going to turn that bloke down, not with that lovely hair and those nice eyes—"

"And don't forget his arse!" Kat chimes in.

"Listen, you two. God, you're both mad. I'll phone him right now and tell him I won't do it. I'm staying here."

"Good. We'll listen in. You can no longer be trusted, Judas."

"Would you stop with that? Do you even know what Judas did?"

"Yes, of course—something horribly traitorous back in the day."

"Yeah, wasn't he the lad with the Trojan horse?" Yasmine chimes in.

"Ugh, don't bother!" Kat shouts. "She's only trying to change the subject!"

I make a big show of getting my mobile out of my bag and waving it in the air.

"Dial him," Kat insists, stepping closer and crossing her arms.

I do, and then she reaches out to put it on speaker.

When Logan answers, he sounds so sexy I sort of wilt. He gives me a hello and I forget my agenda for a moment as I try to think of some way to get over to his flat for a quick lay.

Kat clears her throat with an exaggerated, "AHEM."

"Right, hey Logan…I've got Kat and Yasmine here with me on speaker. Say hello, you loons."

I fully expect him to get the same loathsome treatment they're giving me, but instead, they're positively delightful.

"Hello Logan!" Yasmine says in a chipper tone.

"Hey bud!" Kat adds.

I frown. "What? You aren't going to shout at him like you've been doing with me? How's that fair?"

"Well Logan hooked us up with his lovely mates." Yasmine shrugs.

"And *he's* not the one abandoning us!" Kat says with a narrow-eyed glare in my direction.

"So I guess you haven't made much headway with them?" Logan asks me.

"They've piled all my things in the living room. Kat wants to burn my bras."

He laughs then. "I thought you were joking about them giving you a hard time."

"No, we're quite prepared to cut her out of our lives completely. You know, *excommunicado* style," Kat says, leaning toward my mobile. "But Logan, while we've got you, has Jay said anything to you about me?"

"Yeah, actually. I talked to him today during our workout. He mentioned that he was going to call and ask you out on a date for this weekend."

Kat beams. "Brilliant. I can't wait. Did he look handsome then? At the workout? I'll bet."

"Can you ask him about Marcus?" Yasmine shouts from across the room.

Kat slices her with a hard look. "Not right now, Yasmine! This is important. Logan, your girlfriend is a traitor for abandoning her mates, and we do not accept your offer of partial rent payment. Good day."

Except I don't hang up, and we all go silent. Then finally, Logan laughs.

"Call me later, Candace?"

"Sure, yeah, before bed."

There's that heavy pause again! The one we keep doing at the end of our calls! It happened when I left his flat the other day too. He kissed me then I pulled back, and we looked each other in the eyes. It was like we were right back in primary school, all blushy and awkward.

"Right, well, ta-ta!" I say quickly.

Then I end the call and look up at my flatmates.

They're wearing odd expressions, looking at me like I've grown a second head.

"Why haven't you said you love him?"

"LOVE?!" I bark out a hearty laugh, and then one more for posterity. "Who said anything about *love*?"

Yasmine tilts her head, studying me with a you-poor-sod expression. I hate it.

"Right, well, now that everything is settled...Kat, grab that pile of panties and help me shove all these clothes back into our room. I'm not going anywhere."

"Thank god," she says, walking over to start kicking my garments back to where they belong.

"You know, a real mate wouldn't have done this in the first place," I point out as my blouse flies up into the air and lands on the corner of the telly.

She screws up her face like I've just said the dumbest thing she's ever heard. "What kind of mates have you had before? This is very standard."

"So you've excommunicated people before?"

"Oh *loads*. I'm quite stubborn when I put my mind to it."

Saturday can't come soon enough.

It's like the second half of the week is in cahoots to go really slow, like the days know how eager I am to get to the weekend (the *good* bit) and they want to draw it out for a bit of fun. I've got another shift at District Friday night, and it doesn't go very well. I'm waiting on a group of lads, asking for their drink orders, when I notice the girls one table over start to snap photos of me. They're doing it real sly, so at first, I'm not totally sure what they're doing. They have their mobiles positioned partially behind their water glasses, but when I look over, they all laugh and scramble to shove them away, back down into their purses.

I tell myself I'm just being paranoid, but it only gets worse from there. I'm asked by two different groups to give them my autograph. What in the world do they want with my chicken-scratch letters on a stained cocktail napkin? I laugh and try to play it off as if they're kidding, but they insist, and well…I don't want them to think I'm some snotty brat, so I do it, but I feel crummy afterward, like they think I'm someone more special than I am. I'm a total fraud—or at least that's the way it feels. Neither of the groups leave decent tips, which just goes to show you how annoying people can be sometimes. I've worked my arse off the whole night and I have barely anything to show for it. Still, I count out the bills and set most of them aside in my head to send to Mum in the morning.

I had a long chat with her last night, same ol' same ol': her trying to insist they don't need money, me not budging on the subject. She asked about Logan, and I told her we're proper dating, girlfriend/boyfriend and everything. Even with the press and such, she still didn't quite believe it and made me swear I wasn't pulling her leg.

After I grab my purse and mobile from the employee break room in the back of District, I head for the exit, more than ready to be done with my shift. I've gotten used to seeing Pat waiting out on the curb for me, so when I spot an unfamiliar sleek black SUV in his spot, I frown, assuming he's forgotten to pick me up.

I turn toward my subway stop, a bit mopey that I have to trek home like a normal person, when the front door of the

273

car opens and out walks Logan, rounding the front so he can get to me.

I stand there on the sidewalk like a total knob, just soaking him in.

He's a sight for sore eyes, that's for sure, all hunky and done up in a black button-down and slacks. He's dressed up, and I remember that he had a fancy dinner tonight with Nike. He must not have changed out of his clothes yet. *Yummy.*

"What are you doing here?" I ask with a smile I can't quite keep from spreading across my lips.

"Picking up my girlfriend," he says, with a slight tug of his brows like he's almost offended by the question.

"You didn't have to do this. You're probably dead on your feet. I can make it home on my own."

There's not even an argument from him. He just moves behind me and starts prodding me toward the passenger side of the vehicle.

"I've never seen you drive before," I point out.

"You sound impressed."

"I suppose I am. Is that silly?"

He laughs and helps me up into the seat. I'm quite useless, apparently, because he takes it upon himself to buckle me in place too. He gets really close and leans over to click the seatbelt into the little slotty thing, and well, I take full advantage of his position. I inhale his cologne and melt into the seat. He turns to look at me, his eyes as dark as my thoughts.

I lean in and kiss him, and he must have expected it because there's no shocked delay, just a responsive mouth and a little bite on my bottom lip. *God.* I want him and he bloody well knows it, because when he breaks the kiss (much too soon, if you ask me) and leans back out of the car,

274

he's wearing a cocky grin as if he knows everything I'm thinking.

He shuts my door and heads back to his side. I scan the sidewalk for paparazzi, but for once, we've lucked out.

I don't even ask where we're headed as he pulls away from the curb. I know he'll take me back to his flat, because that's exactly where I want him to go. Usually, I'm a Chatty Cathy with him, but right now, I'm too on edge. I keep glancing over out of the corner of my eye, taking in his profile in repose as he deftly navigates the city streets. His hands on the steering wheel are all big and veined. Not too much, you know, like the scary blokes who resemble the Hulk, but enough to make my belly tighten with desire.

His shirtsleeves are rolled up to his elbows, his forearms tanned and toned. I really stare at him, long enough that he glances over, and I don't even bother looking away to try to feign coolness.

There're no teasing remarks from him. No, he must feel what I feel, because he turns back to the road and reaches his hand out toward me, gripping my thigh and squeezing gently. It's like he's saying, *Me too, Candace.*

And well, it's probably meant to be a nice little touch, a way for him to show affection, but I haven't been alone with him in days and my body seems to have a mind of its own. Instead of sitting there nicely, my legs split apart, just an inch.

He notices.

I can see him swallow in my peripheral vision, so I do it again, another little bit so that cool air rushes up between my thighs from his car's A/C.

I'm still wearing my District uniform, but I've taken off the apron. My black skirt makes it so easy for him to slide his hand in and up, not all the way, just enough to tease me into spreading my thighs more.

We come to a red light, and he hits the brakes harder than normal. I turn my head to stare at him, and he's looking down, between my legs. I reach for the hem of my skirt, watching him the whole time as I start to slide it up...up...*up*.

I know his windows are heavily tinted; I know because they look just like the windows on Pat's SUV, and those were done to help shield Logan from prying eyes. Right now, the tint helps shield me. He doesn't disappoint. His hand follows my skirt as it trails higher, and then he grips my left thigh and tugs so I'm split apart even more on his front seat. I'm wearing silky pink panties, and he must like them because he stares so long the light turns green and a car lays on the horn behind us.

I laugh as he groans and turns his attention back to the road, his hand staying on me.

His fingers dig into my skin when he tightens his grip. City streets whip by us and I know we're getting closer to his building, but for some reason, I don't want that. I want to stay here—suspended on this seat with his hand between my legs.

His fingers skate higher, and I grip the edge of my seat, waiting...wanting...*hoping*. Then the edge of his finger skims my panties, and a lightning bolt of excitement ricochets through me. I must make a little sound because Logan jerks his head toward me, like he can't help but take me in like this. Then his eyes are back on the road and his hand continues, over the silk, over my skin, brushing, rubbing, teasing.

My eyes flutter closed when he tugs the material aside.

I feel deviant doing something like this. I know it's bad and improper and loads of other naughty words, but once his fingers touch me and he feels how ready I am for him, I'm no longer responsible for acting decent.

I blink my eyes open when his SUV whips to the left and then down a slope, into a dark car park. We're back at his building, and my heart starts to hammer in my chest when he takes his hand off me, pulls into his parking spot, and kills the engine.

His seatbelt clicks, then he leans over and undoes mine too. It goes slack across my chest and he's tugging me up and off the seat. I half-expect he'll carry me out of the car and up to his flat, but instead, he props me on his lap and leans in to kiss me—hard.

He's more impatient than I've ever seen him, as if that ride home absolutely killed him. He grips the side of my head and his fingers twine through my hair, our mouths staying in sync, tongues licking as we consume each other.

It's hot and heavy and necessary. It feels absolutely vital that he reach down and gather my skirt up again so it sits high on my waist. Then I reach down for his trousers and start to unzip. I'm fumbling because there's not much space on his front seat, but he helps me, and together, we unsheathe him.

"Condom, condom. Bloody condom," I say, looking around his front seat.

"Fuck. I didn't replace the one we used the other day."

I could kill him in cold blood right there. How dare he do this to us? We're right here and we can't wait, not even long enough to make it up to his flat.

"Please tell me you're clean. Yes? You've been checked?"

He nods. "Last month."

Oh thank god.

"I'm on the pill and I'm clean as a whistle." I want to stop talking about this, but it seems important that he know. "I don't…um…I've never gone *without*."

It sounds like a lie. I mean what girl sits on a guy's lap, grinding down on him, and says she's usually oh so careful even though she's not being that way now? But his gaze catches mine, and he sees the vulnerability there. It doesn't make sense. All the careful decisions I've made in the past, all the rows I've had with boyfriends when they've wanted to go without a condom, and now, here—*poof*—I'm ready and willing to give it a go with Logan. Have I totally lost it?

Maybe.

Maybe I have, because he's kissing me again, and it's like we're telling each other the same thing. *I trust you. I trust your intentions.* And more importantly, *I can't wait either.*

He's so hard underneath me and I'm rocking back and forth, teasing him and using him to rub against my sensitive skin. He lets me continue for another few seconds and then with a rough grip on my waist, he stills my hips and reaches down to align us.

I go up on my knees to give him better access and then we click into place, heartbreakingly perfect.

I sink down on him slowly. Like last time, it's painful for the first bit, and then my body eases around him, accommodating his size until I can't take any more.

He stays there for a moment, buried deep inside me, and he takes my mouth again for a deep kiss. We start to rock together gently, moving our hips in sync, and then he picks up the pace, thrusting in and out of me so that I start to careen toward my release.

Then abruptly, he stops, and I protest, angry.

My fingers dig into his forearms and I squeeze my thighs around him, but he has other plans in mind, and I'm forced to listen when he speaks.

"Get in the back."

"What?"

Oh hell. He doesn't answer. He starts to shove me back there, and I have to climb over the console in the middle of the two front seats. I trip and fall into the back, but he's right after me, contorting his huge frame and making me laugh as he gets stuck for a moment.

"Fuck," he groans, looking down at me lying there, skirt flared up, thighs spread apart.

He manages to push through and then he's on me, pinning me down to the seat with his weight and taking my wrists to press them against the door behind me. He takes hold of my fingers and wraps them around the door handle.

"Hold that," he tells me, and I bloody well listen. He pushes up and off me enough to look down and assess me. I'm his conquest, and he's got me right where he wants me. That's how he looks: scary and beautiful and *mine*. He surveys my top, apparently annoyed that it's still in place. He shoves it up to reveal my bra then tugs the cups down so my breasts spill out over the top. Next he leans down and kisses the peak of each one, teasing me.

I'm dying! He can't do this. We were going at it in the front seat and I was so close, but now he's slowing it down, torturing me.

The air in the car is starting to get humid from our breath, and I feel sticky with sweat when his hips roll over mine. He spreads my thighs again and brushes against me. I moan and he does it once more, not pressing into me even when I beg him to.

My panties are still on, and I hate that they shield me from his thrusts.

I move my hands to take them off, but with whip-fast reflexes, he forces my hands back to the door handle.

"I said, hold that."

His tone has gone dark and possessive, and I'm left complying like an eager student. My fingers tighten around the door handle like my life depends on it, and then he takes the pink silk between his fingers and starts to slide it down my thighs. It gets caught on my knees, but instead of ripping like a brute, he gently fixes it and continues tugging until the material falls off onto the floor of the SUV.

Then his eyes fall between my thighs and his fingers follow, parting me for him.

I arch up off the seat when the pad of his finger brushes against sensitive nerves, and when he does it again, my insides clench.

"Logan," I plead, but he doesn't listen. He withdraws his touch and reaches for his length. He wraps his hand around himself, slowly pumping up and down while he watches me. He's in no hurry to end this, but I am. *I AM!*

He hears my impatient whimper, and it must finally get through to him because he positions himself between my thighs and presses back into me. Finally. This. Again. His weight, his fullness, his hard length seeming to completely fill me and *then some.*

"Candace," he says, tracing his mouth along my chin and letting his body press flush against mine. It's suffocating and wonderful, nearly too much. He covers me completely, but my hands stay on that handle as he starts to rock his hips like gentle waves, pulling out of me and then slowly pressing back in. "You feel…"

His words get lost as he buries himself to the hilt and a deep moan escapes him.

I know how I must feel. Tight. Warm. Wet.

I know how he feels. Hard. Rigid. *Huge*.

"Logan," I say, turning my head to capture his mouth.

Once we kiss again, his hips start to pick up speed, and the shackles of restraint are suddenly thrown off. It's like he's finally having me the way he wants me, pinned underneath him, at his mercy.

We're moaning and arching and thrusting together. My legs lock around his waist as if I'm trying to pin him in place and then I'm lost, totally, as my body starts to quake and I squeeze him inside me in a viselike grip. I come apart and he follows right after me with such force that I have to bite back a cry of pain. As soon as it feels like too much, the wave recedes, replaced with calm oceans.

We're panting and collecting our breath slowly. He props himself up on his elbows and looks down at me with a soul-crushing expression. It's like he's not quite sure I'm real and he has to assure himself I'm here by tracing the line of my jaw.

His lips part and I think he's going to say something, but he doesn't.

The words aren't said, but we both know they're there, lurking just under the surface.

We both know.

"Pass that spatula, will you?" I ask Logan.

"Here," he says, handing it over. "Is the salt over by you?"

"Yeah, catch."

"The eggs are almost done."

"My pancakes need another few minutes. I swear yours cooked faster than mine. Have you given me the bad pan or something?"

I lift it up off the gas burner to look for marks of sabotage.

"They're the exact same pans. Don't try to come up with excuses for why your food is going to suck."

"It won't! You'll be eating your words once you take a bite of my fluffy pancakes!"

"I'm sure."

It's Sunday morning and Logan and I are having a breakfast-off. It's a very mature competition in which we each make the same foods—eggs and pancakes and bacon—

and then we sample some of everything to decide who is the Champion Chef of Breakfast, or something like that. I've used my preschool teacher craft skills to assemble a trophy out of recycling rubbish. On it, I've drawn a stick figure hoisting a spatula into the air. I want that trophy—and so does Logan. He really thinks he's the world's best chef, but he's in for a rude awakening. When he wasn't looking, I over-peppered his eggs and dumped loads more flour into his pancake mix. Poor sod. Some might call it cheating, but I say it's just my competitive nature coming out to play. He really needs to keep his head in the game. Is this how he behaves on the football field? I'd better give him a few pointers.

I check my pancakes again, and they're beautiful, New York's most handsome breakfast cake. I flip them onto a plate to keep warm and then cut off my burner.

"Done!" I say, whipping my towel in the air. It hits Logan in the head and he growls in feigned anger before ripping it out of my hand and trying to smack my arse with it.

"Hey! Ease up, you! That actually hurts!"

He chases me through the kitchen and I have to duck around the island. He's much faster than me—good thing our competition doesn't have an athletic component, because I'd be sorely outmatched.

"Enough! *Hey!*" I groan when he catches me and hoists me up off the ground. "I'm hungry. Let's load up our plates and see who the victor is."

"We know who it's going to be," he taunts.

He's really going to cry once he bites into my perfectly cooked eggs, but I won't even feel bad.

After our plates are loaded with the food cooked by each of us—separated out so we won't get confused—we take our seats at his breakfast table facing one another.

It's all very strict. We've concocted real rules and everything. We have to take a bite of the same type of food at the same time, and we have to be totally honest with our opinions. We can't just vote for ourselves for everything, because where's the fun in that? I tried to convince him to have one of the doormen come up and plate the food for us so we'd be totally blind as to whose food we were eating, but Logan only laughed. I suppose some of us are taking this more seriously than others.

"My eggs first," he says, nodding for me to load some onto my fork.

I do as he says, and then we lift the forks to our mouths at the same time, gazes locked. The moment they touch our tongues, our faces contort in disgust. My pepper trick worked handily.

"Sorry bud," I say, after forcing myself to swallow down the small bite. "Eggs are not your forte, I'm afraid."

"Uh-huh," he says, all knowingly. Damn, he must have caught me adding the pepper then. "Let's try yours."

I'm already smirking with pride as I lift my bite to my mouth—then I immediately spit them out onto my napkin one second after I've tasted them.

"What'd you do to my eggs?!" They're horrid, frankly the worst thing I've ever tasted. Maybe it's too much salt? But then that doesn't explain the bitter aftertaste. "I only added pepper to yours!"

"I have no idea what you're talking about," he says, all smooth and unruffled.

The arrogant jerk! He's not even going to admit to cheating then!

"So my eggs are better?" he asks, already puffed with pride. "Even if *you* over-peppered them?"

I scowl. "Fine. Whatever. We've still got two other categories. I'll obviously win those."

I don't win those. The pancakes and bacon are all inedible thanks to our attempts at sabotage. We've really mucked this up. By tainting each other's food, we've made it so we don't even have a decent breakfast to eat. I nearly gag when I try a bite of my pancakes. He added loads of onion powder to my bowl, and the result is nothing short of disgusting.

"I hope you're proud of yourself," I say as I load our plates into the dishwasher. "I'm still starving!"

"ME? C'mon, admit it, we both got a little competitive."

A little?

He leans in to kiss me but stops short when he's only a centimeter away. "Admit it."

I groan. "Fine. Yes." I kiss him quickly before taking his hand in mine and tugging him toward the door of his flat. "Now let's go get some proper food before I pass out from hunger."

He stops me on our way out so we can grab hats and sunglasses. I'd forgotten for a moment that we aren't just two normal people going out for breakfast. If we're leaving his flat, we have to be prepared.

Logan adjusts his Yankees ball cap on my head then smiles. It's quite big, which means it should do the trick.

We ride the lift down as we try to decide where we want to eat. Logan has a favorite spot only a few blocks away, so we plan to head there, turning left on the sidewalk in front of his building and holding hands as we walk.

It's gorgeous out, brisk but not so cold that I need a coat. The sun is shining and there are loads of people out and about, enjoying their Sunday morning. I stop us at a newsstand so I can buy a paper we can share at breakfast. I like reading the Sunday comics and attempting the crossword, even if I never get very far with it.

When I'm done, I turn to Logan with the newspaper in hand and smile. He nods for me to join him again so we can continue our walk, and it's then that I notice a group of photographers a few yards ahead of us on the street. Instead of keeping their distance, they're hurrying toward us with their cameras already firing away.

Oh great. We've been spotted.

We're at a busy intersection and there are a lot of pedestrians around us. I'm tempted to turn us in the opposite direction and attempt to lose the photographers in the crowd, but then we wouldn't be able to go to Logan's restaurant, and what a crap turn of events that would be. I'm still hungry, after all. We shouldn't let the photographers deter us. We're not doing anything wrong. *They are.*

"Logan! Candace! Where are you guys headed this morning?" one of them asks when they get closer.

Neither of us answers, but that doesn't stop people from turning to take notice of the spectacle. They're curious about why we're drawing so much attention. I hear people start to murmur Logan's name and he tries to grab my hand, but then a passing pedestrian who's trying to hurry away from the crowd knocks into me and I shuffle back to keep from falling. Without bothering to check if I'm okay, a photographer comes closer, shoving a microphone right under my chin.

"Are you headed to breakfast?" he asks me.

Is this allowed?! How can they get away with this?

"Please back up," I say, holding my hand out to block him from coming any closer.

He doesn't listen, and there are too many people starting to surround us. Logan tries to grab my hand again, but I have to step back, out of the way of another photographer who's snapping photos directly in front of my face. The flash keeps going, blinding me.

"Stop!" I shout, angry that they're violating my personal space like this. What are they after, anyway? An up-close shot of my nostrils? They need to stay back, or better yet, go away altogether!

"Candace, are you and Logan an official item?!" another asks impatiently, like *I'm* the one causing them problems.

"Candace," Logan says, his voice more severe than I've ever heard it. I know he's not upset with me—he's just trying to get my attention—but I take another step back, trying to get away from the photographers, and I stumble right over the edge of the curb. I didn't realize I was so close to the street, and well, I've never been the *most* agile person. Once I lose my footing, I'm able to keep myself standing, but then *wham*—I find myself in the direct path of an oncoming cyclist. I turn just in time to see his bike headed toward me, and then I scream as we collide.

I wake up on my back, blinking up against a bright light. A huge figure comes into hazy focus in my periphery.

Oh dear, I've died. And that's God there, coming round to tell me they haven't got any room up in heaven for the likes of me—not since that time in the fourth grade when I stole Patsy Smith's jelly sandwich when she wasn't looking. Suppose it's hell for me. Better get on with it then.

"Candace?"

God sounds a lot like Logan.

I don't find it all that surprising, really. Then I force myself to look to the side and I see Logan there. The first thing I think is, *Wonderful! He's dead too!*

Then my logic kicks in and I realize I'm in hospital, gowned up and in quite a bit of pain.

It's not as if I don't remember getting here; it's just that I'm a bit disoriented. I remember the cyclist and the crash—*OUCH*—and then I remember some of being at the scene of the accident, everyone shouting and crowding around me. There was quite a lot of conflicting advice getting tossed around.

Don't move her!

Well we can't just leave her lying on the street! Someone grab her feet and help me hoist her onto the sidewalk!

Has anyone seen her shoe?!

An ambulance came up quickly with its blinking lights and *weeoo weeoo* siren blaring, and Logan was there the whole time, holding my hand, looking down at me and telling me I'd be all right. I remember feeling safe with him beside me, confident that I wouldn't come to harm as long as he was near.

"How long have I been out?" I ask, aware my throat's a bit dry and scratchy.

"Just a few hours. They said you'd be tired after everything that happened."

"So I wasn't in a coma then? I haven't been out for a decade, have I?"

Wouldn't that be just my luck? Sleeping away the rest of my 20s and waking up 35 and in need of eye cream.

I expect him to smile or laugh. It's a funny question, right? But he only shakes his head.

Right.

I look down and try to assess the damage to my body. My left hand is bandaged, and I think I remember them putting some stitches in for a cut there. I lift the blanket up off my body with my right hand and glance down. Underneath my hospital gown, I can see some mild bruises and scratches on my legs, but nothing too serious. Phew.

"Is it just my hand then?" I ask, suddenly feeling a bit embarrassed to be laid up in hospital with all these IVs and machines beeping round me. I'm quite the wuss, aren't I?

"And a mild concussion." He says it like he's trying not to wince. "The nurses should be back in soon to check on you. They said I was supposed to wake you up if you slept much longer."

"Right. Okay then."

Next I register an odd feeling on my head, like something heavy is weighing it down. I lift my right hand and feel the thick bandage wrapped around my hair a few times. Oh. Lovely.

"You have a bad cut there," Logan says, answering my unasked question. "On the back of your head where you hit the ground. They had to cut away some of your hair."

"I'm bald?!"

Somehow that's the most alarming thing of all.

"No, it's nothing. You won't even be able to tell once it's all healed."

I pat around back there gently.

"It doesn't hurt," I say, a little baffled.

"They have you on pain medicine."

Oh, right. Well then. I swallow down my distress and turn to look at Logan, finally noticing the worry lines near his eyes and the deep furrow between his brows. He has his ball cap in his hands, coiled tight in his grip. He looks like he's been wringing it like that for ages. There's a chair beside my bed, but he's not sitting in it. Instead, he's standing near my knees, glancing down at me.

"Are you all right?" I ask, wondering if he was injured too.

"I'm fine."

"Oh okay. It's just that you look a bit odd standing there. Why don't you sit down?"

He ignores me. "You're probably hungry. We never did get that breakfast, and it's already past lunch. I was going to go down and grab you something from the cafeteria."

I wrinkle my nose. "I'm fine, actually. The meds they have me on must be making my stomach hurt a bit. I don't think I could eat." I pat the bed beside my hip. "Sit by me?"

He doesn't budge from his spot. Instead, he keeps wringing that bloody hat.

"Logan?"

His eyes are on my chest, like he can't quite meet my eyes. I've never seen him like this, and it has me worried. I try to sit up and reach out for him, but the movement messes with my precarious state of equilibrium. My head suddenly starts pounding, and I immediately lie back down.

Logan jumps forward to help me position myself on the pillows.

"Easy, Candace. You're really hurt."

I offer him a lopsided grin. "Oh come on, I bet this happens to you all the time on the field and you handle it like a champ. I'm a big baby with these machines beeping away."

He glowers at me, clearly not appreciating my quip. "I don't think you understand how serious this was…how much worse it could have been."

I frown, not quite sure what he's playing at. It was just a collision with a cyclist. It probably happens all the time in

New York City. Frankly, I'm surprised it hasn't happened to me before with how careless I am.

"Just a bit of a scuffle with a bike. Next time, I'll win," I tease.

His smile is a flat line as he replies, "There was a car too. It nearly hit you both. I watched it swerve out of the way in the nick of time."

The expression on his face contorts as if the memory makes him sick. I understand completely. My stomach tightens too, imagining how much worse off I would be right now if there'd been a car involved as well.

"But it *did* swerve," I remind him. "So there's no sense in worrying about what could have happened."

His gaze flits up to mine and I flinch back, shocked by how much fury I see lurking under the surface.

"You don't get it. This was horrible, Candace. Seeing you lying there on the street, bleeding from your head..."

At that, he turns and shoves his hand through his hair, as if he can't even bear to look at me.

"I'm sorry," I offer weakly. "I'll be more careful next time."

Is that what he's after? An apology? Does he think I willingly put myself in harm's way?

"*Jesus*, don't apologize. *You* don't apologize. None of this was your fault. It was my fault."

"What? What do you mean?"

He wasn't even by me when I stepped off the curb. He was trying to get to me, but there were too many people.

"I never should have let us walk to breakfast like that."

"I walk places all the time!"

"Yeah, *before*."

"Before..."

"Me!" he explodes.

The room fills with the aftershocks of his outburst, and we sit in absolute silence. He thinks this was his fault. He's angry, but not with me.

"You didn't invite those photographers there," I say meekly. "*They're* the ones to blame for all this."

Maybe I should have just kept my mouth shut, because my words only seem to anger him more. His eyes are hot coals when he glances back at me.

"You don't get it, Candace. This is the life I lead. It's what comes with my career. The lack of privacy, the photographers—all the bullshit. It's not just going to magically go away."

"Well so what? I know what I've signed up for. Don't you think I realize how serious this all is?"

"No. I don't think you do. Not after this morning. That—" He shakes his head as if trying to dislodge the memory of it. "That can't happen again."

"Okay…so we won't walk to breakfast for a while. Or y'know, next time we'll use better disguises. Kat actually has these awesome wigs—"

He cuts me off. "Candace, you're not getting it."

His tone is sharper than ever before, and I can't help but feel wounded. Does he think I'm a complete idiot? That I'm not going to be more careful next time?

Then our eyes meet again, and it suddenly clicks.

"What do you mean it 'can't happen again'?"

"I won't let it."

So that's it then? This is how it ends?!

"Jesus, what a coward you've turned out to be! Just say what you're tiptoeing around. I can't stand it!"

"If it weren't for me, this would have never happened."

He's the one with the soft voice now. I'm the one shouting and growing angrier by the second.

"You're kidding me! What a load of piss! You're worried because I've been hurt and now your way of making sure I'm okay is to break it off with me? Too bad! I'm breaking it off with you first. How's that!"

Our voices must have carried out into the hall because there's a knock on the door, followed by a gentle voice. "Hello? Is everything okay in here? Candace, I'd like to do a quick check of your vitals."

Then a nurse walks in with tight braids and green glasses and a gentle smile.

"Yes, that's fine. He was just leaving anyway," I say, jutting my chin out toward Logan.

"Candace—"

"I can come back in a few minutes?" the nurse offers, glancing awkwardly between us. "Though I should warn you, Candace, you've been through quite a lot today, and I don't recommend making it any worse…"

She's trying to tell me to stop shouting at my boyfriend, and that's fine. I'm *done* shouting at him. He can damn well leave for all I care.

"I'll come back later," he tells me as he starts to head out of the room, and because the pain of our argument still stings, I fire back a two-word response that I immediately regret.

"Don't bother."

He nods, turns, and leaves the room.

And just like that, we're over.

The door slams and I let out an angry groan.

"Right, well…good riddance!" I shout in his wake. "Who needs a man like that anyway? I'll show him. I'll have a new boyfriend by the end of the day. Maybe I'll meet a handsome doctor or nurse or janitor. I don't bloody well care who he is. I'll just make sure Logan knows I've moved on and he can go do whatever he damn well pleases. Breaking up with me like that when I'm already in hospital! Who does he think he is?!"

The nurse just blinks at me, a little taken aback. "Boyfriend troubles?"

"Not anymore! Have you got a single brother you could set me up with?"

She actually smiles at that, though she tries to hide it. "I don't think you want to be set up with anyone just yet. Here, lie back and let me see your hand."

"Oh, I assure you I do. I'm as single as they come. Completely solo as of, oh…thirty seconds ago."

"If you ask me, I don't think he was going to break up with you."

"And how would you know?" I ask, all menacing.

She glances behind her and looks back at me, as if weighing her options. Then she shrugs and admits, "Well, I was listening at the door. I was supposed to come in a few minutes ago, but you two were really going at each other."

"What a Nosey Nellie! Can't say I blame you. Actually, it's good that you were listening—you can give me some proper advice. So you don't think he was going to break it off with me?"

She's examining my hand when she replies, "No. It's obvious he feels guilty. He's the one who forced you into the limelight, and now look, it's landed you in the hospital."

I drum the fingers of my good hand against my chin, considering what she's said. "It sounds bad when you put it like that."

"Exactly. So it's natural that he would want to reassess the relationship and make sure you're still up for the challenge after all that's happened. I think it's actually really considerate of him."

Her eyes have gone a bit moony.

"I can't help but feel like you're really taking his side."

She shrugs. "What can I say? I'm a big fan."

I roll my eyes. "You too? Sheesh. What is it with Americans and football? Is it all that interesting?"

"Oh, I don't even watch the sport. I just know him from when he was on the cover of *People* last year. Have you seen it? They did this whole spread where he was only wearing his football pants and nothing else."

Her cheeks have flushed, and I swear she's really heating herself up talking about it. Pretty soon the poor thing will need to go into the loo over there and splash some cold water on her face.

"Oh jeez. Sounds utterly ridiculous." I roll my eyes. Then I lean in close. "Can you pull up the photos and show me?"

I sigh into my mobile, antsy to end the conversation with my parents.

"I'm totally fine," I assure Mum. "You don't need to worry. They're only keeping me here overnight to cover their bases."

"Well that's what it's like being a proper celebrity."

"Mum, I'm not a celebrity."

"Say that to the press! You've been on the telly three times since I started watching this afternoon. They keep calling you the luckiest girl in New York or something like that. I taped one of the stories, but then your Dad mucked it up and rolled some Arsenal footage over it."

"That's okay. I don't really need to see it. I'm *living* it."

"Right, right. So you're sure you're all right? No permanent damage? While you're in hospital, you ought to see if they can check your head, right in the back behind your ear. I dropped you when you were a baby and I'm still a bit concerned I might have done some real damage."

"Mum, I'm sure I'm just fine. And if I'm not, I've lasted this long, so there's no sense in worrying."

"Right. Well, I won't keep you. Give Logan our love, dear."

"Will do. Love you, Mum. Talk soon."

After I hang up, I realize I didn't correct her about giving Logan her love. It's not really something I can do now, not after shouting at him like I did earlier. All afternoon, I've wavered back and forth between feeling as though this is all his fault and he should bloody well be sorry for the damage he's caused then berating myself for taking things too far. I really did think he was going to break it off with me. He looked like men do right before they lay down the death blow to a relationship, all guilty and sad.

Bollocks!

I turn back to the food tray they brought up a little while ago. There's a sandwich, a salad, an apple, and an empty chocolate pudding cup. I ignored most everything and devoured the pudding. When I was finished, I had my nurse—she's called Jada and I think we're proper friends now—sneak me up a second one. Then we looked at a few images of Logan from the *People* magazine shoot and I nearly foamed at the mouth. I mean, I knew he was hot—I did have him naked on top of me just this morning—but I mean, holy moly, someone grab me an ice pack so I can shove it down my gown. They've really turned him into a heartthrob, haven't they?

"Is he good in bed?" Jada asked.

I sighed. "Brilliant, unfortunately. It'll make this whole breakup business even worse, I fear. How am I meant to go from *that*"—I pointed at the image of Logan on her screen— "to a normal bloke off the street? It's not fair, is it?"

"Exactly. I think you should try to make it work. If not for your sake, then for mine. Please, girl, I need to live vicariously through you."

I've been thinking about what she said since she left, and I know I've got to do something. But first, I have other important things to manage. It's past suppertime now and I still haven't phoned Yasmine and Kat. I don't want to worry them, but sooner or later, I'll have to let them know what's happened.

I already phoned Mrs. Halliday to let her know I'll be out tomorrow. She made a big fuss and told me to stay out the first half of the week, just to ensure I'm really taking care of myself. It's a relief; at least I don't have to worry about my job at The Day School on top of everything else.

The door to my room opens, and I'm expecting Jada (though I'm secretly praying it's Logan), but then there's a blur of balloons and teddy bears and my two flatmates blubbering on about how worried they've been about me.

"Yaz! Get out of my way. You're hogging the doorway."

"It's the balloons."

It's quite a struggle for them to get inside, and they sort of fall in together like a comic duo. Then they look up and see me in bed, and their eyes go wide in fear.

"OH MY GOD. HER HEAD IS BANDAGED!" Kat says, rushing toward me. "Are you dying?"

"No. It's just a cut."

"Yasmine, don't just stand there! Get her water! Food! *Something!*"

"I'm fine, really." I have to bat away the sandwich Kat picks up off my tray and tries to shove into my mouth.

"You poor thing. Are you in loads of pain? Want Yasmine to give you a bit of a foot rub? Yaz? Get to it."

"I'm fine! I swear. No one touch my feet."

Yasmine immediately stops trying to untangle them from the blankets.

"Where's Logan? Down getting you something from the gift shop? Tell him not to bother—I think we've cleared out the place," Yasmine says, dropping a load of things onto the end of my bed. There's a box of chocolates, a little charm bracelet wrapped in a clear box, and a teddy bear wearing a pair of scrubs like he's about to go perform surgery—and that's just half of it. There're about twenty balloons filling the air, bobbing up and down. I swat one away when it gets too close to my head.

"Are you two both mad?"

"We're worried!" Kat whines. "You can't even imagine! There we were, enjoying some wine on a Sunday evening, and then we turned on the telly and there's our mate, splayed out on the street with sirens wailing around her!"

"They showed it on TV?!"

I thought Mum was exaggerating.

"Yes! It was part of the news and everything! Very big deal. Now, don't worry. Your knickers were showing for a bit, and in my opinion, they weren't your cutest pair—"

"Don't make the poor girl feel worse," Yasmine groans.

"Right, well, you did look quite nice when they lifted you up on the gurney."

"Yes! Very brave. And of course, Logan looked absolutely handsome, worrying over you like that. For a little while I didn't think they'd let him into the back of the ambulance with you, but then he shouted at them all heroic like. Wasn't that brilliant, Kat?"

"Yes. Like something out of a movie. I cried a bit. And then we rushed here, of course, to be by your side, though I can't stay for too long. Jay's expecting me for a late drink, and Yaz has got to run to see Marcus too."

"Oh good. Abandoning me already?"

"Well we figured you wouldn't want us around anyway," Kat continues. "Just getting in the way. Won't Logan be back soon?"

"No."

They exchange a worried glance. "What do you mean?"

"He's gone. Left earlier after we had a shouting match. I sort of took things too far, I'm afraid."

Kat nearly jumps on me in a panic, grabbing her mobile to shove at me. "Call him! Apologize!"

"I can't. I mean…I don't know if I want to. He really made me mad."

"Who cares?! Swallow your pride and apologize anyway. That man loves you! He was about to fight a paramedic to get to you, I swear it."

"Fine. I'll call when you two clear out."

"Okay, then we're off."

"Already?"

"Like I said, we'll just get in the way."

"Hospitals sort of give me the willies, to be honest," Yasmine says, giving the room a quick look of disgust.

"Whatever. Go on. I'll talk to you later."

"Love you! Heal up!"

When they're gone, I'm left with my mobile taunting me to have some courage and ring Logan. I hesitate at first, worrying about what I'll say, but then finally, I give in.

It rings and my heart thunders in my chest like it never has before. I worry I'm overdoing it. My poor body has been through a lot in one day, and now I'm putting it through even more emotional upheaval. The call rings again and again, but I don't hang up. I will him to answer with a silent plea.

It continues on like that four more times before his voicemail kicks on.

The preprogrammed robotic voice fills the air, and because I'm a total chicken, I hang up right when it beeps for me to leave a message.

Well then…at least I've tried. No sense in crying. Much.

CANDACE
24

"Could someone refill my tea?" I ask, wagging my empty mug from my comfy spot on the couch.

"You've got legs," Kat says, without looking up from her mobile.

"Yasmine?"

Her inaudible gibberish tells me she's not getting up either.

"Oh lovely! Where was this attitude when you two came rushing into my room at the hospital, worried sick?"

Yasmine yawns and stretches out on the other side of the sofa. We're sharing, though she's taking up way too much room. I try to steal a bit more blanket and she yanks it back.

"Yes, well that was before you started milking our sympathy for all it's worth. *Kat, could you please stop shouting on the phone? Kat, could you please put your dish away instead of just letting it collect mold in the sink?* I mean, truly, when will it end?"

"You're right," I drawl, monotone. "I'm practically Mussolini."

"Glad you can see it from our side."

When I stand, prepared to make my own tea even though I've got a head wound (!), Kat holds up her mug. "Oh, grab me some while you're up, will you?"

I snatch it out of her hand and call her a wanker, but she pretends she can't hear me.

"Thanks love."

It's Tuesday. I know because I've looked at the calendar on the fridge one thousand times since waking up. I haven't spoken to Logan since Sunday, since he left my room at the hospital. He didn't phone me yesterday, though I did a good bit of staring down at my mobile, willing it to ring. It got so bad that I locked it in my room for the afternoon, though even then, my gaze kept pinging to the door. I'd hear a phantom vibration and shoot to my feet, dashing into my bedroom, only to be disappointed by the fact that he hadn't phoned me back. Once, Mum phoned, and I nearly chewed her head off for not being Logan. Then I felt bad and relented and had to sit and chat with her for ages to make up for my meanness. She walked me through the entire spring garden she's planting, down to the type of soil she's using to fertilize her delphiniums. *You see, I've put a good bit of eggshells down in the dirt.* Oh good Lord.

I put the kettle on and drum the fingers of my uninjured hand on the edge of the counter.

What is Logan up to anyway? Leaving me high and dry like this? I'd ask Yasmine and Kat, but they've banned any talk having to do with him. I suppose it's fair. I did do a good bit of whinging yesterday, but can't they understand? I lov—

No!

I cut off the tail end of that thought with a sharp axe.

Then I have a brilliant idea to circumvent their rules about discussing Logan.

"I read this interesting article today in the newspaper," I muse aloud.

Yasmine frowns in disbelief. "No, you haven't. You've been sitting on the sofa all day, watching horrible daytime telly like a sad sack."

"Yes, well, this was earlier. Uh, when I was in the loo. The article was an advice column, actually. Very interesting."

"I suppose you'll tell us even if we don't want to hear it?"

I ignore Kat and continue on. "In the article, this girl...*Candy*, she um, asked the columnist how she should go about winning her boyfriend—er, *girlfriend* back after she royally mucked up."

I think I've done a brilliant job disguising my true intent, but Kat only rolls her eyes at me.

"I'll bet the columnist told *Candy* exactly what we've been telling you: either call him again or move on. You're the one who went off the deep end. Logan probably thinks you're not worth all the trouble."

"No!" I hiss. "She actually told Candy to go out and find better mates, the kind who will let her complain for as long as she wants about the guy who's broken her heart!"

"Right, well, bring me my tea before you go find these new wonderful mates of yours."

It's utterly hopeless. I'm on my own. Neither of them seems to understand how desperate I've become. Logan and I can't be over. We just can't be. Had I known, I would have really savored the last time we were together, Sunday morning in his bed. When we had sex, it was quick and hard and we kissed like we were trying to bruise each other, but now I wish it'd been longer, sweeter…

I feel sick.

Wednesday is no better than Tuesday, but at least I've got a doctor's appointment in the late morning to keep me distracted. When I arrive downstairs, prepared to head out onto the sidewalk toward my subway stop, a huge man steps away from his post against the brick and introduces himself to me.

"Candace Williams, I'm Ryan Kline. Mr. Matthews has employed me as part of your security team."

"*Security team?*" I nearly bark out a laugh. "What are you on about?"

He tugs a wallet out of his black suit jacket to reveal a small certificate. I have no idea what it means, but I nod like I do. It's got a gold seal, so that must count for something.

"So you're…what?" I ask, peering up at him. I've got a long way to go before I meet his gaze. He's quite a large bloke. "My bodyguard?"

"Yes ma'am."

I nearly laugh. Me? With a bodyguard? It's got to be a joke.

"How many others are there?"

He did mention a *team*.

"Three in total. We've been taking shifts outside your building since Sunday evening."

"What?! How am I just hearing about this now?"

"We haven't made contact because you haven't left your building until now."

Oh right. Okay, let's not go into details. I've been a little busy, y'know, *convalescing*, not just being a lazy git.

"Mr. Matthews gave us strict instructions not to intrude on your privacy," he continues, and I nod along, utterly baffled.

Logan hasn't phoned me back, but he's set up a security team for me? What in the world is he playing at?

"Right, well, it was nice to meet you. I'm off to the doctor now."

"Of course. Lead the way."

I frown. "What do you mean?"

"Mr. Matthews has instructed that we're to remain with you, without breaching your personal space."

What?!

I don't even bother arguing with him; he's only doing the job he's been employed to do. Instead, I grab my mobile out of my purse and phone Logan.

This time, he answers.

I don't bother with a greeting. This isn't a friendly chat, after all. He could have had that if he'd ever bothered to phone me back in the previous three days. Now, he'll get my temper.

"What on earth have you done hiring a team of people to follow me around the city?"

"*Hello*, Candace," he says pointedly, sounding amused. "How are you feeling?"

"Now's not the time for that. I'm still upset with you. Answer me, will you?"

"They're highly qualified and trained to remain out of sight. I've used them myself on and off for the last few years. I assure you, you won't even notice them."

"Not bloody likely! They're security guards!"

"Yes, and after Sunday, their presence is absolutely necessary. In fact, I should have done it when we first started dating."

"But we aren't dating anymore, so you can call them off."

"That's debatable."

"Oh is it?!"

"Candace, are you on the way to the doctor?" he asks, sounding exasperated with me. Tough luck, bucko! *I'm* the one who's exasperated!

"Yes, and how do *you* know that?"

"Because I've been in contact with your medical team, just to ensure everything is going well."

"Isn't that illegal?!"

"No. I was with you at the hospital. I'm listed as your emergency contact, and you signed papers to allow me access to your ongoing care information."

"Right, well I must have been a bit out of it when I did that. Anyway, it doesn't matter. I can't believe you've been in contact with them but not me!"

"I thought you needed some time to cool off."

"Well you're wrong. I'm not cooled off. Not in the least. In fact, I feel like I'm about to—"

Instead of giving him a piece of my mind like I want to, I pull the mobile away from my ear and end the call quickly. It feels good. So good, in fact, that I wish I could phone him again and hang up on him a second time.

I glance back at Ryan, who's been following me on the sidewalk this whole time, and sure enough, he's acting completely oblivious to the conversation he just overheard. *Huh.* So maybe he *is* good at his job.

I continue walking toward my subway stop then turn my head to see him trailing a few feet behind me. I stop. He stops. I take a step forward. He takes a step forward. I lift my right hand to wave it in the air. His right hand stays by his side. Right, well then.

"Come on. If you'll be walking with me, there's no sense in trailing me like a shadow. I'd rather chat anyway. I get quite bored on these walks."

He nods and picks up his pace until he's right beside me.

"Have you got a girlfriend?" I ask, because at heart, I am incredibly nosey. I want to know everything about everyone.

"Wife," he says, all business.

"And what's she called?"

"Bianca."

"Can I see a photo?"

He tugs out his wallet again and flashes me a small photo of him and her, along with a little baby girl. It's so sweet that he carries the image around like that, especially when everyone's got their mobiles these days.

"Is that your daughter?" I ask, pointing to the baby.

"Yes. That's Hope."

"She's lovely. So cute. She takes after your wife, I think."

"Absolutely. They could be twins."

We carry on like that, chatting and getting to know each other better until we reach my subway stop. It's there that I spot the first photographer. I wouldn't be surprised to find out a few of them had been trailing me since I left my flat, but this is the first one to try to get in my face.

"Candace! How are you feeling?!" he shouts. "Is it true that you needed brain surgery when you were in the hospital?"

He barely gets the words out before Ryan steps up to him and stretches out his arms, blocking me from view.

"Back up. Farther. Give her space."

The photographer nearly pees his trousers when he gets a load of Ryan. This is brilliant! I can already tell I'm going to abuse my power. Maybe I could use Ryan to cut the queue at my favorite coffee shop. I'll have him march in and terrorize everyone waiting in front of me so they all scream and run out, leaving me at the front. Voilà.

After my doctor's appointment, I text Logan.

CANDACE: Not that it's any of your business, but everything is healing up nicely. They think I can get my stitches out on Friday. Oh wait…what am I telling you for? They've probably already phoned to tell you the news!

LOGAN: I'm glad. Are you back at work already?

CANDACE: Tomorrow.

LOGAN: You aren't working at District, are you?

I'm not. I've called in for the whole week, but I don't feel like telling him that.

CANDACE: I don't think that's your business.

He phones me then! My mobile starts ringing and I shove it into my purse.

Then Ryan's mobile goes off and he, of course, answers it.

"Hello—yes—I'll tell her—yes—of course."

Then he hangs up.

"Well?! What's he said?" I demand.

"He doesn't think you should be waitressing anymore, but if you insist on it, a member of my team should be there with you the whole time."

Oh good grief!

I throw up my hands and walk on. "Let's go, you. Where should we eat lunch? Do you like sandwiches?"

He seems extremely confused, like I've just asked him to do the worm down the middle of the sidewalk. "I don't usually eat on the job."

"Right, well, you will with me. I'm not going to have you watching me chew my crisps like a weirdo."

"Okay then, there's a good place around the corner."

I motion for him to lead the way.

Thursday is my first day back at school since last Friday, and the kids must have decorated the room yesterday so I'd see it all when I arrived. There're big letters that say "Get Well Soon, Ms. Candace!" and loads of streamers. They've even tidied it up (I'm sure with the help of the temp), and it's a really lovely way to start the day.

When they start to arrive, each of them rushes to give me a hug and asks me how I'm feeling. I don't have the bandage on my head anymore, which is quite a relief as it was getting a bit itchy under there. I've still got my hand wrapped up to protect the stitches, but they all think it's quite cool and I even let them decorate on it so it ends up a colorful mess by the time they're set to leave for the afternoon.

I start to gather their things and load them up with their lunch sacks. One by one, they leave, until Briggs is the only one left.

"Don't worry, Ms. Candace. My uncle didn't forget about me," he says with a huge smile. "He said he'd be a little late for pick-up today."

"Oh, did he?"

All day, I've told myself I wasn't excited to see Logan, but it's no use. I didn't slip out to the loo and freshen up my makeup during naptime just for the fun of it. I am eagerly anticipating his arrival at my door, so much so that I'm a nervous wreck.

I tidy up the pillows in the reading corner. Then, suddenly, I hate how they're arranged and decide to completely redo them. That'll do...for now. Next, I rewash the brushes in the sink that we used during art class. It takes quite a long time using only the one hand.

I'm nearly finished when there's a knock on the door, and I turn to glance over my shoulder. Logan's standing on the other side of the half-opened Dutch door with a bouquet of white peonies in his hand. He's dressed to the nines: black suit, black tie, crisp white shirt underneath his unbuttoned fitted jacket.

He is, in short...*divine*.

I don't even have enough sense to walk over to greet him, but fortunately Briggs is there as a distraction.

"You look like a secret agent, Uncle Logan!"

Yes, very 007 of him to show up here like that.

I dry my hand with a towel and head for the door, highly aware of every step I take that carries me toward him. He's watching me with a little smile, every bit as confident as he's ever been.

"Who are the flowers for?" I ask, crossing my arms once I'm close enough to him to feel that little tug of energy that seems to exist between us.

"Briggs' teacher. I've got a thing for her."

Briggs gags like he might throw up. "Girls are so gross!"

Right. I accept the flowers when he holds them out for me and try hard to ignore their beauty, but they're quite huge and there are enough of them that they're heavy in my hand.

"Where are you off to?" I ask, nodding toward his clothes.

"A dinner with the team from Gatorade. I wanted to invite you."

"I can't go. I've got plans."

With my sofa.

"You didn't answer my call yesterday."

"I'm a busy girl."

He tips his head, looking at me like he can't get enough. His eyes crinkle and he's not mad, even though he should be. Why isn't he mad?

"So do you have plans all weekend?" he asks.

Yes. Tomorrow night, I'm going round to Jay's for dinner. Kat's been telling me about it nonstop, droning on about what she and Jay plan on cooking, how great Jay is in the kitchen, what dress she plans on wearing...*la de dah.* Now I know how she and Yasmine must have felt when I wouldn't shut up about Logan.

Anyway, he asked me a question, so I'll answer.

"Yes, I do have plans, as a matter of fact. Plans tonight. Plans tomorrow. Plans straight through the weekend. Do you?"

His smile widens. "Yeah."

"You two are being weird," Briggs declares. "Are you going to get married?"

I nearly choke.

"What?! Why would you—"

"Should I ask her to marry me, Briggs?" Logan asks with a lazy smile.

"LOGAN!"

"Yeah, she's cool. Not like the girls in my class who are scared of worms."

"I'll take that into consideration," Logan says, glancing back up to me with mischief in his gaze. "We'd better get going so Candace isn't late for her plans."

"Yes, thank you." I nod. "Very considerate. Bye, Briggs."

"See you later, alligator!"

"In a while, crocodile."

Later that evening, I'm lying in bed trying to force myself to get into a book that's been sitting on my nightstand for ages. It's not that I don't like to read; it's that my brain doesn't seem to want to concentrate lately.

Kat is gone, off at Jay's just like she's been the last two nights. They must be getting on well then. I turn a page—having not absorbed a single thing from the previous one—and I continue on like that until my mobile rings on my nightstand.

It's Logan, and I answer it because I'm weak and in love. Sue me.

"Hello."

"Hi. How were your plans?"

"Wonderful. I've just finished making out with a hunk. What about you?"

"I'm home from my dinner. It was boring without you."

"Well of course it was. What did you expect?"

"Are you in bed?"

"'Course not. I'm at a huge party."

"Sounds like you're lying down."

"That's 'cause I am, you knob. Are you happy then? I'm lying here in my pajamas like I have been for the last three hours. I hope you're pleased."

"I am. Now, do you want me to come get you?"

"Absolutely not!"

"How long are we going to do this then?"

314

"Do what?"

"The back and forth where you pretend you aren't crazy about me. We had a fight. It happens."

"Yes, well it was a pretty big one, I'd say!"

"I agree, but it was warranted. Things between us turned serious pretty fast, and I hadn't stopped to consider how best to protect you. On top of the security guards, I still think it makes sense to have you move in here with me. Ryan isn't impressed with your building, and he doesn't think it's the best place for you to live."

"Oh, I *see*. You've got Ryan agreeing with you, then? How convenient that he sides with the man *paying* him."

"Like that matters. He likes you more than he likes me. He says you talk a lot."

"Of course I do. He's my mate. I think he'd follow me around all day even if it wasn't his job."

"Uh-huh."

"Is that the reason you've phoned? To bother me?"

"Am I bothering you?"

No. Please never hang up.

"I suppose not."

There's a long pause, and then he sort of sighs like he's exhausted. "I miss you, Candace."

"Yes, well, that's good. Maybe you'll appreciate me more in the future then."

"This is the last night," he says, all confident.

"The last night of what?"

"That I'll let you do this. I'm not going through the entire weekend without seeing you."

"Well, sounds like you have your work cut out for you! Nice chatting. Talk soon!"

I hang up then stare down at the mobile, my stomach in knots.

I shouldn't be so excited by his threat. I should be extremely worried about what he intends to do before the weekend is through.

I'm outside Jay's apartment, about to go in. Before I do, I glance down at my clothes, assessing them like I've never cared to do before. I'm nervous tonight, on edge.

With a groan of annoyance, I force myself to knock on Jay's door, and he shouts for me to come in.

In all the years I've known him, he's never invited me over for a dinner party. There've been club outings, dinners at steakhouses, parties with models, sure. Tonight, I have no idea what he's planning, but I know Candace will be here, so I didn't hesitate to accept his invitation—even if it was sent over on formal letterhead.

His apartment is nice and ultramodern, lots of sharp edges and white furniture. Or at least it is usually...

Now, I notice feminine touches that weren't here the last time I came over: a porcelain cat statue near the door, a little framed watercolor of a bouquet of roses, pink hand towels hanging on a hook in the hall bathroom. I peer in and see there's also a new fuzzy pink mat near the sink.

I find Jay and Kat in the kitchen. They're wearing matching aprons that say "Mr. Chef" and "Mrs. Chef". There's a crystal vase with roses sitting on the island. Jay's wearing slacks and a pink shirt.

What the fuck have I walked in on?

"Logan! Hi! Lovely of you to join us," Kat says, hurrying around the island so she can take the bottle of wine out of my hands. "Oh, a merlot! Perfect. We're having steak, so this will go really well with dinner." She turns back to Jay. "Sweetums, how are the potatoes coming?"

"They look good. Just a few more minutes, I think."

I haven't known Jay to cook. Ever.

I look behind me, worried I might have stepped into a twilight zone back by the door. There are candles lit everywhere, and soft jazz playing. Either he's been abducted by aliens or he's totally in love.

"Make yourself comfortable, Logan," Kat says, patting one of the new paisley-print bar stools. "I'll open this and let it air out."

Right.

"Things between you two seem to be going well," I point out.

Kat and Jay look at each other then reach their hands out to touch, as if the small distance between them is too much.

"They are. Aren't they, Pookie?" Jay says.

Pookie?!

Kat blushes and nods in agreement.

There's another knock on the front door, and Kat squeals. "That'll be Candace!"

She hurries to answer it, and I lean forward.

"Jay, man…do you need help? Blink twice if you want me to call the police."

He only laughs and shakes his head as if I couldn't possibly understand how happy and in love he is.

I hear voices in the hall and turn to watch Candace walk in wearing a short sky blue dress and flats. Her blonde hair is down and straight, and her eyes seem to be even brighter than usual.

"What's with the personalized doormat out front?" she asks Kat. "It has your name on it and everything."

"Oh yes. Sweetums got me that for our anniversary."

"Anniversary?" Candace asks with a confused frown.

"Yes. Our one-week."

"Oh jeez. You've gone absolutely mad. And wait, did I just hear you say *Sweetums*?"

Candace finally notices me in the kitchen and stops dead in her tracks.

I smile.

She narrows her eyes.

I walk toward her and she stays stock-still, peering up at me skeptically as I approach.

"Hi Candace. You look lovely."

I bend down to kiss her cheek, and she sucks in an audible breath.

"Logan. *Hello*. I didn't realize you'd be here."

"Surprised?"

"More than a little."

"You look better. Did you have that doctor's appointment today?"

I look down and see that the bandage covering her hand is gone and there's a small Band-Aid in its place, where the cut must still be healing.

"Yes, but of course, *you* know that."

"Pookie, could you come help me pour the wine?" Jay asks.

Kat skitters away, and Candace scrunches her face.

"Pookie?" she mouths at me.

"Don't ask."

"Did you see the doormat?" she whispers.

"I missed it."

"Make sure you look on the way out. It's totally whacko!" she continues, keeping her voice down. "Have they fallen off the deep end?"

There's a groan of pleasure behind us, and we both turn to see Jay spooning some potatoes into Kat's mouth while she flutters her eyes in ecstasy.

"Oh, blech," Candace groans. "I've totally lost my appetite."

"That's fine. Let me take you on a quick tour while they finish dinner."

"I don't think I want—"

I'm already taking her purse from her and setting it on the couch. Then I push her down the closest hallway, shouting back at Kat and Jay, "We'll be right back! I just want to show Candace your view, Jay."

"Cool, man. Dinner will be ready in about ten."

"All right, easy there," Candace says once we're walking down the hall. "Sheesh, you haven't got to push me around like that. I'll call one of my bodyguards and have them come up here if I have to."

"I gave them the evening off since you'll be with me."

"Oh my gosh. The arrogance! How do you manage to fit that big head of yours into a football helmet? I'm surprised your brain doesn't explode out of the sides."

I laugh at the visual and prod her along.

She looks so hot in her dress, and now that I know she's healed up, I don't feel so guilty about the plans I have for us.

We reach a door at the end of the hallway and I push it open. It's Jay's lounge, where a group of us usually gathers to watch basketball and golf. It has sweeping floor-to-ceiling windows covering the side wall, showcasing an expansive view of New York City.

Candace gasps. "Oh, wow. You weren't kidding about the view! Look at it."

"Yeah, it's great," I say, sounding bored as I turn her away from the windows so she's facing me instead of them.

"What are you doing?" she asks hurriedly. "Don't kick the door shut!"

Too late.

"Are you still mad at me?" I ask, tightening my hold on her waist as I start to walk us backward.

"What?" Her blue eyes widen in alarm. "Yes! Of course."

She looks panicky, like she's trying to figure out some way to bolt.

I bend down and kiss her cheek, gathering her close. "Are you still mad at me?" I ask again, this time quietly against the shell of her ear.

"I suppose...yes..."

Her voice has turned soft and less convincing.

I move lower, letting my mouth fall to the sensitive skin at the base of her neck, right beside the thin strap holding up her dress. Then I kiss her there before repeating my question.

"I... Maybe we could talk it over..." she answers.

"I don't feel like talking."

We have ten minutes, and I haven't touched her in a week. I'm going crazy. Pretty soon I'll be ordering *her* personalized doormats and calling *her* Pookie.

Her hands slide up over my arms and she grips my shoulders. "I suppose I could find it in my heart to forgive you," she says, her gaze heavy on my lips.

She wants me to kiss her.

I think she's dying for it as much as I am.

"And you'll consider moving in with me," I add, lowering my head.

"Maybe," she says, pressing up on her tiptoes to kiss me before I can kiss her.

She doesn't kiss like she's still harboring any ill will toward me. She kisses me hard and presses her small body up against mine like she wants to fuse us together. I gather her dress in my hands and let it slide up around her waist so I have better access to her body. My hands drift down, over her butt, and I squeeze. She lets out a little squeal, and I smile against her lips.

We don't waste any time. Our mouths go right back together, and I deepen the kiss, demanding she let me sweep my tongue against hers. She rubs her body against me, and I'm hard. Of course I'm hard. I've been desperate for her all week, and now here she is, pliant in my hands, ripe for the taking.

She groans impatiently then quickly shoves away from me, breaking the kiss.

She presses the back of her hand up to her mouth and looks at me with a wild, unreadable expression.

"I absolutely *cannot* stay for dinner."

I frown. "What?"

"Yeah. I just can't. I can't sit across from you at the table for an hour and pretend I'm not imagining you totally naked, on top of me. And worse! I'll have to listen to those two drone on." She points to the door. "Take me back to your place so we can have proper sex."

322

"We can't just leave."

I say it just so it gets said, though I don't really mean it. I want to leave as much as she does.

"Like hell we can't. C'mon, let's go. Either you take me to your flat or we're having sex on Jay's sofa while they listen, and if I were him, I know which one I'd prefer."

Then she scurries over, yanks my hand, and starts to drag me back into the hall. She's pretty strong when she puts her mind to it.

"Hey, listen gang," she says once we're back in the kitchen. "Something's come up and we've got to go actually."

"Are you serious?! We cooked all this food," Kat protests, throwing her hands up in the air.

"Yes, sorry about that. Logan's got the runs. He didn't want me telling everybody, but well, there you have it. Don't want him soiling his knickers at the dinner table, now do we? We'll just take a few of these rolls for the road—they smell great. Good job, both of you. Jay, lovely place you have here. Love all the pink. We'll be seeing you soon!"

"You're lying!" Kat shouts as we hurry to leave.

"Am not! Logan will shove down his trousers and show you if you insist!"

Jesus. This girl will be the end of me.

"Quick, grab my purse there, Logan," Candace says before forcing us to take off toward the door. She can't get it herself because her arms are overloaded with rolls. "Bye now!" she shouts to them. "See you both soon!"

We don't stop even once we're out the door. We're both laughing, and it only gets worse when Candace points down to the doormat. Sure enough, it reads "Welcome to Kat and Jay's love nest!"

It sends her over the edge, laughing so hard she has tears in her eyes. I watch her, totally enamored, wondering what I did before she came into my life. Was I even alive?

I kiss her there in the hall, squashing her up against the wall so the rolls flatten out between us. She moans that they're ruined, but I don't care. I have to kiss her. I have to tell her I love her. Here in this hallway.

She blinks up at me totally stunned after I say it.

"What have you just said?!" She sounds a little hysterical.

"I love you," I repeat, holding her gaze.

"Oh my god!" She throws a roll at me so it bounces off my head and lands with a dull thud on the floor. "You've just said it *now*—*here*, of all places?! I've got mascara running down my cheeks from laughing so hard."

"Yes, well, you're always laughing. It would be hard to find a time to tell you when you're being serious," I say, yanking her back toward me. "But that's just it—it's part of the reason I can't get you out of my head. You're crazy," I say, wiping her cheeks. "And I love you."

"Right." She pats my chest. "Well, sorry you're so in love with me! Wish I could say the same, but I have loads of boys running after me and I—"

"Candace, say it."

"I really can't."

"Yes you can."

One of Jay's neighbors walks out of their apartment, an old woman with a scarf tied around her head and a yappy little dog at her feet.

"No canoodling in the halls!" she chides us as she passes to head for the stairs nearby.

Once she's gone, Candace locks eyes with me again and presses her lips together to keep from laughing.

"It's fine if you can't say it," I say, turning away and walking off without her.

"Oh no you don't!" Another roll hits me square in the back. She's got a pretty good arm. "No reverse psychology here, mister! I love you, do you hear me?! I love you!"

"Hey! Keep it down out there!" another neighbor shouts.

Candace runs and takes my hand so we can hurry off to the elevator together.

I make her say it again before I kiss her against the back wall as the elevator slides down to ground level.

"I can't believe you want me to say it again," she teases. "Isn't it obvious? I'm totally mad about you! You're so handsome and sweet and not at all how a professional foosball player should be."

"*Football* player," I correct.

"What's the difference?" she asks before rising up and pressing her mouth to mine.

CANDACE

00

Epilogue

"SACK HIM, YOU BLITHERING IDIOTS! *DO SOMETHING!*"

Our defense is asleep. They have to be. That's the only reason Green Bay's quarterback manages to complete a twenty-yard pass, which is caught far too close to the end zone. I shout in anger and try not to resort to any more curse words. I've already met my yearly quota.

Then I look back at Yasmine and Kat, hoping to get some assistance or at least see they're as upset by the game's turn of events as I am, but the two of them are sitting on their arses, munching away on all the food provided in our private suite at the stadium, completely unbothered that we're close to letting Green Bay score and take the lead.

"Aren't you two going to get up and help me?!"

"Help with what? You shouting your head off won't change anything. Just tell your fiancé to start throwing some touchdowns. How about that?" Kat says, sucking the mustard off her fingers. This is her second hot dog of the quarter.

"Right. Some help you two are."

"I can't get up. What do you want me to do? The doctor says shouting is bad for the baby. You shouldn't be shouting either. I'm sure she's in my belly listening and thinking her auntie is a loon."

Right. Kat is knocked up. She's only about four months along, but the way she whinges on, you'd think she was 43 1/2 months pregnant.

She's over there with her feet elevated and a heating pad stuffed behind her lower back. Oh good grief. She doesn't even have a proper bump yet!

I shouldn't have been so surprised that she got herself into this position. It's just like her. She and Jay have been married for a while. Oh yes, *married.* They flew to Vegas the night after we bailed on their dinner party and tied the knot. Kid you not. We thought they were insane, and well, they are, but oddly enough, it seems to be working. They still refer to each other as Sweetums and Pookie, and I still gag every time I hear it. Yasmine and Marcus are together still too, though they've had a rocky few months. They're both so bloody dramatic. They love the back and forth and the fighting, and I swear their relationship changes with the lunar cycle. *Oh, full moon—guess they're off again.* This time seems to be it, though. I know from Logan that Marcus is totally smitten with her and has bought a ring and everything. I bet they'll be engaged by this time next year, just in time for my wedding.

WEDDING.

YES! I've managed to convince Logan to spend eternity with me. *Ha ha ha.* Joke's on him!

I've been planning the wedding for a few weeks already, and it will be small and tasteful and modest. JOKING. Oh my god. No. I'm only planning on getting married once, so we're blowing it out of the water. We're heading to the Caribbean, and we want all our friends and family there, loads of food, a huge band, lots of cake, fireworks, dancing until we've all got feet covered in blisters—you get the idea.

I glance down at my ring and smile. Even *it's* totally ridiculous, but that's Logan's fault. After five months together, he surprised me one evening back at our flat.

I'd just arrived home from work. I quit my job at District and I don't help Kat clean very often either, but I love my work at The Day School, even if I am knackered at the end of every day.

Anyway, I strolled in, set my purse down, and noticed a trail of rose petals leading me into the kitchen. Then, CANDLES—so many I think Logan might have bought out the entire city's stock. I'm surprised the fire sprinklers weren't going off.

He was standing in the middle of them with the ring in his hand, as handsome as ever.

"Marry me?" he asked.

"Oh my" is all I managed before I started crying, real big sobby tears so that I had to grab for a dish towel and wipe away the snot. Fortunately, he got the gist of my reply. He came toward me, gathered me up in his arms, and then slipped the ring on my finger. I haven't taken it off since.

It's obscenely sparkly and could knock out someone's eye if I'm not careful…but well…I love it, of course.

"Would you fetch me another little shrimp cocktail?" Kat asks me.

"Get it yourself!" I groan, turning back to the game. There're only a few minutes left in the fourth quarter. New

York is up by six, which is a horrible spot to be in because if Green Bay manages a touchdown, we're screwed!

"I can't get up. You'll have to help me."

"You're not *that* pregnant."

"I'll have you know that back in the day, women were basically put on bedrest for their entire pregnancy."

"Yes, well, nowadays, they compete in the Olympics. I don't see your point."

"Fine! I'll get it myself, but I'm not naming the baby after you anymore."

"You were never planning to name her after me," I point out, knowing full well they've decided to call her Cassie, after Jay's mum.

"Well…you don't get the middle name now either!"

I'm too busy watching the game to care about her threats. Green Bay is on their fourth down. They're going for a field goal. OR maybe they're tricking us into *thinking* they're going for a field goal and they're really going to try to run the ball in for a touchdown. Oh my god, they're putting in their special teams.

"BLOCK THEM," I scream.

Apparently, they hear me, because they don't let Green Bay score, and then the game is over. WE WON! It's just a regular season game, nothing to go crazy about, but I'm still hopping around with glee. Not only do I like winning, Logan likes winning too. I can't stand when he comes home all down and upset after a hard-lost game.

Now, we'll have a lovely weekend together! We'll be celebrating. Oh yes! That reminds me.

"Right, well, I'm off, you two," I say, grabbing my purse and jumper. "Yasmine, roll Kat out of here if she can't manage to walk anymore."

"Where are you rushing off to?" Kat asks, mouth full of shrimp.

"Home! Duh. We won!"

That means one thing: sweet, sweet victory sex.

At the start of the season, I assumed Logan would be utterly knackered after a game. I expected he'd arrive home and face-plant down onto our bed, not stirring until morning, but boy was I wrong.

When he wins, when he plays a good game or throws a great pass, it's like he's got more energy than he knows what to do with. He's positively brimming with endorphins and pheromones and whatever else it is that makes a woman want a man. I've learned now: after a win, be prepared.

I rush out of the private suite. Out there, in the hall, I meet up with Ryan. He's always here for home games—watching in another suite with a group of bodyguards—just in case the fans get a little rowdy, not that I see many of them. Sure, there are a few with private suites up on this level too, but they mostly mind their own business.

"Good game," Ryan says.

I beam. "*Great* game."

"Logan will be happy."

You bet your arse he will be. I'm positively overflowing with giddy excitement as the lift sweeps us down to the ground level of the car park underneath the stadium. From there, Ryan leads me to where he has the SUV parked, and we move along in the queue of cars toward the exit. There's no point in waiting for Logan to join me before I leave the stadium. He'll have to do postgame press on the field then have a shower in the locker room. Sometimes he has to do more interviews after that as well. Still, it'll only be about an hour or so before he gets back to the flat.

An hour! Hardly any time, really.

Once Ryan drops me in front of our building, I dash off toward the lifts, waving at the doorman and receptionist. They congratulate me on the good game and I thank them without stopping. I officially moved in with Logan only a few weeks after we started dating. Kat had a wild change of heart about the whole living together situation after she and Jay had their shotgun wedding, and it's not like she could keep me from moving out once she had. We offered to cover our portion of the rent for Yasmine, but she could easily afford the entire thing, and she was happy to convert our bedroom into a home office for herself. It all worked out really well, actually. No need to burn anyone's bras!

Speaking of bras, right when I make it up to our flat, I head for our bedroom. Decisions, decisions. I've got quite a bit of lingerie in here. Logan's got a sweet spot for it. He says it makes it so I'm a present he gets to unwrap slowly. *Ooh la la.* I pass over the red set he got me for Valentine's Day, and the black set I wore for him the night he proposed. I settle on a pale blue lacy bra and panties. There are matching stockings and a garter belt too.

With an indulgent smile, I lay the lingerie out on the little bench in the closet and then head for the kitchen. I couldn't eat dinner earlier—nervous stomach—so I grab a protein bar and chow down, knowing I'll need my strength for the night ahead. I check my mobile while I eat, scrolling through photos of the game that have already been posted. I linger too long, staring at each one, studying them while I chew slowly. There's this one close-up shot of Logan on the field, about to throw a pass. His arm is cocked back and his body is stretched taut. In spite of the helmet and pads and uniform (or maybe *because* of them), he looks absolutely mouthwatering. I love when he's in his element, all intense. He completely zones out. I could be standing on the sidelines

332

in a cheerleading costume, waving pom-poms, and he wouldn't even notice. I could strip *off* the cheerleading costume on the sidelines and wave around my ta-tas, and still, nothing. He only has one goal while he's on that field, and it's to win at all costs.

I get a little hot just thinking about it. All that severe, determined concentration…it's the same way he gets in the bedroom.

I'm forced to use the empty protein bar wrapper to fan my face, but it doesn't do the trick. Oh well, I need a shower anyway. Just a quick rinse. I got quite sweaty when I was leaping up and down back at the stadium, shouting at our team *and* their team—anyone, really—and getting a little carried away. It's a wonder I still have a voice.

In our bathroom, I wrap my hair up in a bun so it doesn't get wet and step under the hot water in the shower. I use my floral-scented body wash to lather up my arms. There's nervous energy humming inside me, like I'm a little kid waiting for Santa to leave me presents on Christmas Eve. I exfoliate my arms and legs until my skin is silky smooth. It gets quite steamy in there because the water feels so good and I'm in no rush to get out.

Then, I hear a noise.

The bathroom door opens.

I scream and splay out against the cold marble wall behind me, reaching for anything within my grasp—a loofah. *Oh good, that'll really hurt a robber. Nice going, Candace.*

"It's just me," Logan says, strolling into the bathroom all cocksure and pleased with himself. He's wearing athletic shorts and his team's t-shirt. His hair is still damp with sweat, so it looks inky black.

"What are you doing home already?!" I ask, stepping forward and wiping the glass so I can get a proper look at him.

He reaches back to tug off his t-shirt. "No postgame interviews, just a quick conversation on the field with that ESPN correspondent you like then I hopped in my car."

"No shower?" I ask as my mouth drops open. Getting a good look at his naked chest will never *not* stop me in my tracks, even now, when there's a fresh bruise on his ribs and a red line across his abs. Marks of war.

"No shower," he replies, pushing his shorts down along with his boxer briefs and stepping out of them. My jaw drops farther.

"Well I'm just about to get out," I say, like a total git who hasn't got a clue.

He glances up and locks eyes with me through the glass. "I'll just join you."

My heart kicks up as if sending out a signal to my body: *Full steam ahead, lads!*

"But, I've pulled out lingerie," I say weakly, pointing toward our shared closet.

He doesn't reply. He moves toward the shower, swings open the glass door, and steps inside. It's like he's just sucked all the air out with a vacuum. I struggle to breathe as he comes closer. I think he's headed for me, but he stops under the stream, letting it soak him from head to toe. He watches me while he does it, or rather, he *devours* me while he does it. There's no hiding his true intent as his eyes glide down my body, pausing at my chest and the shadow between my legs.

I know it's Logan, my fiancé, *my best mate*, for heaven's sake! But my body doesn't seem to catch on. It's pumping adrenaline through my veins like I need to prepare to escape.

I take a step back so I can put a bit more space between us, and in a flash, his hand reaches out and he grasps me by the neck.

I yelp, and he loves it. He tugs me toward him until I'm under the stream too, but there's no water in my eyes. He's blocking it with his head so that it rolls down our shoulders and stomach. We're not touching, but we're a hair's breadth away. His soft grip stays on my neck, and his thumb brushes back and forth over my quickening pulse.

"Maybe I'll let you put the lingerie on later," he says.

His dark eyes are so hot I feel charred.

He's looking down at me like he's concocting all sorts of wicked ideas in his head.

"But first, I need to clean off."

He nods to the side of the shower, toward the niche where we keep our shampoo and soap bottles.

"Get me some body wash."

No politeness in his tone. How rude! I shouldn't listen, but I do, because...well, look at the man.

I get some soap and don't wait for him to tell me what to do. I know what he wants. I start at his broad shoulders, dragging my hands over his arms. At times, it feels like there's so much of him compared to me, like I'll be here for days washing him off. *With arms that size, sheesh.* I get some more soap and move to his chest. He winces gently when I brush my hand over the bruise at his ribs and then I bend down to kiss the skin, letting him know I'm sorry he's hurt.

I know he likes my lips on him. I can see it for myself, the way he starts to harden the farther I go down. The soap slides down his rippling abs, coating his skin as I bend lower. I kiss a trail down to his hips, and then gently, I touch him, soaping up his hardness, pretending to clean him off.

It's really a guise. I don't need to be nearly this thorough. After two passes, one could argue that he's properly clean down there, but I have no plans on stopping. He doesn't say a word as he watches me continue. I look up and he eclipses the shower light, casting me in shadow. He looks like the devil.

I pause for a moment, and his mouth twitches.

"Keep going," he instructs brusquely.

Oh, tsk tsk. Someone needs to learn a little patience.

I stand up and pump more soap into my hands, then I bend back down to wash his thighs and calves. His muscles stiffen under my soft touch and I know he's growing antsy. I'm not doing what he wants me to do, but he needs to be clean, doesn't he? I wash his feet and his toes, and this is really a fun little game I'm playing. I'm even smiling to myself when suddenly he bends down to grip me under my arms and hauls me up against the marble wall.

I go completely still as he pushes himself between my legs—not so nicely, I might add—leaving me no choice but to wrap them around his hips.

"I don't have the patience for you sometimes," he says, bending to kiss my neck. He's in a frenzy as he moves lower, taking the tip of my breast between his teeth.

Ow!

Punishment, I see.

In return, I drag my nails down his back. No more gentle caresses for the man who's had a hard night on the field. If he wants to play rough, so will I.

It feels like a sauna in our shower with him pushed up against me, but the cool marble balances it out. My head falls back as his mouth moves to my other breast, and then his hands seem to be everywhere—neck, breasts, waist, hips—before they move lower. He touches me between my legs, swirling circles and working me up, but just like I did to him, he doesn't continue nearly long enough before he takes himself in his hands and guides his length inside me.

I'm a little too tight, not quite ready for him, especially at this angle, but I know we're still playing the punishment game because he doesn't ease up as my fingers tighten on his arms, warning him that he's walking a dangerous tightrope.

He presses into me slowly as his body crushes mine. Our mouths find each other, and we kiss rough and hard and passionately, like this might be it for us, like this shower will be the last time I feel him this way. He pushes in farther and my thighs quake.

"I love you," he whispers against my mouth, but it's not a delicate confession. It's a volatile truth: *I love you and it feels like too much sometimes. I love you to an extreme.*

I know how he feels. My arms tighten around his neck as he starts to pump into me faster. I hold on for dear life, like at any moment he could be stripped away from me. Loving Logan is as painful as it is painless. He's the anchor in my life, the partner I want by my side forever.

"I love you too," I whisper back.

"Say it again," he insists, like he's hungry for it.

"I love you," I tease, kissing his cheek.

"You're mine," he warns, though the softness in his gaze belies his rough tone.

"Well, of course I am." I laugh. "Who else would put up with me?"

Find other R.S. Grey Books on Amazon!

Love the One You Hate
Doctor Dearest
His Royal Highness
Coldhearted Boss
Make Me Bad
Hotshot Doc
Not So Nice Guy
Arrogant Devil
The Beau & the Belle
The Fortunate Ones
The Foxe & the Hound
Anything You Can Do
A Place in the Sun
The Summer Games: Out of Bounds
The Summer Games: Settling the Score
The Allure of Dean Harper
The Allure of Julian Lefray
The Design
The Duet
Scoring Wilder
Chasing Spring
With This Heart
Behind His Lens